Call Me QUEEN
a novel

Chi
Thank so
much for
your support

Renee

ISBN-13: 978-1542306645
ISBN-10: 1542306647

Editor: Adrienne Horn
Graphic Designer: Edifyin Graphix
Proof Reader: Tonya Harris
Author Photo: Chuckee Henderson
Cover Image: iStock by Getty Images

This is a work of fiction. Names, characters, places and incidents either are the product of the author's imagination or are used fictitiously. Any resemblance to actual persons, living or dead, events, or locales is entirely coincidental.

First Edition

The Stories…

Every next level of your life will demand a different you…

Unknown

To my first Queen, my grandmother, Maude, and my only Princess, my daughter, Alyssa

CRYSTAL

Innocence
The sweetest fragility
This world
This heart
Has ever known
My innocence at its fullest
Short lived
But when it lived
It surely did
Surely the unicorns
Flew in purple skies
And I
Would float like feathers
Caught in the breeze
Drifting into the seven seas
Just to catch a closer glimpse of horizon
I'm flying
I'm higher than I could ever be
Because my wings
They stretch further than my eyes can see
And that is pretty far
With vision of 20/15
I can dare to dream
Dare to be what I want to be
Even now
Even Queen
Even now I dare
I stare reality in its face and say
My innocence won't be replaced
With your darkness
My light will glow
And I will show you
I will show you my growth
I will spread my wings for you to see
And I will spread my innocence

I will shed your indifference
Just please
Please spare me a little of your time
As I fight to remember that nursery rhyme
It was my favorite you know
That one with the cow jumping over the moon
Where are my stars
May you shine for me
I ask politely
I was raised with manners
And I know what matters
I know that I matter
Still
Even if you don't think I do
Even if you never thought I did
My innocence
I acknowledge
Carefully
It's a treasure you see
It's still deep inside of me

Chapter 1

Summer in New York City was always a good time. Crystal woke up that morning with a new-found excitement. *It's my birthday*, she thought as she giggled to herself. On the Fourth of July in 1986, Crystal had turned 5 years old and she was letting everyone know. It was warm, but not so hot that you couldn't breathe. As if they didn't know already. She was just beginning to understand the importance of the day. The whole Independence Day was a bit intriguing to her.

The fireworks had not yet begun, but the grill was hot. She could hear aunts in the kitchen at her grandmother's house prepping for the barbecue. "This is all for me!" At that point, she paid no never mind to that Independence Day thing. She had no clue what the actual holiday was about anyway. She also didn't really care.

"Grandma, will there be fireworks today?" Crystal asked her grandmother with a quizzing look.

Grandma Marie knew from her expression that this would not be the end of the question in this conversation. "Yes, dear heart, there will be fireworks this evening."

"When will they start, Grandma?" Crystal immediately followed with another question.

"When the sun goes down." Marie always had an answer for her little love.

"Why do we have to wait so long, Grandma?" Crystal continued to quiz her grandmother. This was, of course, her very special day and these were very important questions. Crystal was well aware and understood the concept of birthdays now. You only get one a year so make it as special as you can.

"Well, honey, we won't be able to see them very good if we have them during the daylight," Marie said with a grand smile.

Crystal paused. "Well that makes sense!"

"Mmmhhhmmm." Marie kept busying herself in the kitchen in preparation for the rest of the family to arrive.

"Hey Grandma, I have a question." Crystal put her little hand on her chin. "I know there will be fireworks. I know that it will be tonight. But why do we have fireworks?"

"Oh, honey, because it's your birthday. We love you and want to celebrate such a special little girl." Marie said as a matter of fact.

"All for me, Grandma?" Crystal was now as excited as any little girl could be with a Fourth of July birthday.

"All for you, dear heart." Marie gave Crystal a big hug and watched as she skipped happily, down the hall.

"Crystal, can you please come here for a second?" Uncle Scott called down the hall to Crystal as she was playing with a new Barbie she had just opened for her birthday gift. She got up to see her Uncle Scott. With her face beaming with pure joy and innocence, she smiled and gave him a big hug. "So, Crystal you know today is a special day, huh?"

"Yes, it's my birthday and I am 5 years old!" Crystal exclaimed proudly. Raising her hand, she counted on her fingers.

"I have a very big gift for you, but it will have to wait until tonight after you blow out your candles and sing you your song."

"Oh, wow really? Grandma, just told me that fireworks start at night," Crystal said brightly showing her two missing front teeth.

"Well, that's your surprise. I am giving you fireworks!" Uncle Scott had a huge smile on his face as he watched his niece.

Crystal could not contain her joy. She jumped and hopped and squealed. "Oh, thank you, Uncle Scott. That is the best gift ever! I have to go tell mommy." She found her mother in the kitchen talking to her Aunt Stacy. "Mommy, guess what?"

"What's up birthday girl?" her mother replied in the kitchen as she finished up the preparation for the barbecue.

"Uncle Scott is going to give me fireworks for my birthday gift tonight!" Crystal squealed. She was a natural loving and happy little girl. Her innocent smile beamed. She ran to tell her cousins and other relatives about the gift as she gave hugs to everyone. She was a loveable child. She loved hugs and everyone knew it and everyone loved her for it.

The biggest surprise of all was when she saw her father, Tony, in the distance. She saw Tony talking to Uncle Scott as Uncle Scott handed him money. "Daddy!" Crystal exclaimed. Tony and Crystal's mother, Eva, were no longer together. She didn't see him as much as she wished, and now that they lived with Marie, she saw him less and less.

Tony turned around and smiled at the little girl in her purple dress. "Birthday girl!" Tony loved his daughter and would not have missed her birthday for the world. Even though it was a shock for everyone else who witnessed the heartfelt reunion. His absences had been becoming more frequent as the months went by. It had nothing to do with him not being welcomed. The door was always open for him to come by. It was his fault.

Tony didn't stay long. He told Crystal that he would return with a big surprise. Eva looked at him with questionable eyes and returned to the kitchen. After that moment, it seemed as though everything became a blur for Crystal. By the time she knew it, she had eaten her hamburger, birthday cake and opened her gifts. She absolutely adored when her family sung "Happy Birthday" to her. She had a sweet tooth unlike any other child anyone had ever known. Her other grandmother, Clara, had made her a cake in the shape of a carousel and it tasted as good as it looked. The sun was about to set and the anticipation of Uncle Scott's gift was so overwhelming. All she could think of was the loud pops that would be in the dark sky as it lit up with fairy twinkles from her magical gift. Her favorite color was purple. Like the dress and jellies that she wore that day. Other neighbors had started their displays so Crystal and her cousins sat on Marie's steps staring into the rapidly darkened sky.

The children could hear whispers from the adults. As the day progressed, the whispers were increasingly turning into shouts. Crystal could not understand what could be so hard pressing on such a wonderful day. Everyone was being so nice to her. It was in fact her birthday. She was finally five! She would be starting school in September. She would be a kindergartener like the big girls she sees at the park. She looked up and saw her Uncle Scott with tears in his eyes. *I think Uncle Scott is crying,* she thought to herself and she began to worry her little heart.

"Crystal, I am really sorry. I won't be able to get you those fireworks like I promised you. I don't have a gift for you today." Uncle Scott choked on his words as he struggled to get them out. The last thing he wanted to do was disappoint Crystal on her most important day. She was the little girl that didn't ask for anything and was grateful for everything.

"Oh no, Uncle Scott. Well it's okay. You can sit down with me here and watch the other fireworks. They've started and they're really pretty." Just then a bright white light shot into the sky and sprinkled the clouds. "See Uncle Scott, we still have fireworks. Grandma told me earlier that all fireworks were for me anyway. So, see everything is good! Thank you, Uncle Scott!" The night sky was clear without a cloud in sight. We could see the beauty of the sparkling twinkles from blocks away.

That little conversation with that little 5-year-old warmed Uncle Scott's heart. There was still a piece that was broken. Still a piece that will never be mended. Still the memory from just a few hours ago of making her the happiest little girl in New York City. Still the memory of giving Tony $300.00 of his hard-earned cash to buy the fireworks for Crystal's gift. Then the realization that Tony would not return that night. He would probably not return the next night or months of nights after that. It was at that moment that Tony told the family not in words, but in his selfish actions, that he was using drugs again. Not only was he taking from family, but he had also started taking from his daughter. He had stolen his daughter's fireworks. He had taken her special gift. Crystal didn't know the details of that day until she was much older. She did remember she fell asleep on Marie's lap that night like she had done many nights after. Marie's lap turned in Crystal's safe place.

Crystal remembered seeing Uncle Scott give her dad money. She remembered that he had left shortly after that as quickly as he had come by. As quick as he could utter the words "Happy birthday." She didn't understand why Tony would break a promise, and although she didn't tell anyone, she was upset with him. She honestly didn't think that the adults would understand. She didn't think the adults would know what to do. So, it was her first of many secrets. The secret that she knew something was wrong and acted like everything was okay. She thought, *the adults will tell me when they are ready and right now, they just aren't ready.*

Chapter 2

The adults wouldn't be ready until Crystal was 8 years old. Three years had passed since the exchange of the $300.00 from her Uncle Scott to her father Tony. She had figured out the details as she got older over the years. It also helped that her and her cousin, David, would sneak around their grandmother's house while the adults would talk. The adults normally consisted of her mother, Eva, David's mom, Stacy, and Uncle Joe as the core. Anyone else around would just be extra. The real gossip started after Grandma Marie and Grandfather Jose would go to sleep. Their grandfather was from Honduras and barely spoke English, but he knew enough to know what should and shouldn't be said around the kids.

On one of those faithful nights, the adults were in the living room drinking alcohol, talking and socializing. They had no clue that the kids had literally crawled by the door and hid behind the couch giggling as they would try to sing an oldie but goodie Jackson 5 or Temptations song with the variants of hair brushes, combs and anything else they could get their hands on to use a microphone. They couldn't sing at all, but they were having fun, and the kids liked the entertainment. On this particular night, the conversation changed rather quickly. It wasn't the normal who-was-dating-who-and-who-got-divorced conversation. It was a different kind of gossip. This time it was a little more personal and effected Crystal directly.

She could hear her Aunt Stacy mention something about Tony. It was a name she had rarely heard, especially since her mom was in a different relationship.

Eva had moved Crystal in to live with her boyfriend, Clarence, right after the 5th birthday incident. At first, she didn't want to get to know Clarence, but she had grown to love him as she had loved her own father. She only saw Tony once after her birthday barbecue. It was almost a year later and he randomly stopped by to visit her with her first pair of Barbie skates. She was so excited to see him that she didn't really care about the skates at the time. Soon, the skates were too small and became the only reminder she had of him. She kept those skates for a long time.

"Is Tony still out of the streets? Have you heard from him at all?" Stacy asked without any hesitation. She had no clue the children were eavesdropping.

"I don't know. He is probably in jail," Eva said in a casual tone. What seemed as simple as pouring water in a glass was the first devastating moment in Crystal's life.

Daddy is homeless? Daddy is in jail? Daddy is on… drugs? Her words poured out like lava. The smoldering sense of the reality that came out as clear as day forced Crystal to have to hold back tears. David saw it and he felt it. At 10 years, old, he saw his 6-year-old cousin's heart shatter into a million pieces. Immediately he turned to her and started shoving her out of the room, but it was too late. Her smile faded and her dreams were gone. She had become more like the adults on the other side of the sofa. At 6 years, old, she was all grown up. She knew what drugs were from the talks she had at school and the "Just Say No" campaign that was plastered all over the inner city.

"Crystal, sit down. There is something that I want to tell you," Eva told Crystal in her concerning mother voice. Crystal sat on the sofa and clasped her hands. She didn't say a word. She knew whatever she needed to hear was serious and she wanted to hear it all. "Your father wants to see you. He is in a rehabilitation facility for drug use…" Eva had said more words, but at that point Crystal shut down. She sat there and began to cry in an attempt to drown out the words she never thought she would hear. "I know you are sad, but you needed to know. He wants you to—"

Crystal cut her mother off and said, "I know, Mommy. I know Daddy is on drugs and I have been waiting for someone, anyone to tell me. I am not crying because I am sad. I am crying because I no longer have to keep the secret anymore." At that point, Eva started to cry. She called Tony and told him that Crystal had kept her secret for two years.

Crystal did get to visit Tony. The rehabilitation facility was hours away. She didn't know where she was going, but she was curious. When most children were going on Disney World vacations, she was on a 5:00 am bus to somewhere to visit her father who was on drugs. The weekend was as pleasant as it could be. She sat in on her first drug rehab group session. She sat there as stiff as a board and quiet as the paper that lay on her lap. She felt like an object, not quite human and definitely not a child.

It seemed as though everyone around her was able to express how they felt and what they had gone through. Everyone, but her. None of the counselors had ever asked her how it felt for her to have a father that had chosen drugs over her. Essentially, that is what he did. He chose a substance that would only equal death over the life of his child. Crystal was hurt and confused. Everyone wanted to know how he felt. What was going on in his mind and heart. Everyone again had forgotten about her. She could have really used one of those big, warm and loving grandma's hugs right about then. If she could just go back to being 5 years old when everything was simple and easy. When she knew nothing but the truth of the fireworks for her. She still wanted to believe the fireworks were just for her. Something had to be for her. It just couldn't be this.

She left the rehab facility silent. She left a little quieter than when she had arrived. At some point, she wanted to believe she had heard wrong while she was hiding behind the sofa, but this confirmed it all. Daddy was a drug addict. Daddy stole her birthday money. She had to grow up. She had to know to expect the unexpected and that days won't always be so happy. Take the pleasant moments as they come, even if there are some bad times.

Chapter 3

After the stay at the rehabilitation center, that was pretty much it for the next couple of years with Tony. To her, he was still Daddy, but Daddy had other obligations that didn't involve her. The thought of knowing that hurt deeply, but it was something she accepted. When Tony had successfully completed his program, it wasn't any time wasted before he was back on the street.

She would spend every other weekend with his mother, her grandmother, Clara. She heard the adults talking again and found out Clara had taken her mother to court for visitation under Grandparents' rights. For a while, it was cool for Crystal to spend time with her father's side of the family. She didn't do much when she was at her house. Sometimes her Aunt Sydney would come by and take her to a movie or lunch, but for the most part, she spent it playing her Nintendo or Sega Genesis. Her mother didn't allow her to have one. She complained it would be too distracting and wanted her to focus on school.

Crystal didn't mind. It gave her something to look forward to when she visited Clara. There were a few times they would do things like when Clara tried to teach Crystal how to roller skate. Crystal ended up flying down a hill scared for her life and threw herself in the grass before she hit the street. However scary it was, they were able to laugh about it. "As long as you didn't get hurt that is all that matters," Clara said after the ordeal was over. Crystal thought it would be a good idea to walk the rest of the way back home in her socks. They laughed all the way back.

Another cool thing about staying at Clara's house was she never had milk. Each morning Crystal was able to eat her cereal with ice cream. It was more of a topping than breakfast and she loved every bite of it. She liked hanging with her grandmother. It gave her a nice break from being at home with her mom all the time. The arrangement worked out nicely until the next Tony incident occurred.

Crystal had arrived at her grandmother's house at 7:00 p.m. as arranged. They walked over to the video rental store, which was about three blocks away and she picked out two VHS cartoon movies and a new game for her Nintendo. They had both stayed up pretty late eating ice cream and watching movies so they fell asleep on the pull-out sofa in the living room. This set up became a ritual for the first night.

Crystal woke up first. "Grandma, what did you do to the TV?" It was odd that her grandmother would remove the TV and the VCR in the middle of the night. "What are you talking about, Crystal? I didn't touch the TV." Clara was talking to Crystal with her eyes closed. "Well, Grandma where did the TV go then? It's gone," Crystal said again now completely confused. Clara sat up in bed to the same horror Crystal had awakened to.

Clara called Sydney and Scott. Neither one of them had any clue what had happened to the TV or VCR. The family gathered in the dining area. Crystal was told to go to the bedroom and wait. The two-bedroom apartment was small so she was able to hear every word.

"Tony must have taken it!" Uncle Scott exclaimed. "I can't believe he came in here when you all were sleeping and stole the TV! He stole it right from under your nose!"

"He has really lost his mind now! How could he do this with Crystal here?" Sydney was now upset. Everyone was upset. Crystal was forced to listen from the other room. She was the only one not allowed to express her own frustrations. Again. What about Crystal and what she had to say? *My daddy stole something else?* Crystal was so sad.

She was called out of the bedroom and witnessed her grandmother cry for the first time in her life. The sunken feeling in Crystal's chest seemed to further shatter her already broken heart into a million more pieces. "What about the movie? The movie was in the VHS. I am really sorry for not taking it out. I was tired and wanted to watch it again with my ice cream and cereal. I didn't mean to leave it in there. I didn't know I had to take it out!"

Crystal had always read the sign at the movie rental store that stated if a movie or game was missing or lost, the renter would have to pay a $25.00 penalty. Not only did Tony steal the TV and the VHS player, he also stole the movie and her grandmother would have to pay for. Sydney took Crystal home shortly after. When she showed up early, Eva knew something was wrong and immediately called Clara. Crystal wasn't sure what was being said on the other line, but she clearly heard the cursing from her mother. Crystal went into her room, curled up in a ball and cried herself to sleep.

A few months later during another visit, there was a *bang bang bang bang* on the door. Crystal jumped up out of bed first. She was scared and woke up her grandmother. The TV was replaced and they were back on the pull-out sofa like old times. Even though Crystal didn't come over every other weekend as much, she did come by about once a month after the theft. *Bang bang bang...* It happened again. Crystal's heart was racing. She could feel her breaths shortening, and she was scared. Shortly after, Clara jumped out of bed too.

Clara grabbed a bat that was nearby and walked up to the door. *Bang bang bang* "Help!" Someone on the other side was calling for help. It sounded like a man's voice. The pounding continued. Crystal stayed in bed looking for something to grab too. She eyed the lamp. That would be her weapon of choice. There was nothing else in her reach and she had to think quickly.

Clara crept up to the door and looked though the peep hole. "Oh, my God!" She screamed and opened the door. It was Tony.

Tony had been badly beaten and was bloody. He could barely stand up. He could barely breathe. Crystal thought he was going to die right there in front of her. "Tony, what happened to you? Who did this to you?!?" Clara had a thousand questions, but Tony had no answers.

He crawled to the pull-out sofa where Crystal was. Crystal barely recognized him. She wondered if he even knew she was there. "Crystal, go get me a hot rag from the bathroom." Crystal heard her grandmother, but she was stuck. She sat in pure fear staring at Tony as tears seeped from his closed lids. Even in the darkness, she could see that his face was bruised in multiple places. His blood completely covered the sheets.

"Crystal, go get me that rag now!" Clara yelled snapping Crystal out of her trance. Crystal ran to the bathroom and did just that. Clara was a registered nurse that worked in a nursing home. If anyone could patch him up, it was her. Crystal came back with the rag and gave it to her grandmother.

Tony calmed down a bit and was able to get words out. "I was sleeping on the park bench and some guys came out of nowhere and started beating me up for fun. There were too many of them and I couldn't fight them all. I came here. I have no place to go."

Did Crystal hear him correctly? He was sleeping on a park bench? This was the first time she had seen Tony since the rehab visit. Tony was very tall and muscular, but right now he appeared small and frail. There was nothing she could do to help her father. She felt helpless. She felt hopeless. *This is the life he chose over me.* That was the realization she came up with. Tony had a mother, brother, sister, daughter and many other family members that loved him, but he chose to be on the streets for drugs.

Tears streamed down Crystal's face, yet no one in the room knew. Everyone, as always, was preoccupied with the problem at hand. Uncle Scott and Sydney were summoned again. They came at once. In the middle of the night she was taken home. Early. All because of Tony. Again. This was a habit that somehow happened whenever she was around.

By the morning, Crystal told her mother she didn't want to go back to Clara's house. No one knew it, but Crystal blamed herself for everything. *It's only when I am there that these things happen. I won't go back and no one can make me.* And at the tender age of nine, that is exactly what happened. Crystal didn't spend another night at her grandmother's house for months. And she didn't hear from Tony for years.

Chapter 4

Another Fourth of July had rolled around like clockwork. Crystal still viewed her birthday as a special day, but it was more of a holiday that everyone celebrated. It had lost its magic during the 1986 ordeal. This year was 1993 and she was turning 12 years old.

After having just graduated from elementary school, she was surprised that Tony had showed up. Of course, he showed up late. Very late. She had spent the entire day before constantly calling him, reminding him what time to arrive. He said he was coming. "He said he was coming, Mommy! You know what, Mommy? I am going to call him again." She could no longer trust his word anymore, so she needed to make sure for her own sanity that he was actually going to do what he said he would do.

Her mom had taken her to get her hair done at the salon and she felt pretty. Feeling pretty was not something she normally experienced. She had a beautiful dress, a great hair style and her cap and gown hung neatly in the closet. "Is he really going to come?" Crystal started to doubt he would come and began to worry. "Let me call him again!"

She had every right to doubt. Not too long ago he called and said he wanted her to spend the weekend with her. Eva allowed it since he was off of drugs for the 800th time. Crystal went down to her lobby and waited for him. She had done this before and he was normally there within fifteen minutes to get her. He didn't live that far away. This time however, it was different. This time he was late. Very late.

Crystal waited. Three hours went by and it was late. At this point, she was still waiting more for the reason. Of course, she knew she would get in trouble for staying in the lobby so long. She could hear her mother now, yelling at her for not coming upstairs at a reasonable time. She just wanted to believe that her father was telling her the truth. She needed to believe that her father was telling her the truth.

Tony lied to Crystal. It was now five hours later and Crystal was not only heartbroken, but she was scared. Scared at how her mother would react since it was now 10:00 p.m. Just then, her stepfather, Paul got off the elevator and saw her in the lobby waiting. Tears filled Crystal's eyes and she knew she was caught. She knew Tony was caught. She knew her mother and stepfather would be angry.

Paul came into the picture right after Crystal's fifth birthday. At first, Crystal wasn't pleased that her mother was seeing another man. She wanted her parents to be together. After a while, Crystal warmed up to Paul and they had a good relationship. Sometimes she was able to go to him with situations before she could go to her mother. They would go on day trips to places as far out as Pennsylvania and as close as the neighborhood diner for breakfast.

"Crystal, what are you doing out here this late? Tony never showed up?" Paul asked in full concern. There was no excuse for her not coming upstairs sooner. "Why didn't you come up earlier? Why did you wait so long?"

Just then, Crystal started crying. She always waited to cry when she was near brink of exhaustion and couldn't hold it in any longer. "I just thought he would come and when he didn't I knew Mommy would be mad. Then I waited because I was scared I would get in trouble for waiting so long and now you're here." She was crying even harder now.

Paul was well aware of Tony's drug issues. He was actually a counselor himself and was able to place him in the original program where Crystal had visited. Paul never got in the way of Tony and Crystal's relationship. He knew Tony was her father and it would be Crystal's decision of what kind of relationship they would have. It would not be based off of bad mouthing from either him or her mother.

"Eva, I have a surprise for you!" Paul called out at the door of their apartment. Crystal was standing on the other side of the doorway.

"Surprise? What are you talking about?" She was tired and she didn't feel like playing guessing games. She was getting ready to go to bed. Just then Crystal came around the corner with her head hanging low and tears streaming down her face.

"What the hell? Did Tony never come to get you? You were down there that long waiting on his black ass? Oh, hell no! He can't have my 9-year-old child waiting for him at 10:00 p.m. Absolutely not!" Eva was furious and started making calls. Paul told Crystal to go in her room. Crystal could now hear him telling Eva to calm down because Crystal didn't need to hear her that upset. Eva called Tony and cursed him out.

"Daddy, are you *really* coming to my graduation?" It was now 9:30 p.m. and Crystal needed to go to bed, but not before she called her father one last time.

"Yes, I will be there. I told you I wouldn't miss this for the world," Tony said sweetly to his only daughter.

Crystal woke up bright and early. She had to get ready and be at the school before everyone else for ceremony preparation. She was both nervous and excited at the same time. She put on her light peach dress and small jacket to cover the thin straps. She was wearing her first pair of two-inch heels for the special occasion. Her long, thick hair laid straight and covered her back leaving just enough room for her cap to stay on.

"Looks like you're all set. You look very pretty, Crystal," Eva said to her daughter.

"Thank you, Mommy. Have you heard from Daddy? Is he coming?" After all of that, the only concern for Crystal was that her father would actually show up. She was tired of being disappointed by him and really needed him to be there.

Throughout the ceremony, Crystal spent most the time looking for her father to come through the door. She barely caught her name being called for her girls' basketball team trophies and her academic Historian medal. She was beyond discouraged and depression was settling in. Yes, all her other family was there, but she *needed* Tony to be there too.

The graduation was almost over. She heard him before she saw him. Tony had arrived interrupting the ceremony being loud and obnoxious. She didn't care. All that mattered was that he made it.

"Hey Crystal who is that?" her best friend Jocelyn asked her.

"That's my father, J. He actually came," she whispered.

"Your father? I have never seen him before! I have known you for years! I have known you since kindergarten!" Jocelyn didn't know what to think of the whole thing.

"Yeah I know. He isn't around much, but he made it today." Crystal beamed in her chair. She wasn't sure why Tony was being so loud, but her thoughts were cut off when she heard her principal congratulate the graduates and the caps flew in the air.

Tony was drunk. Crystal could tell and she was disappointed all over again. The short-lived moment she shared with Jocelyn was just what it was. Short lived. Eva didn't want to, but she did extend the invitation to Tony to attend her luncheon. They were going to Crystal's favorite restaurant, The Sizzler, for all-you-can-eat shrimp. Tony declined and left just as quickly as he had appeared. He was becoming more and more of a magician with his disappearing act.

Crystal was sure he wouldn't show for her birthday this year, and she was okay with that. He would normally call her on his birthday, July 25th, and not July 4th. That way he could get his happy birthday wish from her, and he would then be able to wish her a happy belated. That actually hurt her feelings although she never told anyone that it did.

Her barbecue this year would be at Crotona Park, one of the biggest parks in the Bronx and the closest to her grandmother's house. Crystal, Jocelyn and Crystal's cousin, Nicole, were practicing a song for the better part of the night to sing at the birthday gathering. They all had the same favorite song, *Weak* by Sisters with Voices. Crystal and Jocelyn had pretty decent voices to be almost 12 years old. Nicole, not being able to sing at all, didn't stop them one bit. They were going to have their mini concert in the park no matter what.

The performance was cute, and they got a standing ovation. Crystal was in rare form that day. She didn't like being center of attention, but it helped that she shared it with her best friend and cousin. Later that night, things turned for the worst right after the fireworks display.

Nicole was making fun of Crystal. The teasing was mostly because Crystal didn't live in as nice of a neighborhood as she did. Crystal was able to ignore it for the most part, but it didn't help that their older cousin, David, was instigating the entire ordeal.

"I live in a better everything than you. You live in the dirty Bronx. My life is better than yours!" Nicole teased. Crystal wasn't sure where all of this was coming from, but she wasn't in the mood for it. Besides, she hated arguing with anyone, so she did her best to tune her out.

"Oooooooh!!! Are you going to let her talk to you like that, Crystal? She said you lived in the dirty Bronx!" David mimicked, not realizing that he also lives in the same exact place and should have been offended as well.

"I don't care what she has to say, D. She is stupid and I don't deal with stupid people." Crystal had her fair share of people making fun of her. At this point it didn't matter where it came from.

"I won't shut up! *Make* me! And it doesn't matter no way. Your father ain't nothing but a crack head anyway!" Nicole shot back.

"Wait, Nicole! That was a low blow. You shouldn't have said that." David knew that was way too far below the belt. He was the one that was there when Crystal found out about her father's substance abuse problems. He saw his little cousin's heart break right before his eyes for the first time.

Crystal stared at Nicole. She knew she could beat up Nicole. She had done it before, and she was about to do it again.

Crystal calmly got up and stood over Nicole who was sitting on the bed. David, at this point, was nervous, but was going to let Crystal do whatever she wanted to do because Nicole had no right to call Tony a crack head even if it was true.

"What are you going to do, Crystal? You can't do shit to me!" Nicole taunted, but Crystal didn't say a word. Instead, she swiftly grabbed Nicole's shirt and ripped it right off her back without hesitation. Crystal had manhandled her so quickly that David didn't even have a fight to break up.

Nicole tearfully ran down the hall to tell on Crystal. Crystal sat back in her chair quietly not caring about any of it. She figured she would get in trouble, but she didn't care about that either.

David looked at Crystal and said "You are going to get in trouble for this one, but you did the right thing. She shouldn't have said that and that shirt was God awful ugly."

"Crystal! Get your black ass down here right now!" Eva called out to her. It had begun. Her mom, aunts, uncles and grandmother were in the living room. Crystal entered the room with a blank expression on her face as David followed closely behind her.

"Yes, Mommy?" Crystal was still eerily calm and had no care in the world.

"Did you rip Nicole's shirt off her in the backroom?" Nicole's mother, Kim, asked Crystal sternly.

"Yes, Titi I did." Crystal's grandfather was from Honduras. Titi meant *auntie* in Spanish.

"Why would you do such a thing?" Eva questioned. Crystal was not a violent person, so something terrible must have happened for her daughter to step out of character.

"Well, Nicole said that she was better than me because I lived in the dirty Bronx and she lived in a nice neighborhood. Then she added that Tony was a crack head." For the first time in her life she had gone numb. It would be a feeling she would get used to.

"You said what?!?" Kim exclaimed. She was so embarrassed at her daughter's actions. "Do you realize that your mother and father come from the same place that Crystal and all the family lives in? Who the hell do you think you are?!?"

Nicole was confused. Her plan had backfired. Crystal didn't get in trouble at all. David was there to cosign on everything that was said in the backroom. They did make Crystal apologize for ripping the shirt, which she did halfheartedly. That was the end of that battle. David gave Crystal a hug. Those came far and few in between, but he knew she needed one that night.

Chapter 5

Briefly when Crystal was in middle school, Tony had made another appearance in her life, but it had been the longest stretch since birth. He was back in rehab. He had a new girlfriend, and Crystal once again had hope. Hope that her father would stay clean long enough to finally love her. She would even spend some nights with them. It was during those weekends she would go to different clubs in New York City. She was sure she had no business being there at 12 years old, but it was quality time with her father, and they were making up for a lot of lost time.

Tony was a musician. He was one of the best percussionists in New York. It was this musical gift that led him on the downhill spiral with his drug addiction. Crystal had been to so many clubs and met so many live bands in the NYC music circuit that they all knew who she was even though she couldn't remember any of their names. It didn't matter. She was just Tony's kid that didn't bother anyone.

He would also get Eva and Crystal free tickets to the world-famous Apollo Theater during amateur night for ShowTime at the Apollo. He was a part of the house band, Ray Chew and the Crew, at the time. Crystal was allowed to go backstage and meet the celebrities who performed. Her and her mom met SWV, Brian McKnight, Full Force, Brandy and Another Bad Creation. There were other times in the clubs where she would run into different celebrities like the comedian, Flex, and Queen Latifah, who introduced herself as Dana Owens. Meeting Queen Latifah was her favorite. She actually stopped and had a small conversation with her in the comedy club where Flex was performing.

Before the heavy drug habit, Tony was the drummer for artists like Roy Ayers, Phyllis Hyman and Chaka Khan. Her mother told Crystal that Chaka came to see her when she was born. Crystal screamed in her face. Crystal was known to be a crier when she was a baby. Chaka said to Eva, "Watch out for your daughter. With a set of pipes like that, she was born to be a singer." She always wondered if that is where it began. A sad tale of money and fame with no proper guidance. Tony had started his drug abuse right after Crystal was born in 1981. He had been battling the addiction ever since.

At those clubs is where she discovered her first virgin strawberry daiquiri. "What will it be, little lady?" The bartender, also known as the evening's babysitter, asked.

"Oh, I don't know. Make it special. But no alcohol please," Crystal said with a smile. The bartender threw a purple straw in the tall pink drink and she sipped and loved it. "Oh, this is so good. I think this is my favorite!" Tony was playing with the funk band that night. She liked the band and loved the music, but it was the longest set. She knew she was in for the long haul and would probably find herself sleeping in a booth before long.

Tony and Crystal's relationship blossomed like never before during that time. It was then that Crystal discovered her own musical talent. She couldn't play any instruments like her father, but Tony couldn't sing at all. Crystal however, could sing just about anything. *One day I will let him hear me sing,* she thought to herself proudly. She was starting to see they had more in common than she had ever realized.

33

The next night would be the jazz band and maybe a studio set in the morning. Crystal now fully loved music.

Tony took Clara and Crystal to a store. This store had everything. It was a place she had never been to, and she was excited to go. "Pick out any two things you want, and they are yours," Tony said to Crystal. Her eyes were brightly shining, and she was ecstatic. "Daddy, Daddy, I like that and that," Crystal said pointing at the glass. "Are you sure that is what you want, honey?" Clara asked smiling as she walked up to Crystal.

Crystal wanted a small gold diamond ring and a gold crucifix. The clerk rang up the items, and Crystal skipped out the pawn shop as the happiest girl in New York. She was so excited to show her mother what her father had gotten her. It was the first time he had gotten her anything since she was 6 years old. *I will never take this off,* smiling to herself.

There were times when she had to take it off though. Tony would drive to Clara's home and to Crystal's school so they could go get the jewelry cleaned. By the time they arrived to Crystal's other grandmother's house, Crystal's diamond would be sparkling and the gold cross would be shining.

Crystal would spend the better part of her day staring at her ring. She loved the way the sun's rays would bounce off of the diamond. It was the prettiest thing she owned and her daddy had gotten it for her.

"Crystal, please report to the front office. You have a visitor," Mrs. Doyle, Crystals homeroom and Social Studies teacher, announced. Crystal grabbed her things and went downstairs. She saw Tony standing with the secretary, but Clara was not with him. "Hi, Daddy. Where is Grandma?" Crystal asked cautiously. Tony had never showed up without her grandmother before. Why on earth would he be doing it now?

"Your grandmother is in the car waiting for me. I had to double park and couldn't find parking. I ran in so I could get the jewelry and get it cleaned," Tony said.

"Oh, am I going with you guys this time?" Sometimes they would pull her out of school early if it was close to the end of the day. She only had about twenty minutes left in the school day.

"No, not this time. I have a gig and I need to get to the city tonight. I am playing at the jazz club, Sweet Waters." Tony had his story down pat. It was then that Crystal felt comfortable handing over her ring and necklace. It had been a while since it had been cleaned. Tony gave Crystal a hug and kiss and left. Crystal went back to Mrs. Doyle's class.

She sat there uneasy for the next 20 minutes. A couple of times Mrs. Doyle asked if she was okay. Crystal was a quiet child, but she had stopped participating completely since she was called down to the office. Crystal didn't realize her behavior had changed that much. *I hope he meets me at Grandma's house soon.*

Chapter 6

"Hi honey, are you okay?" Crystal's grandmother opened the door for her as she came in and sensed something was wrong.

"Yes, Grandma, I am fine." Crystal hurried up the stairs, ate her snack and did her homework in silence.

"You are awfully quiet, young lady. Are you sure you are okay? Did anything happen at school today?" It was not like Crystal to be so isolated, and Marie was starting to worry.

"I am okay, Grandma. I just have a lot of homework to get done. That's all." Crystal wasn't completely telling a lie. She did have a lot of homework, but something was definitely wrong. She spent the better part of the afternoon peering out the second-floor window looking for Tony to drive up. *Please God, let him hurry up!*

"Crystal, where is your ring and necklace?" Marie didn't miss anything. The one thing she prided herself on was knowing her kids. Those kids included her grandchildren. As soon as Marie asked the question, Crystal cried. She could no longer keep her tears from falling from her eyes. She had tried to call her father, and his number was disconnected. She had no way of getting in contact with him, and she knew he had taken her jewelry. The same jewelry he bought for her as a special gift.

The tears she had been trying to hide all day streamed down her face in that instance. "Daddy came to my school, and I gave it to him. I am so sorry, Grandma. I thought he was going to clean it. I thought Grandma Clara was in the car waiting for him. He said she was there. I believed him, Grandma. I am so sorry. I should not have trusted him. I tried to call him, but it won't go through. Grandma, my daddy stole it!" That was the most Crystal said to anyone since Tony left her school. Her grandmother reached out to her and held her in an effort to console her, but that was to no avail.

Shortly after Crystal broke the news to Marie, Eva came in from work. She saw Crystal crying and immediately became concerned. "What's the matter? What is wrong?" Eva asked quickly.

"Something *terrible* has happened." Marie told Eva what happened just as Crystal told her. Eva ran to the phone and tried to call Tony again. Marie was well aware that her daughter would be furious with Tony. She had been in the middle of many disturbances dealing with them. She feared this would be one where she would be of little help. Her only focus was her granddaughter. "This child sees too much."

"The number you have reached is disconnected," the operator said. Eva slammed the phone down and then called Clara. Clara had no clue that Tony had gone to Crystal's school that day. She admitted she thought Tony was back on drugs and had not heard from him in a few weeks.

Eva was furious and started yelling at Clara. "If you thought that bastard was back on drugs, you should have warned us!" That was the first-time Eva had openly spoken bad about Tony in front of Crystal. Crystal was still crying in Marie's lap.

Eva called the entire family, and told them what Tony had done to Crystal. She was irate! They called everyone they could think of that may have known where Tony was. "Have you seen Tony?" Eva was now on the phone with Tony's girlfriend, Debbie.

"I am so sorry, Eva. I would have never thought he would have stooped so low. I haven't heard from him, and today, I came home and my entire apartment was cleaned out. I have nothing left. Please give Crystal my love. I am so sorry. I have nothing left. He took everything I had." Debbie tearfully hung up the phone.

"That black bastard!" Eva was so angry. She threw the phone in the corner. Everyone was allowed to show their frustration. Everyone, but Crystal that is.

Repeatedly, she was told, "Don't cry. Calm down. Don't worry yourself," by various people at various times. They all told her the same thing, as if they were all reading the same script.

Crystal was done. Tony had stolen directly from her. How was she to get over this? "Daddy doesn't love me," she said to herself. That was the last day she would ever call him "Daddy." He was not her *daddy*. He was just a man that she thought she knew. That day he became Tony, and no one would ever be able to change her mind. This was a far cry from the Cosby show that was playing on the TV behind her. That fantasy of having the same type of doting fatherly love that Mr. Cosby showed to his family was whisked away as her rainbow faded in the clouds.

Crystal dreaded going to school the next day, but she had to. Her mother went with her this time, and they all had a meeting with the principal. Tony was officially no longer allowed to come to Crystal's school. Her mother had filed a Do Not Contact notice against him and needed the school to have the paperwork on file. Crystal was embarrassed. The principal looked at her with concerning eyes. *Now everyone knows Tony is a drug addict.*

Mrs. Doyle was notified of the situation as well since she was Crystal's primary teacher. Crystal could feel so many eyes looking at her. The nurse asked her if she wanted a counseling session. There was no way she was going to talk to this woman. She didn't even know who she was. In the two years, she had been going to her junior high school, she had never stepped foot in the nurse's office. If she wasn't feeling well, her grandmother took care of her. She wasn't going to start the trend now under these circumstances.

"Hey Crystal, where have you been all day? I saw you come into school this morning and go to the principal's office. You get in trouble or something?" Jared, one of her longtime friends from elementary school, asked. They had been in each other's class since kindergarten.

"I am not in trouble. My mom just had to give some paperwork to the school. I just had to sit there during it." Sitting there wishing the building could blow away the whole time. Crystal hoped Jared didn't ask any more questions. He didn't.

"Well, I'll say this. You're quiet, but today you are *really* quiet. I hope everything is okay," Jared said running away to play with his other friends during recess.

The conversation with Jared was the only one she had all day. Other than answering a few questions during class, she had hardly said anything at all. She just wanted to leave. It was Friday and she wanted her weekend to start. She needed a break. *Hopefully Grandma will let me spend the night.*

The much-needed mini vacation from all the drama is just what Crystal needed. Her mother was still fuming about what Tony did to her. She overheard from the adults that Uncle Scott was looking for him. He had left the house the night he found out about the robbery. It was just him and his bike. He still had not returned home, and the family was hoping that he wouldn't find Tony.

Eva called Crystal's godfather, Trevor, to find him first. He was an undercover policeman for the New York Police Department. The plan was for Trevor to find Tony and put him in jail for a couple of weeks until the family calmed down. It worked. Trevor found Tony before Uncle Scott did. That was the last Crystal had known of his whereabouts for years. She preferred it this way. Tony was nothing more than a thief to her. He had stolen more than just her birthday gift money, the TV and VCR. Tony had stolen Crystal's childhood. He was the first man to love her and the first man to break her heart.

CELESTE

I dream often
Of the way you used to be
I wonder where she went
I wonder why she left
I wonder if she will ever return
I wish she would
So I could
Wrap my arms around her and say
I love you
I've missed you
Can we start over?
I can be better
I will do better
Just don't leave
Again
My heart can't take that again
But if you never return
Just know
I even still love you now

Chapter 1

It was the beginning of the school year and Celeste had just started the 5th grade. One more year to go and she would be in Junior High. She always looked forward to the future. In her mind, she could do absolutely anything she set her mind to do. One day she asked her mother for a dresser for her dolls. Without a doubt or hesitation her mother replied, "No!" With Celeste being who she was, she took that "No!" as a challenge. Instead of viewing it as "No, you cannot have one," she saw it as "No, I will not get you one."

It was right after Christmas so she collected all of the left-over boxes from the gifts and made a dresser for her doll clothes. It consisted of duct tape, scotch tape, water color paint, crayons and glue. It had drawers, flaps and anything else she could imagine a dream doll dresser would have. She has always been a determined child. She completed that project in just less than three hours. It was one of those the-kid-is-too-quiet-what-on-earth-could-she-be-doing moments. Her mother, Sara, took a step back, laughed, told her she did a good job, and then walked away. There was really nothing else she could have done with Celeste. She was just that kind of child.

Celeste came home from school, prepared her snack and started her homework. She always came right to her grandmother's house and stayed there until her mother got home from work. As the time passed, she noticed it was half past 7:00 p.m. Her mother was late again. She wasn't exactly sure where her mother would go between her 5:00 p.m. and 7:00 p.m., but she knew on the late night's home, it would be an even later night for her to cope. It was Friday night, which means nothing but trouble. At least she wouldn't be alone. Her cousin had started at the same school she did and would be visiting for a couple of months. Celeste is an only child, so her cousins are more like siblings than anything else. She could hear mom stagger up the stairs. She grew increasingly embarrassed with each step her mother took. It didn't matter that it was in front of family. Celeste never wanted anyone to see her mom in that condition.

Sara walked in and didn't acknowledge Celeste sitting in the room. Her cousin, Jenny, was there and looked puzzled. She could not imagine what would be in store for the duration of the evening. "Jenny, do you want to spend the weekend with us at home?"

Celeste loved the idea and loved her cousin, but she had hoped Jenny would have declined the invitation. Hope would be for the weary on this one because Jenny excitedly replied, "Yes!" Celeste dropped her head. The look of despair for the average person would have never noticed. However, her grandmother, Kora, noticed it right away. Even though they were many years apart, Kora and Celeste were kindred spirits. One would always feel the other even in a crowded room. Kora made a mental note and continued to watch TV.

"Are you sure you want to come to my apartment, Jenny? I can just stay here with you. I am sure we would have more fun." Celeste uttered those words in a solemn voice.

"Of course, I do! Why wouldn't I want to spend the weekend with you?" Jenny retorted in her perky tone. "This is going to be so much fun!"

Celeste never answered her. She packed up her belongings and waited for the cab to arrive to take them home.

"What do you girls want to eat?" asked Sara. Her words were slurred and they could smell the alcohol on her breath.

"Mommy, we already ate dinner at Grandma's house." Celeste wanted as little contact with her mother as possible. If they could just get to her room, close the door and giggle like 11-year-old girls. Once the cab arrived, it was around 8:00 p.m. There were still too many hours left in the evening, in Celeste's opinion, which left way too much time to get into unwarranted trouble.

As they got into the elevator to go up to their 18th floor apartment, Celeste prepared herself for the drill. Her mother began to squirm, doing her famous "pee dance" as the elevator crept up the floors. In Sara fashion, however, there wasn't much time left and she began to urinate on herself cursing the whole way up "This goddamned elevator is too damn slow! I have to fucking pee!"

Jenny just stood there and didn't say one word. Celeste wasn't sure if she was actually breathing. She just figured she was because she had yet to pass out. Slowly, Jenny turned to look at Celeste. Celeste lowered her eyes and then her head. They exited the elevator with a huge puddle left by Sara. The door closed behind them as if part of the décor. "Someone better clean that shit up! Hahahhaha!" Sara hysterically laughed all the way down the hall. The girls were trying to find the humor in the ordeal.

"What did you say you wanted to eat?" Sara asked Celeste again. She was bothered at this point.

"Mommy, I already told you we ate dinner at Grandma's house. We are not hungry." Celeste attempted once again to reason with her mother.

"No, the hell, you didn't. You're always lying to me," Sara said very angrily. Jenny still quiet now had a look of confusion as she tried to figure out this entire ordeal. For Celeste, it was just another Friday night with an unfortunate audience to bear witness. Celeste finally went in her room after Sara fumbled her keys to get them in the door for almost two minutes.

"Uh Celeste, what's wrong with your mom? Why is she acting that way to us?" This question had been on Jenny's mind since the cab ride and now she understood why Celeste protested the visit in the first place.

"Jenny, it's Friday. It's not like every day, just every other day. She can't handle being drunk like that every single day. She still has to work and stuff." Celeste answered nonchalantly. There was nothing to hide now. Jenny was in the thick of it.

Jenny looked afraid. "Wait, your mom has a drinking schedule? Maybe we shouldn't be talking about this so loudly."

Celeste brushed off the notion that it was a conversation that shouldn't be had. She knew Sara was paying no mind to them to say the least. "No, it's okay. She can't hear us. And yup she drinks every other day. It wasn't always this way, but now it is." Jenny had seen what she was hoping would be the worst of it. She knew it could get really bad really quickly, so she would turn her focus on her new-found hobby, poetry, or just make something creative.

"Bitches! Get your asses out here now!" Sara screamed at them from the living room. *Bitch.* It was something reserved for Celeste, but with the addition of her niece, she simply clumped them both together.

It was that moment when Jenny couldn't take it anymore. She cried so hard she could barely breathe. Celeste didn't know what to do at this point. Both Sara and Celeste looked at Jenny as if her actions baffled them both. Celeste had been used to this kind of name calling. She actually expected it since she only got an 85% on her spelling test. Even when she got a 90% or better, her mother would ask her where the rest of whatever percentage points were that she needed to make the perfect score. "Why the hell are you crying?" At this point, Sara was annoyed and didn't want to be bothered with the little girl. Even if the little girl happened to be her niece.

"You cursed at us!" Jenny was so distraught she could not hide it, and she didn't understand why Celeste was just standing there as if it were business as usual. Jenny ran to the phone and called her father to pick her up immediately. It was then Celeste began to panic. She knew it was a bad idea for her cousin to spend the night on a Friday. It would have been better on a Saturday. That was the day her mother would spend all day in bed recouping from the previous night's excursions. Saturdays were Sara's off days.

Celeste was completely embarrassed and wanted desperately to go with Jenny to Grandma's house. She knew as soon as the door closed it would had been all her fault for what had happened that night, and she didn't want to find out how creatively mean her mother could get with her words and actions. Thirty minutes later, Jenny's dad came to pick her up. Reluctantly, Celeste went as well. She knew there would be consequences for choosing the wrong side. Where had the loving Sara gone? Seems like her love was locked and loaded at the bottom of a dark rum and coke glass. It was that late ride back to Grandma's house where she decided she would never take a drink in her life for any reason, at anytime, anywhere for anything. She never wanted her future children to feel trapped by curse words held together with cruelty all because for a third time, she had forgotten that the girls had already eaten dinner.

"Is it like this all the time when she drinks?" Jenny's tears had dried like plaster to her face. She still managed to speak through the quivering.

"Yes, Jenny. Every single time." She avoided eye contact when she whispered her response. Her attention was focused on the darkness through the window that reflected her life at that moment. "I am never going to drink," she said, speaking to herself in a barely audible tone. She didn't know what questions she would face when she opened the door, but she knew they would be there. She also knew that she would have no definitive answers. She would spend the majority of the night awake startling herself with the shadows as the

47

car lights peaked through the room. *When did it become this?* she questioned. Celeste and her mother used to have a great relationship. She remembered going to libraries in different parts of the city and having lunch at Woolworth on Saturday afternoons. There was her introduction to the Civil Rights Movement as her mom talked to her about diner sit-ins. She didn't know what happened to their relationship. All she knew was the schedule. Now not only she was aware, but Jenny was too.

Chapter 2

The schedule continued and Celeste coped the best way she could. She tried to ignore the issues at home by throwing herself into school. Middle school was not as easy as she had hoped. The school work wasn't too hard, but the children made life terrible at times. Celeste was a tall 13-year-old with newly braced teeth, who was also very slender and under developed compared to the other girls in school. "Leste two-backs!" This little name calling gem was given by her best friend, Tyra. It caught on like wild fire and the rest was history.

Celeste's refuge became poetry. What was just a hobby to pass those Friday nights became her day and night and her before and after school release. It was as if she needed the pen and the paper. No one else had the mind to listen to her. Jenny was living in Illinois, at that time, and she saw her less and less. Most of the friends she had in school and in her building, she found hard to trust, and her mother's relationship was null and void. She was seemingly alone.

There was a small glimmer of hope the night that she finally got her menstrual cycle. She was the last of her friends to get it, and she was just relieved that she was actually as normal as everyone else for a change. It was a Saturday night when the epic event occurred.

Sara was mellow and had slept Friday night off for the better part of the day.

Celeste approached her mother gingerly. "Mommy, I got my period." She didn't know what her mother would say to her. Surprisingly, Sara was happy and supportive about the ordeal. She talked to her friend, Ella's mom, to see if she could spend the night. It was fun with movies and ice cream. For the first time in a long time, Celeste smiled sweetly and wholeheartedly. She needed that night for however short it would be. There weren't many moments where she felt special. Only a few people made her feel loved. That evening she was both.

Chapter 3

Her graduation year from middle school from an academic stand point was amazing. However, her home life had deteriorated since the faithful night when Jenny needed to cut her weekend visits short to a dismal ten minutes. Her mother was drinking very heavily. Things got to the point where she wondered if it was just alcohol anymore. Celeste excelled at school. It seemed to go unnoticed to many, but her teachers noticed, and it reflected well on her report card. She even did so well that she was able to participate in the Dream Team. The Dream Team was the academic achievement group that needed to maintain a consistent grade point average of 3.7. It wasn't even for Sara. If Celeste could maintain a 3.7, then she should have a 4.0.

Nothing she did was good enough for her mother. She knew her grandmother was supporting her. In elementary school, Celeste was a part of a lot of active clubs and sports. Cheerleading, basketball, jump rope, accelerated reading, and track and field to name a few. Middle school didn't have the same amenities, and it showed in her expression or lack thereof.

"I have to give the money to Greg, your father's mechanic, for the work he did on the car. Hold the elevator door and don't you move!" Sara yelled at Celeste even though a decent tone would have been acceptable. They were only in a small compact elevator. Celeste hated that elevator. She had come to know it all too well during those faithful Friday nights after leaving Grandma's house. She stood and held the elevator for upwards of thirty minutes. She could see urine and other fluids stuck in the corners along with the dirt and grime.

"This smells like pee," Celeste thought to herself. Her greatest fear was someone would come and see her holding the elevator door alone and she would be helpless. She has no idea what her mother could be doing. After the tenth time with this same tired story, she definitely knew not to believe what she said about Greg. She wasn't even sure if Greg lived in this building, and sure as hell didn't believe her father would have given her the money for her to pay him. "Why couldn't he pay Greg himself?" She had asked her mother that question only one time. Sara cursed Celeste out so badly she never asked the question again. She also never got a direct answer either.

Her father was absent. Not in the sense where he wasn't around. He was very much there without being there. So much that at this point in her life he just might as well remain nameless. Once Sara's drinking got bad, he threw himself into work. That was great for him! He had a refuge. He had peace. He would sleep and eat there. The biggest problem? If he was there at work day in and day out, where was Celeste? Home alone with her mother to fend for herself. The abuse was racking up and getting bad. The family had somewhat known about the drinking issues and no one stepped in to intervene. What would be the point of telling them these details? Celeste was on her own. Other than her homework and poetry, she was left to fend for herself. Her childhood was ripped to shreds and there was no one to turn to. There weren't many she trusted.

"God if you can hear me… please protect me," Celeste prayed. Prayer for her didn't happen too often. Other than Palm Sunday and

Easter, her mother didn't make a big deal about church. Sunday mornings were set aside to clean what would start out as her room and then evolve into cleaning the entire apartment. She knew that God existed, but she was not really sure if He, It, They or She existed for her. Those nights in the elevator she was scared. She figured she might as well try, what does she have to lose now?

Sara exits the apartment as if business as usual. Celeste always wanted to ask her mother what went on behind the door of apartment 302. One Friday night she even let the elevator door go and walked up to the front of the apartment and just stood there. Taking shallow breaths, but breathing nonetheless. She had always thought she would hear loud music, talking, laughter or something audible, but it was silent. The brown door was disgusting. It was filled with just as much grime as the elevator.

She walked so close to the door that her breath blew back in her face. She could never bring herself to ask. She could never bring herself to knock. The fear of knowing was greater than the fear of not knowing. Celeste walked back to the elevator undetected. The elevator was even waiting for her when she pressed the button. It had never moved. It was as God himself held it there for her. There wasn't any other way to explain the fact no tenant in that building had to use the elevator for any amount of time.

Her mother exited the apartment without any idea of Celeste disobeying her. They went home in silence as usual, and Celeste, knowing not to stare at her mother, found refuge in her feet. To look at her could bring conflict. Celeste wanted nothing more than to just make it to Saturday. To just go in her room and close the door drowning out the sounds of her mother rummaging through the night at crazy hours until the alcohol would take hold and send her to her sobering sleep.

Sara put the key in the door and walked in with an attitude. *Maybe the meeting didn't go so well after all,* Celeste thought. She then prepared herself for what would be a very long night.

53

"Bitch, what are you looking at?" Sara screamed at Celeste. *Bitch...* There it goes again. She was called a "bitch" every other day and sometimes on the off days too. It didn't matter what her mother's alcohol content was at the time. She was what she was.

"Nothing Mommy, I am just tired and I want to go to sleep," Celeste responded. Her voice was shaking. She knew what could be in store for her, but she was desperately trying to avoid it. *Maybe I should call Grandma*, she thought. Jenny was visiting again, but she dared not ask if she could spend the night. She was left alone once again to fend for herself.

"You think you are so cute, don't you?" Sara approached Celeste slowly with an evil scowl on her face. You would have thought Celeste was the most disgusting thing Sara had ever seen. There was no love or joy in her eyes. For the first time, Celeste thought her mother hated her.

"No, Mommy. I just want to go to sleep. That's all I want to do." Celeste was actually exhausted. She was barely sleeping these days and the anticipation of Friday nights was the culprit. Sara, at this time (even though Celeste was only thirteen), was shorter than her. Celeste had sprouted and was beginning to mature in her looks as a beautiful young woman. Sara wasn't a fan of these changes. Sara was jealous.

Sara had been jealous of Celeste for years. How could she not be? Here was a person that had her whole life ahead of her and had made none of the mistakes her mother had made. Celeste had a clean slate that Sara just didn't have anymore. Celeste had the nerve to take the best attributes of Sara and make them even better. How dare Celeste be better, smarter, taller, prettier, and wiser than Sara was at such a young age.

"You ain't got no titties. Are you fucking, Bitch?" Sara spewed at Celeste. Celeste didn't know what to do. She was so insecure about her body that all she wanted to do in that instant was cry, but she knew that she couldn't show that kind of emotion. She had to take whatever Sara was giving her. She had to make it to Sunday. She was definitely a virgin, and to call out her under development in such a mean-spirited way hurt her feelings. Celeste had yet to even be into boys. She didn't think any liked her because of her lack of development. There were so many other girls that were in real bras in school. She could have worn a tank top, but she wanted the strap to show in certain clothes so she could appear to be like everyone else.

"No, Mommy. I am not having sex. I am a virgin," Celeste pleaded to her mother. The tears she fought so hard to hide had begun to slide down her cheeks.

"You're a fucking liar, you hoe! You are a goddamn hoe!" As Sara screamed those hateful words, she swung at Celeste. Celeste didn't see it coming. She felt it before she knew what had really happened. It wasn't often that Sara resorted in physical violence. She had preferred name calling and other obscenities. Her right cheek stung and her heart was pounding. As a natural reaction, she swung back. It was the first-time Celeste had ever defended herself from her mom in any way. She hit her mother back harder than the blow she received. Until that moment, she had not realized how much she had grown and how much stronger she really was. Sara glared at her. "You Bitch! How dare you put your hands on me? I am your mother. 'Thou shall honor thy mother and thou father'..." Celeste couldn't believe that her mother was actually quoting the Bible knowing the last time they went to church was on Easter Sunday, especially on a Friday night.

Celeste walked in her room, closed the door and got ready to go to bed. She had assumed that was the end of it. She thought everything would calm down. She had done enough, more than enough to stop the abuse. She never wanted to raise her hand to her mom. She still loved her mother even if, for some reason, her mother no longer loved her. *What did she do that was so wrong? Where was her father? Why was she always alone? God, are you there?* Celeste took her thoughts and laid down with them in her all too quiet room. There was no peace there.

The silence was interrupted by Sara storming into Celeste's room in rage with no comparison to anything Celeste had ever witnessed before. The fury in her eyes was so piercing that Celeste knew the fight would not be over and she had to defend herself. Sara grabbed Celeste by her hair and dragged her out of bed while trying to rip off her scarf. "I will pull the hair out your head! I hate you! You stupid bitch! How dare you put your hands on me!! I am your mother!" Celeste was being dragged across her wooden floor. She found the strength to get up and made the fight even. Other than playing with her cousins, this would be her first fight.

"Stop it, Mommy! I don't want to do this!" Celeste screamed, but it was too late. Sara had kicked her in the stomach. Celeste kicked her back and slapped her. Sara flew into the nearby wall and almost knocked herself out. Sara got up and tried to kick Celeste again. The fact that Sara was drunk was to Celeste's advantage. Her fighting strategy was sloppy and she had no balance. Sara spent the better part of the fight trying to keep herself up.

The agility of Celeste was too much for Sara to compete with in the end. Sara tried to hit Celeste over and over, but she kept missing her. Celeste didn't hit her mother again. There was no need to. As long as she kept ducking and running, she would be okay. Celeste was tired, but she knew she would outlast Sara. She had to just keep moving.

Celeste hurried to put on her sneakers and ran out of the apartment. She didn't have a quarter for the payphone to call anyone. It was midnight. She was alone. She was scared. She was thirteen. Her grandmother lived thirty minutes away by bus. She had no bus money. Celeste walked. She walked under the 1994 New York night sky. It was July. It was warm. There was a surprisingly sweet breeze in the air. She was scared, but not scared enough to go back to her mother's home. It was Saturday now. Saturdays were always so much better. Friday nights were the bad nights. *Why couldn't I just make it to Saturday morning?* she thought to herself. She would have gotten up and made herself breakfast, watched a little TV, and did some cleaning. Maybe even finish folding her laundry.

Instead, she walked alone from one end of the Bronx to the next. No one bothered her. No one asked if she was okay. There were no police officers. There were no homeless people. It was as if the path was cleared just for her. The park where she had spent her birthday and shared so many smiles while singing her favorite songs seemed so quiet now. The trees whistled in the wind. The bugs fluttered by the light poles, illuminating the sidewalk. "God, are you there? Have You ever been there?" She had to question it. She just had to ask.

Reaching her grandmother's house by 2:45 a.m., she reluctantly rang the doorbell. Her grandmother opened the door. "Child, what are you doing here this time of morning? Where is your mother? Oh, my God! Are you okay?" *Child.* She wasn't a child anymore. She didn't respond. She walked in and draped her body onto her grandmother and cried. Jenny and her mother woke up. Celeste told them what happened. She was surprised to know the family had no clue she was missing in the first place. Sara never bothered to call anyone. There was no concern for the young girl's whereabouts.

Jenny tearfully hugged Celeste. Celeste didn't have any more words to say. She lay in Jenny's lap. *Child.* That was how her grandmother described her. She didn't know that girl anymore. She didn't know herself anymore. She had changed. She had to change. She had to survive. That was the last thought before drifting to sleep.

She could hear her grandmother and aunts yelling at her mother the next morning. She was surprised her mother was up that early. On a normal Saturday, her mother wouldn't wake up until about two in the afternoon. It was 8:00 a.m. then.

"I want to see my child!" Sara screamed from the other room. "You people can't keep me from MY daughter. I will call the cops on you. Just you wait. You all are kidnapping!"

"Kidnapping? This child walked here in the middle of the night by herself because you abused her. She didn't just hit you. She defended herself. You can't just beat on her. You can't just treat this child like this," Celeste's grandmother retorted. The screams from the next room felt as if the house had no walls. It was so loud and clear that Jenny and Celeste heard everything.

Celeste thought to herself, *there goes that word again*. That day she was finally protected. Her family didn't allow it and Sara left. Later on, her father came by. She refused to see him and went back to sleep. A few weeks prior she had walked in on her father choking her mother. At the time, she judged him and vowed no man would ever put her hands on her and see the light of day. Now all of a sudden, she thought maybe there was reason for the altercation. She knows first-hand what Sara was capable of doing. Eventually, she knew she would have to return home. She knew that her protective shield would fizzle and no real change would come about. And that is what happened two days later. Her father came and told her it was time to go home. *Home.* Another word she had no clue as to why people were tossing around as if it were real. She simply got her things and gave her grandmother a hug goodbye.

"I love you, child," her grandmother said in a somber voice.

"I love you too, Grandma, but I am not a *child* anymore."

Chapter 4

Celeste secretly resented her family for allowing her mother to take her back home. She didn't think they fought hard enough for her. *Maybe I am not worth the fight. Maybe I am not worth the effort. Maybe I deserve this.* After a while, Celeste didn't make a big deal out of anything. After her first night with Sara, she made the family aware and no one did anything.

She figured she might as well get used to what life would have until she found a way to leave. She would never run to her family again. She would keep this to herself and deal with it the best way she knew how. She would keep this not-so-much-a secret private and to herself. If she could just get good grades and keep herself occupied, then she knew she could keep her mind off of what was going on at home and be okay. At least she would be okay for a little while.

In her eyes, not many people loved her. *If they loved me, they would protect me.* There wasn't much for her to do or any place she could go. Her mother kept beating her. She stopped fighting back. She would find ways to defend herself passively. Celeste would sleep with four scarves at night to protect her hair. Sara would always threaten to shave Celeste's hair while she slept. That was her favorite threat.

As time went on, the schedule became more detailed. It would depend not on when her mother drank, but who she was drinking with. If she drank with her aunt and at her grandmother's house, she knew she would pee on herself in the elevator. They would also be alone long enough for there to be physical violence against Celeste. If she drank with her next-door neighbor, she knew she would be in for a long night, but her mother would be too preoccupied to deal with her. She would be too busy entertaining and providing the money for the alcohol. When Sara stopped buying, they would stop drinking and go home.

She didn't like the fact of Mary, the next-door neighbor, coming over to hang out with her mom on those nights. Sometimes, the visits didn't end on Fridays. Mary didn't work and had nine kids living next door in a two-bedroom apartment. Celeste was, however, best friends with her daughter, Sasha. Sasha and Celeste were one year apart. Sasha was very much aware of Sara's alcohol abuse. Unfortunately, her mother was abusing it also.

It was different for Mary, though. Mary didn't work and lived off of welfare. They had lied to the state saying that her husband, Earl, was estranged, but he was very much a part of the picture. If the state found out Earl was still living there, they would be cut off of from their benefits. Celeste hated the scam and thought her mother should find another friend. Mary was always nice to Celeste, though. She just thought she was using her mom for her paycheck.

Sara would buy all of Mary's kids snacks and other things when they went to the store. Celeste was the only child, and very rarely, did they offer her anything. These were the little things Celeste noticed but dare not speak on. She knew she would be beaten if she ever brought it up and didn't think it was worth it in the least.

Chapter 5

Sometimes Sasha would hear the commotion in Celeste's room. It wasn't hard to hide the fights. The yelling and screaming was so loud that anyone on their side of the eighteenth floor of their building could hear it. It didn't help that Celeste and Sasha's room had an adjoining wall that connected the two apartments. To make the matter even more embarrassing, Sasha shared her room with all of her brothers and sisters.

Sasha had her own problems to deal with within her family. Not only was she the oldest girl in a family of nine kids and had a mother and father who both abused alcohol, but her father was abusive to her mother as well. Celeste stopped going over there as much after the incident happened while she was visiting her friend. She wasn't sure what Mary did wrong to Earl, but out of nowhere, he leapt over the sofa placed in the middle of the living room and punched her in the face. It was like something out of the arcade game, *Street Fighter*, that she had seen Ryu or Ken do. They existed as if they were a couple of the main characters in the game.

Celeste was so devastated she didn't want to go back. Either they would go to Celeste's room and hang out there or they would sit in the doorways of each other's apartments and whisper. It was that time when Celeste realized that she wasn't the only one going through a rough life. That no one was perfect. If they were, they surely didn't live in 1680 Minnieford Ave.

Sara, at this point, had no boundaries and the fury against her daughter mounted. Celeste never understood what she did to deserve the treatment. She blamed herself for the treatment and told herself that she wasn't a good kid. What else could be the cause of this? Why would anyone want to drink themselves to death? That was what she figured her mother was doing.

Sara was too busy trying to keep up with her nonworking friends to realize that her life was crumbling all around her. She didn't care. Celeste desperately hoped someone would intervene, but they never did. She was left to deal with it on her own. Fighting for her peace had not worked. It only brought her more shame in the end. By this time, Celeste had been called a bitch more than she had been called her own name.

She remembered one day she was at her grandmother's house and one of those don't-do-drugs commercials came on. It was the iconic one with the narrator cracking the egg in the hot pan. The egg sizzled as it cooked. The narrator then asked the viewers, "Do you want to get high?" She distinctively heard Sara say, "Yes." Had no one else in the crowded room heard her mother admit that she wanted to get high right then and there after coming home from work? The narrator continued "This is your brain," referring to the egg. "This is your brain on drugs," now referring to the egg cracked and being cooked sunny side up in the pan. "Any questions?" Just that quickly the thirty-second commercial was complete. Celeste had so many questions that she would never ask.

She wanted to disappear. She wanted to fade somewhere in the background where no one knew who she was. She imagined running away a few times, but she had never been a street kid. She was the little girl that made good grades in school and did what people expected of her. Even though nothing she did was right in the eyes of her mother. To her, that equated to her family as well. No one was reaching out to support her. Why should she trust them?

After everything, her aunts and uncles still let her mother babysit the younger cousins. This always baffled Celeste. She loved her baby cousins, yes, but it wasn't Sara who was taking care of them. Celeste would make sure the baby girls were fed, bathed, clothed and entertained. If Sara could barely take care of Celeste, how could she take care of anyone else's kids? It was during this time that Celeste's own maternal instincts would take flight. It didn't matter her young age. She had a responsibility to protect them in the way that she was not.

Celeste fought hard to maintain the appearance that everything was fine. As the sober one in the house, that was her additional duty. She secretly loved compliments. She didn't get them often, so when she did get them, she would cherish them and make them last forever. She would take those compliments and turn them into poetry. Rereading her own rhythmic lines gave her soul the peace it yearned for. It was confirmation that she was able to do something right. *One day I want to write a book of poems*, Celeste thought to herself. Throughout all of the stress and turmoil, she was still able to dream.

CAMILLE

I know you aren't good for me
I know this
I am not stupid
But you are all I have
Here with me
For me
So I will just
Sit down beside you
Quietly
Sing myself songs
Drowning out the sound of your voice
I will let my own sweetness engulf my ears
Hiding my tears
My fear
Wrapped in lyrics
And rhymes
Soliloquy
Poetry
My destiny
Rests in words
Not yours
But the chords
Symphonies
Engage within me
I cannot hear you
You are drowned by my beauty
Hidden from you to see
My song
It's all mine
You can't take it from me

Chapter 1

"Do you want to come outside and hang with us Camille?" Karen asked. Camille was excited for some reason. Even though Camille didn't really want to go, she knew she didn't want to stay in the house either.

"Fine, I will go," she replied with as much excitement as she possibly could. She didn't know why Karen wanted her to go, and to be honest, she didn't want to find out. Karen always had something up her sleeve, and Camille... well she wasn't in the mood for it.

"I didn't have to pry you from your mom's house. You never want to come out. Are you feeling okay?" Karen asked with a hint of actual care and concern or she was just being nosey.

Camille didn't feel like trying to figure out which one it was so she lied. "I just felt like going out today, that's all." Even though that wasn't all. She needed to get out of the house and get some air and to figure out what she was going to do with her life. She had just turned fourteen and would be starting high school in September. She had been accepted to a very high academic school and knew she had a lot of work ahead of her. "So, what are you so excited about, Karen? I am really not in the mood for any of your shenanigans today." As soon as the words left Camille's lips, Karen had walked to the basketball court to approach a boy. *Oh, gosh there is always some boy*, Camille thought. She didn't remember seeing this one around though, as she did the others. He was alone on the court shooting his basketball. *I think I remember him walking a dog a couple times*, she thought to herself.

Karen was the type of girl that had this sweet and innocent persona, but in actuality, that wasn't the case at all. She had a devious streak that went far beyond the *Baby-Sitters Club* books that she read day in and day out. Camille didn't understand it one bit. Karen had a seemingly normal life, but then again so did she. She tried not to judge anyone, because she already knew from her own experiences that people have many faces. Karen developed a bad habit of stealing things out of corner stores. It started out as a bad habit of taking a bag of potato chips or a Hostess cake. It soon escalated to clothes and other accessories. She would even offer to steal things for Camille. Camille always declined and would pay for it herself.

Karen interrupted her thoughts. "Camille meet Stanley; Stanley meet Camille."

Oh crap, what is this about? Why is she introducing me to this boy? Camille's thoughts were racing. She didn't know what Karen was up to, but she should not have trusted her to begin with. She was stuck.

Stanley seemed nice in the first fifteen seconds of their meeting. He wasn't very tall. He was actually shorter than her by about two or three inches. He said a very flat, "Hi." He seemed just as thrilled to meet Camille as she him. The feeling is definitely mutual.

"Well, you guys should talk and get to know each other. Bye!" Karen walked toward the exit to the park.

"Uhhhh, where are you *going*, Karen?" By this time, Camille was annoyed, and Karen didn't bother to answer. She smiled and walked away.

So, there they were. Stanley and Camille, quiet and awkward and annoyed. Well, Camille was annoyed. Stanley continued to play his game. "So, can you play? Do you shoot?" Stanley asked Camille breaking the silence.

"I can. I just don't anymore. I never was very good at dribbling, but I can shoot and my defense is really good." The last thing Camille wanted to do was to play anything. She had her future on her mind and he was not it. She hadn't played basketball in about three years when she was on her school's team. She was a great shooter and defensive player.

Stanley bounce passed her the ball. She caught it, stopped, shot and made the basket. The nets on all the basketball hoops were long gone. It was nothing, but a rim and backboard left. He ran to get the rebound and passed it to her again. She scored again. He challenged her to a game of H.O.R.S.E. H.O.R.S.E. is a simple game where at least two people can challenge the next while shooting in different areas of the court and in a particular way. As long as the challenger makes the shot the opponent must complete the task. If the opponent misses the opportunity, he or she has to add a letter to their tally. Whoever spells H.O.R.S.E. first, loses. After a few minutes, she beat him and he was impressed. She didn't realize that the sun was soon to set.

"Hey, what time do you have to be home?" Stanley, also 14 years old, asked Camille.

"Ummm, actually I don't know. I never have a curfew." After the words left Camille's mouth, she noticed how odd that was. A 14-year-old in New York City not having a curfew.

"Wait, you don't have a curfew?" Stanley was really shocked at this revelation. Either Camille was a good girl or her mother didn't care. After they spent the afternoon together, he concluded that she was a good girl.

Camille never had a curfew because Camille never went out. There was no need to monitor what didn't need to be. She was a homebody and always had been. She would rather stay in the house and make an arts and craft project than deal with the foolishness her friends were doing. Camille's mother and father often pushed for her to be more sociable. What Camille didn't bother to tell her parents was that most of the kids they wanted her to hang out with were smoking weed and drinking alcohol. She chose to separate herself from all of those things. She found solace in her home.

Stanley was cute. He had what he had told people was a birthmark on his face, but it was really a burn mark from when he was an infant. His mother was negligent in watching him and he fell between the radiator and the wall. He had a very dark complexion, braids in his hair and broad shoulders. His smile was sweet, and he looked like he was becoming more comfortable with hanging out with Camille. Camille was actually enjoying his company as well.

Camille could see Karen crossing the street back to the court. "Oh, wow! You guys are still here? You know you two make a cute couple." It had never dawned on Camille that this was the plan all along. She could never understand why Karen needed to meddle in everyone's business. "I mean try it out for a little bit. If it doesn't work out, it doesn't. What do y'all have to lose?" Karen was laying it on thick.

Camille didn't understand why Karen hadn't tried to date Stanley herself since she thought he was so great. Karen was always into some boy. She wouldn't say anything though. Camille wasn't mean and spiteful, but the thought did cross her mind.

Stanley and Camille looked at each other and shrugged their shoulders. From that moment, they were inseparable. She knew she wasn't allowed to have an official boyfriend until she was sixteen, but she didn't think her mom and dad would mind too much. Camille was right. Stanley was allowed to come by for dinner the next week. Her dad cooked dinner for them and made sweet Italian sausage with peppers, onions and fresh cut fries.

Camille's mom, Aleida, did embarrass her completely when she falsely attempted to moonwalk out of the living room on the carpet. If the earth could have just opened up and swallowed her whole at that very moment, I would have rejoiced for her sake. Aleida looked more like she was going to break both her ankles more than she was doing a celestial anything. Michael Jackson would not have been pleased. The visit was pleasant and turned into an everyday thing. Camille didn't know too much about Stanley's home life other than his mom had a boyfriend he didn't like. Stanley lived across the street from her on the first floor. When they would walk by on the way to the store, she would hear yelling and screaming that, seemingly, came from a man and a woman. From the look on Stanley's face she could tell that was his mom.

When Camille finally did meet Stanley's mom, she wasn't too nice to her. She didn't know what she had done, but the meeting was not as warm as the meeting had been for Stanley and her parents. She wasn't offered anything to drink or a seat to sit down and was asked nothing more about herself other than her name.

The apartment seamed drab and dark. It was clean, but didn't have many furnishings. Stanley's room just consisted of twin bunk beds, a small dresser and a TV. Camille didn't feel comfortable there and didn't think she would spend much time there either. The introductions only took about five minutes. She had told her mother that they would be gone a while, but they quickly returned. They were quite comfortable going to her apartment. Stanley accepted that Camille was a homebody and either they were on the basketball court shooting around or they were in her house hanging out. Aleida didn't mind because she was able to keep an eye on them and she knew exactly where they were.

Chapter 2

They had been dating for about 3 months, and Stanley had not kissed Camille. The most contact they had was the hug he would give when he would leave and go home. By now, the whole neighborhood had knowledge of Camille and Stanley's relationship. One day, Karen and Camille were on their way back from the store. Karen lived in Camille's building on the seventh floor. The elevator stopped on the third floor. Barry, another boy, and Clarence, his friend, joined them on the elevator.

"Camille, you go with that boy, Stanley now, right?" Barry asked. Barry had never spoken to her before and for the life of her she didn't understand why he would be speaking to her now.

"Yes, Barry, I am with Stanley now. Why are you asking me that? You don't talk to me ever." Just then Barry leaped onto Camille. Karen was in the other corner stunned and started screaming at Barry. Camille was stuck in the corner with Barry as he was trying to force her to kiss him. Camille had to fight him off with all her strength. Barry was much bigger than Camille. He was much taller and stronger than she was, even though they were the same age. Finally, she pushed him so hard to the other side that the elevator shook. The last thing they wanted was to be stuck with them after what had happened. The boys angrily got off and ran down the hall. Camille and Karen were visibly upset. She was happy that no one was home when she walked into her apartment.

"Oh, my God! I can't believe that just happened!" Karen vocalized her feelings a little too loudly for Camille's taste at the moment, but she understood her excitement. She didn't want her mother to hear what had just happened.

"Hey, Karen, don't mention this to Stanley. I don't want anyone to know. Please shut up about it." Camille knew that eventually word would get out, but it didn't have to be today. Besides, Camille knew that Stanley had a mean streak about him. From their previous conversations, she knew Stanley was a fighter. He had never been mean to her, but she saw him be not so nice to others. Especially to those who weren't nice to her. That was the day that he was supposed to see his father in jail. His father, Big Stanley, had been locked up in Upstate NY for years. She knew that after their reunion he would not want to hear that some guy tried to kiss his girlfriend. The same girlfriend he had yet to kiss himself.

The next day Stanley came by Camille's house. Karen was there also. She was nervous at first, but Karen didn't mention the horrid elevator incident. That put her at ease after a while.

"Are you okay? You seem like something is wrong," Stanley asked Camille. He could tell something was off about her, but he was thinking it was because of him going to the prison to visit his father. Karen grew very quiet when he asked the question, which wasn't like her at all.

"Nope, I'm good. Are you hungry?" Camille knew she could always change the subject with food. Stanley was always hungry. Karen left shortly after that which relieved Camille. She wasn't sure, but it didn't seem as though he ate at home. If he was eating at home, it surely wasn't enough. She had only met his mother that one time and would see her boyfriend randomly walking the dog in the neighborhood. When she did see him, he barely said "Hello" and acted as if he didn't know who she was. It wasn't too bad. He would treat Stanley the same way.

"My dad wants to meet you," Stanley said a little too casually eating the burger Camille had just made for him.

"Your dad is in prison. You want me to go to the jail and meet him?" Camille didn't like this plan much and it made her uncomfortable. She was aware that had been Stanley's life for almost all his life, but it was not hers. The most she had seen of a prison was what she saw in the movies or on the TV show, *Cops*. That was about as close as she ever wanted to get. Besides, she doubted her mother would allow her to go anyway. The thought was quickly dismissed.

Everything was calm until a month later. Karen and Camille were walking down the street and saw Barry from a distance. Camille clammed up noticeably. Tray, Stanley's friend, saw the exchange. He asked if she was alright and Karen blabbed the whole ordeal in full detail as if it was burning inside her to let out. Against Camille's protest, Tray went right to Stanley's apartment to tell him what happened without hesitation.

From the outside window Camille could hear the commotion along with Stanley's mother, Josephine, screaming at him. "You better claim what's yours. You better whoop that boy's ass. Don't come back here without doing just that. We ain't from the Bronx. We from Brooklyn! Show them Brooklyn!" Stanley had told Camille stories of how he would have to fight every day in Brooklyn for one reason or another. That was part of the reason they moved to the Bronx. He was getting in trouble there with his father's history in the neighborhood. Although Camille didn't see Stanley as a bad kid, it didn't take much to turn that corner and go back to his old ways.

Camille calmed Stanley. She was his peace. She was the one that calmed the rage that he fought to keep down inside of him. He had basketball and he had Camille. She knew that much. She also knew anyone that messed with her would feel the wrath she was able to quell inside of him. Not that day though. That day Stanley went outside with one mission. Find Barry and beat his ass.

Camille ran behind him. She needed to at least try to calm him down. She had never seen him so angry and didn't like it one bit. "No, Stanley. It's okay. You don't have to do this! Just let it go!"

"Did he try to kiss you? Did he try to force you to kiss him? Did you have to fight him off? I haven't kissed you yet! Did he try to kiss you when you haven't had your first true kiss yet?!?" Stanley was furious and yelling at Camille at the top of his lungs. It was then the people around realized the severity of the situation. It wasn't just about the kiss. It was also about the principle. Barry had tried to steal something special from Camille, and Stanley was going to protect it. That was the first-time Stanley had ever yelled at Camille. He knew he had hurt her feelings, but he had to. "Go upstairs now!" The vigor in his voice Camille reluctantly obliged. She tearfully made her way home worried about what would happen next.

Hours had passed and she could hear commotion coming from the elevator. It was Karen and Claudette running to her apartment. She opened the door and they told her that Stanley and Barry were in the lobby, and she needed to get down there quickly. She didn't care about the instructions from Stanley at that moment. She ran to the same elevator where the violation had occurred. She pressed L for the lobby. Camille's nerves were on edge and she wished they would calm down. The elevator wasn't moving fast enough so she jumped out and took the stairs the rest of the way with her friends following closely behind her. By the time she got to the lobby, the damage was done. Stanley had waited for Barry to get him. He had been looking for him for over six hours. Barry had a large group of boys with him. Stanley didn't care; he only had two. From what she had heard, the exchange was brief.

"Did you try to kiss my girl?" Stanley asked Barry. Stanley stepped to him even and calmly. He didn't yell or make any sudden moves at the time. He wanted an answer. He wanted confirmation that this boy had violated his girlfriend.

75

"I don't know maybe. Who's your girl?" Barry replied with a sly grin. Barry had heard all day that Stanley was looking for him. He went out of his way to avoid home for as long as he could, but it was his curfew. He had no choice but to face whatever punishment that waited for him at his building. Barry was bigger than Stanley, but Barry was aware of Stanley's strength from playing basketball against him. He couldn't beat him.

"Don't play with me. Did you try to kiss Camille?" Stanley's fist was balled up tight. His breathing intensified. It would only be a matter of time before Stanley struck him.

"Oh, that bitch! Fuck that bitch!" Barry was barely able to finish his sentence. Stanley punched him in the face and then lifted him up and threw him into the wall. The entire wall was made of glass, and shattered with the force of Stanley's rage. It was then that everyone just stopped and stared. A piece of glass cut Stanley near his eye. Someone ran to get his mother. He didn't care. He didn't see the blood. He just kept beating on Barry. Finally, it stopped. Finally, it was over.

Camille made it to the lobby and saw the crowd of people. She heard small chatter about broken glass, and Stanley being cut. She ran outside to find him bloody. "Oh my God!" Camille exclaimed.

"I thought I told you to go upstairs," Stanley said to Camille much calmer now. The rage was released. He was holding a rag over his eye.

"I will go to the hospital with you!" Camille wanted to do something. She wanted to help in some way.

"No, it's late. Your mom will be worried. I will call you later." He hugged her and walked off as if nothing had happened.

"That boy is crazy." She had heard someone say that, amongst other things, as she returned to the lobby and everyone just looked at her. She knew at the moment no one would mess with her. She knew at that moment she was protected unlike any other time in her life. Karen and Claudette agreed with the crowd.

"Damn Cam," Claudette said. "He smashed a whole person through glass for you. He really might be crazy. I guess as long as you stay on his good side you will always be okay. Something is telling me you won't have any problems with anyone else around here."

The next day, Stanley came by to see her. The first thing he did was apologize for yelling at her. He apologized to her mom and dad for breaking the glass wall in the building. He had a private chat with her father about what happened.

He sat down next to her and smiled. "I love you, Camille, and I am not going to let anyone hurt you."

"I love you too, Stanley. You scared me yesterday," Camille said to him in a soft calming tone. *"That boy is crazy!"* The words rang out as if they were just spoken. A memory she would not forget.

"You won't ever see me that angry again. As long as no one else tries to hurt you." He added that slight disclaimer. He gave her a hug and they watched TV for a while. He needed twelve stitches over his eye. Barry never laid a hand on Stanley and he never retaliated.

After the incident, Barry never spoke to Camille again. If she was on the same sidewalk, he would cross the street. If she was on the elevator, he would wait for the next one. If she was on the basketball court, he would go to the other court. Barry avoided Camille at all costs. This was life now and how it always would be. Camille felt protected. No one had every stood up for her in that way before. She didn't like the tactic, but it was still appreciated. She was honest when she shared her first "I love you" with him. She was thankful she had him in her life.

Chapter 3

After the incident, they managed to spend even more time together. As if it was humanly possible to do so. They had just started high school and Stanley was having trouble with some of his studies. Camille was having issues with math. She was never good with numbers and the new material was too much for her to grasp. They decided to tutor each other on their weak subjects. That was when she realized one of Stanley's many secrets. He was not a good reader. It turned out that he could barely read at all. Camille had heard of kids being passed through grades just to get them out of the class, but it was the first time she had ever seen it for herself. This is why Stanley focused so much on numbers. Words just didn't make sense and he didn't have the patience to figure it out.

Camille didn't make fun of him. She didn't tease or joke about it. Two to three times a week they would go to the library and practice. They wouldn't go to the neighborhood library, but the one a little further away. That way people who knew him wouldn't be there to see him reading the children's books. It didn't take him long to grasp reading. He just needed someone to take the time to help him. Camille had been reading since she was 3 years old. Her mother, aunt, or cousin was always there to help her with things like that. She realized in those few months that Stanley didn't have many people that looked out for him in this world. She had prepared herself to be just that.

They had been together now for about six months. The incident with Barry was behind them. His eye had healed. The neighborhood knew not to mess with Camille. And Stanley was secretly reading much better now. His mother, Jayla, was busy bragging about his math scores, yet she knew nothing about her son not being able to read basic words or formulate a proper sentence. Camille understood more and more how detached his family really was as time went on. However, soon he would be reading his grade level. One day after the library, Stanley was taking Camille home. It had been a long day for the both of them. Since Camille went to school in Manhattan and she traveled two hours a day to get to and from there, Stanley would meet her at the train station. Instead of taking the bus home, they would take the long walk together and stop at the library on the way.

On this particular day, he hugged her. The hug itself wasn't rare. It is what they did often, but this time he didn't let go and she didn't pull away. It was just then he placed his face in front of hers and slowly kissed her. She kissed him back. It was her first, and it was magical even though she had nothing really to compare it with. She would never forget it. He ended it with a kiss on the cheek and a smile. He walked her to her door, gave her another hug, and went home.

Camille spent just as much time with Stanley on the phone. Sometimes that is how they would study. Especially on the days where he would say he couldn't make it to the library. She didn't understand why someone would be prohibited from going there, but sometimes Jayla wouldn't let him. After the first time it happened, Camille made the decision to check out two of the same books. This was so just in case he couldn't make it, they would still be able to study. He was doing much better, and he had no one but Camille to thank. He too started writing poetry and lyrics to songs, which was great because now they had even more in common. They would sometimes switch their poetry books for the day just to read what the other was feel.

Chapter 4

As time went on, Stanley and Camille's relationship grew. They started going to church together. They were recruited to join the youth choir at a local church. It was good for them to be involved in a positive activity. They were both gifted musically. Singing in the choir helped Camille find the depths of her vocal range. She had known for years that she could sing, but it was her secret. She wasn't sure why she kept it to herself. Stanley was a great song writer for his age. The choir allowed them the freedom to express life in a way nothing else had up until that point.

Camille was one of two sopranos along with Karen. Claudette was the alto of the choir. Larry, the pastor's grandson and pianist, along with Stanley and Stanley's best friend, Matt, were the tenors. Matt also doubled as the choir director. He was the oldest of the group. This was the core of the choir. There were other members that had come and gone, but at the heart, this was it.

The group was very close knit. Most Sundays, the group (with the exception of Larry) would spend the day with Camille while she cooked brunch. It was as if she ran a restaurant. She made everything to order. Omelets, pancakes, French toast, muffins. It didn't matter.

What they wanted she made happily while dancing to Goodie Mob's song, *Soul Food*. Those were her best days. Those were her best times.

As for Camille and Stanley, if they were not at school, the basketball court, and if not the court, then Camille's couch. They spent a lot of time at church because they were in charge of the youth. There weren't many members. There were times when the choir, which had spent the entire week practicing their selections, would only have the angels to sing to on Sunday morning. On occasion, their parents would come to hear them, but that was normally only during special occasions. As baffling as it was, it wasn't the adults dragging the kids to church. Instead, it was the kids trying to get the parents to attend.

The pastors of the church, better known as the Browns, were known in the neighborhood for being anything but holy. But as the Bible says, who are we to judge? The teens liked the family atmosphere that came along with being members. Even if they were the only members. Slowly, the church grew. The small Sunday morning service that was held in the building's community center on the second floor was about to move to their own private location. There would be no more hauling furniture and Bibles up and down the stairs before and after service. In order for that to happen, the youth had to raise money, paint, and help decorate, and they were happy to do it. Each of them was going through their own personal teenage trials and the church was the safe haven.

Camille left to go on vacation with her aunt, uncle and baby cousins to Disney World. She was to be gone for two weeks. This was the longest time her and Stanley had been apart since they started dating the previous summer. Before she left, everything was as it was. Everything was just right and she was happy. They were happy. It was upon her return that everything went upside down.

She had tried to call Stanley a couple times when she was away, but his mother always said he was busy and couldn't come to the phone. She knew she wasn't telling the truth because Jayla didn't like her. During her vacation, they had only spoken twice. During both conversations, she found herself asking him if he was okay. She could hear something different in his voice. Camille knew Stanley so well. She had no idea why he wouldn't be honest with her. It was almost as if he had become uninterested in her that quickly.

Camille was now home and saw Stanley on the basketball court. She was blindsided by another neighborhood boy. "Oh, I guess now that you back he won't be spending time with Janet... Hahaha." Did she hear him say he was spending time with Janet? Janet was a girl that had joined the choir a couple months back. Camille had been very nice to her and taught her the cues and the songs even though Janet was an alto. Through the choir, Camille found out she could sing both parts.

Why would Stanley be spending time with her? She questioned to herself walking up to him as he gave her a half hug.

"Wow, you're dark." The first thing Stanley noticed was Camille's Florida tan. Not the fact that they had not seen or spoken to each other for two weeks, but rather that her skin had darkened.

This alarmed Camille. He had not ever taken this tone with her before. "So, what? So are you. What's your problem? I have a tan. Florida is hot you know? Besides, I like my tan. Thank you very much!"

"Nothing is my problem. When did you get back?" Stanley asked nonchalantly.

"Stanley, I was due back today. Remember, I told you what day I was to land." Camille was confused. Stanley was aware of her whole life schedule. If anyone knew when she was due to return, it was him. This was not the boyfriend she had left. Why was he acting this way? *Doesn't he care if I had a good time on my trip?*

Bible study was in thirty minutes. She left the court to get ready. She headed to the church and saw Stanley laughing and talking to Janet. At that moment, she knew what happened. She walked right up to him and said, "So what is this about?"

"Nothing. You left and she stepped in. Next time don't leave. Someone else just might take your spot!" Stanley said with an attitude.

She had only seen this version of him when he interacted with other people. He had never acted this way with her in the one year they were together.

Camille was floored and hurt. "Next time? There won't be a next time. Go away from me!" She walked away at a fast pace. Mainly because she was crying. She could hear her father's advice ring in her ears. *Never let them see you cry*. It's what he told her when she had their first conversation about dating and relationships. The rules were simple:

1. *Never let them see you cry.*
2. *Never go out without your hair combed and looking your best. Especially if you are going to see your ex along the way.*
3. *You are raised to be a good woman. You are going to get your heart broken. You are what we guys call "wife material". The wives are normally the ones that get hurt the most.*
4. *Men are not as expressive as woman so take your time. A man may not say it much with his words, but he will show you in his actions. Trust that.*
5. *You're a smart woman. Trust your gut instincts. If your gut tells you to leave, it's over, or he's cheating, then you're probably right.*
6. *If a man is not showing you all the attention, then it's probably because the attention has gone somewhere else. Don't stick around for that shit. Leave. You can do better.*

Stanley didn't run after her. "If she wants to leave, then fine," he said shrugging his shoulders. He walked off with Janet in the opposite direction.

Claudette and Karen were in church waiting for Camille. Everyone had heard the news about her and Stanley. The argument had taken place by the pizza shop across the street from the church. Matt didn't say much to Camille other than he was sorry. Matt was still

Stanley's best friend. He was caught between a rock and a hard place. He knew about the Janet saga and told Stanley he was being dumb.

Everything changed after that. Camille stuck with the choir and Stanley hardly showed up. She needed her choir and her Bible to get her through it. She would see Stanley just about every day and she would not say a word. Her first broken heart by a boy and she didn't know what she had done wrong. Camille didn't show her sadness to her friends or her family. She didn't want anyone running back and telling him anything. If she cried, it was in the shower. She spent even more time in her room. Mainly blasting Brandy's big hit at the time, *Only Broken Hearted*. Pretty fitting for her situation.

Finally, Stanley approached her when she was going to the corner store a little too late for her liking. They had a huge argument in the middle of the street. The real issue was that other boys in the neighborhood realized that Camille was single. He didn't like that they were plotting to get her since he ended things on a terrible note. Camille was very pretty. She was growing even taller and her looks were maturing. She had a very small figure and a statuesque appearance. She wasn't ashamed of her height like others. She always had her back straight and held high confidence. This was attributed by her grandmother. That was the only time she was ever fussed at. *Make sure you always keep your back straight*. She could hear her grandmother's words with every step she took.

"What do you care what I do or where I go or what time I am out. Go find Janet! By the way, you keep bringing up my tan, but that chick is black as night! You make no sense. You are just too dumb for words and she is not even pretty. It must be her titties because that is all she has going for herself. I heard what you did to her in the pool. I was only gone two days and you were fingering her dirty ugly ass in a public pool. If that's what you want, then go ahead. I don't care. Some hoe that will let you do something like that in a public pool has no respect for herself! And to make matters worse, people saw you do it. You have no damn shame! All I did was go on vacation and this is what I get in return. Go to hell, Stanley!" It was that moment where Camille ripped off the necklace he had brought her for Valentine's Day. She had never taken it off until then. It wasn't much but it was from him and that meant it was everything.

Stanley saw the gold necklace glisten on the concrete. "Why would you do that? I gave that to you!"

"Fuck you, Stanley!" Camille stormed away crying. He didn't deny the incident in the pool. She knew when he was lying and when he was telling the truth. Everything she heard via gossip was true.

They broke up for months. After a while, Camille got used to him not being around every waking hour. It also helped that Stanley moved back to Brooklyn. His mother and boyfriend got in a terrible fight, and he threw them out. Camille didn't reach out to Stanley. There wasn't anything left to say. He had long stopped reaching out to her.

School had started and Camille got off the train like clockwork. Stanley was waiting for her at the station. "What the hell do you want?" Camille walked by him asking him the question without waiting for a reply. Stanley tried to apologize, but it was too late. Stanley had hit a growth spurt, but Camille was still taller than him and her legs seemed twice his length, especially when she began speed walking. Camille wanted nothing to do with him. To her, he was an ass, and she had no time for asses.

For three weeks Stanley waited for Camille at the train station. "What do you want from me? Go find, Janet!" Camille was still very much hurt by Stanley's actions. If that was all it took for him to find someone else, then she couldn't trust him.

"She doesn't mean anything to me. She never did. I am so sorry," Stanley pleaded. All he wanted was his Camille back. He couldn't bear the thought of her dating someone else. He had heard rumors that she had given her number to another boy on 161st street by the movie theater. He had eyes and ears watching her every move, and she didn't even know it. He was controlling.

"Kiss my ass, Stanley! Go take her to another pool!" Camille was frustrated and just wanted to go home. Stanley cried. Camille stopped. This was the first time she had ever seen him cry. She walked with him and listened. He was going through a lot of things with his mom's boyfriend, which led to them getting kicked out. Reluctantly, she forgave him.

Camille's mother was pushing for them to get back together. She liked Stanley for the most part. Sometimes, however, she would tell Camille that her and Stanley's relationship was too intense and they needed breathing room. In this way, Camille was a bit confused. However, she kept seeing Stanley.

That wasn't the first time he had cheated on her. There were countless others. One relationship she found out had been going on for two years. She, at the time, had been with him for a little over three years. She was scared to confront him. Scared they would break up. Scared he would leave, and she would have no one to lean on. She was the only one to know that all wasn't fairytales and rainbows. Her home life was growing more and more dysfunctional. She was ashamed and had no one. No one but Stanley. Even if Stanley was not good to her, she had him. He may have cheated on her, but he was there and he didn't judge her. There were mini breakups, but nothing substantial. Anytime Stanley would hear of a boy pushing up on Camille, he would beg for her back. It didn't matter that he had been with other girls. Camille was his in his mind and no one else would have her. He knew he was all she had and he played on that insecurity.

Chapter 5

The church wasn't what it was wrapped up to be. As time passed, the youth ministry found out some devastating news. The pastor of the church was spreading the kid's business to anyone that would listen, and her husband, the co-pastor, was spending his Sunday afternoons smoking crack in the stairwell of Camille's building where the Browns also lived. All of the children cried. They found out during their special anniversary service they had planned for the Browns. The Browns were having a major argument in the back of the church. The children waited in the pews to get service started. The service was running late which didn't matter much, they had no visitors. They were the only ones there for the festivities.

Matt had left the church a couple months prior to the explosion. Camille and Stanley saw him after the service and told him what happened leaving out not one detail. Matt wasn't surprised. He had left because he had heard the pastors talking about him behind his back. He had enough, but he never tried to keep the others from continuing to go. These were the same people who baptized them in the name of the Father, Son and Holy Spirit. *Where was the Holy Spirit when he was in the stairways smoking his drugs,* he wondered?

It all came crumbling down when during the argument, the Browns failed to turn off the church microphone. The children were horrified at the things they were saying to each other. These were not the words of a loving married couple. They were all old enough to know that people have difficulties, but these were unbearable. This was too much.

"Hurry we need to get out there and deal with these damn kids! You are always waiting 'til the last minute to get your crap together! Twenty years later and not a damn thing has changed. You sicken me woman!" Kevin said to his wife.

"I sicken you? Oh, those little bastards can wait! They ain't going nowhere. I don't see you rushing after service with your damn crack pipe! No, you take your time when it comes to that!" Shirley yelled at the top of her lungs.

"Oh okay, well I might be a crack head, but you ain't no better! You call yo' damn girlfriends up as soon as one of those kids leave the house for a counseling session and laugh at them." Kevin paused for a moment collecting his thoughts. "All you do is gossip, woman. I wish you would just hurry up so we can get this damn business over with!"

They cried for the church, themselves, Jesus, their hearts and their families. "What do we do now?" Camille was the first to stand up and walk away. She vowed to never trust a church again. Their betrayal was worse than anything Stanley or her mother, for that matter, could conjure up.

This all happened around the time Camille's mother told her she was dying of cancer. It was all too much to grasp. Camille secretly had a nervous breakdown. A breakdown that only Stanley bore witness to. She was in her room with Stanley thinking about how everything had happened. All of it. To include Stanley. Then, Camille started to cry uncontrollably. She wanted to stop, but she couldn't stop. She could no longer control herself or her emotions. It lasted for over thirty minutes. Stanley sat there with her, holding her until she finally calmed down. She didn't scream or say a word she just cried and accepted her breakdown. A breakdown for what seemed to be for no reason. Camille's mother blatantly lied about the cancer scare. She didn't know why her mother would stoop that low. She didn't know why anyone would do something like that. What she did know was that she was inherently ashamed.

The rumors of the church spread like a wildfire and it seemed as though all of the teens that participated in the youth ministry went on a spiraling downhill slope. Nothing went right for them. Evil had been let in and welcomed. The very people who blasphemed and blessed them with oil were the same ones who opened their spirits up to damnation. When Camille would run into the Browns, they judged her for leaving. It was horrible what they would say to a young girl. These were not people of God. These were people for profit.

Karen had begun to be sexually active. It was with Larry that she lost her virginity. Camille didn't know what Karen saw in him, but she was crazy about him. Shortly after their sexual encounter, Larry was sent to a juvenile detention center. The Browns were very quiet as to why he was sent away, but whatever he had done had been very serious. Karen was sad for a while, but eventually found another boy to crush on. That was her way to cope with all that was going on. Everyone had their crosses to bear.

Claudette had been skipping school, hanging with the wrong crowd and smoking weed, so she had heard. She wasn't sure about the weed, but she did know Claudette was stealing her mother's Newport cigarettes when she wasn't looking. Camille was allergic to smoke, so she had to limit her time with her after that. Even though she lived next door to her, she barely saw her anymore. Claudette had a few boyfriends in different neighborhoods. Some knew about the next and others thought they were the only one. Somehow, she kept them all in line. Everyone was growing up in their own direction.

One night Stanley and Camille were in the kitchen of her apartment while she cooked. Stanley walked up behind her and started rubbing her. They were alone. By that time, Camille had already given her virginity to him. The first time they had sex it was awkward. They had been sexual in some of their activities, but waited a while before they had actual intercourse. Stanley was aware that Camille was a virgin and wanted to make sure she felt she was ready to go to the next level before they had crossed that line. Up until a year prior, Stanley would just kiss her on her special places. He was fine with it since he was new at oral sex himself. She didn't reciprocate. He didn't want her to, and she didn't ask.

They were seventeen now, and in their senior year of high school. "Stop it, Stanley. I have to finish this before my mom gets home." By that time, Camille was the caretaker of the house. She cooked all the meals, cleaned the apartment, completed all chores and did all the grocery shopping. If she wasn't done by the time her mother got home from work, she would get in trouble. "Stanley! Stop it!"

He didn't stop. Why didn't he stop? He covered her mouth with his hand and kept repeating, "You know you want this. You know you want this…" Camille began to cry and could not fight him off of her. "Stop fighting me. I can take this pussy whenever I want it!" The yellow painted walls didn't seem so bright anymore. They were far from cheerful. All the good memories she had made while creating her fanciful delights were slowly being stripped away. He pulled up her skirt and ripped her panties. Camille gripping the counter for balance, tried to move but she was wedged between it and him firmly. She was paralyzed. He shoved his penis into her vagina. There had been no previous stimulation. There was no moistness to ease the insertion, and it hurt. It felt as if he was stabbing her constantly, over and over. The tears streamed down her face. She tried to bite his hand but he cupped his hands and pulled her closer by the waist. Camille didn't weigh much. She was barely over 100 pounds, even though she was tall. By now Stanley had towered over her and he wasn't the same scrawny kid he had been when they first met.

Stanley had raped her in her own kitchen. The same kitchen where the sausage and peppers were cooked by her father for their first dinner. The same kitchen where she flipped him pancakes for brunch after church with all their friends. The same kitchen where she made him his special chocolate birthday cake when his mom forgot about it. *How could this be happening?* Camille thought. She couldn't say another word. She cried. He came. He stopped, zipped up his pants, let go of her, pushed himself out of her and left her to clean herself up.

Stanley wasn't a virgin when they started dating. He had sex plenty of times. Camille was aware of this, and she didn't make a big deal about it. When she did decide to give her virginity to him, he showed his experience. There was nothing clumsy about it, and he knew what he was doing. He never pressured her and he took his time. Those days were over for good. This was not the same boy that pushed Barry through the glass over a hopeful kiss. He had now succumbed to violating her in the worse way possible.

"Why would you steal something that is freely given to you?" Camille asked Stanley and he never replied. He just sat on the sofa and watched TV. She asked him to leave. "Please just go, Stanley. Just leave me alone!"

Stanley simply replied, "Make me. Make me leave." He shrugged his shoulders sitting comfortably on her sofa. "You can't do anything about it. Like I told you, it's my pussy and has been my pussy." She never looked at him the same way again. Wiping off the fingerprints and every evidence from the counter. She finished making dinner with tears silently running down her cheeks.

The part that loved him was beginning to hate him. The poetry that rhymed in rhythmic romance had changed to dismal despair. Camille saw less and less of him. She would rather not see him at all. She wanted to forget that night, but didn't think anyone would believe her. She wanted to break up with him, but didn't have any answers to any questions she knew she would be asked. She never told anyone. Not her mother, Matt, Karen or Claudette. She hid her shame. How could she let him go when he was the only one that knew what really went on in her home? Her mother hated her. She had to. All she did was curse and yell at her. Her self-esteem was low. She hated looking at herself in the mirror. It was summer so she had to stay in the shade. Stanley didn't like her dark. She had to keep her light caramel complexion.

What if I get pregnant? She wasn't sure if Stanley had used a condom when he raped her. She assumed he didn't since she didn't think most rapists stopped to protect their victims. There was a time when Stanley protected her. Now all she could think of was his breath breathing down her neck as he whispered his lies to her. Covering up her mouth with his hand to muffle her screams. The smell of his Cool Water cologne. The smell that she used to love, she now feared. It made her gag. She didn't know what had changed. She didn't know what she had done so wrong to him to make him do these things. The one that would fight for her had turned into her violator.

Maybe he was on drugs, she wondered. His behavior was so erratic and so devastating. She had never experienced that with him before. There was no reason for it. She knew his mother was back on drugs since they had moved to Brooklyn. He came to her crying one day and broke the news to her. He cried more often now. She wasn't sure if it was because he was trying to get sympathy from her or not. He lived with his aunt and younger cousins for a while before moving in with Matt and his family back in the Bronx. It was easier for him to go to and from school. It was also easier to keep an eye on Camille. Even though he was out doing everything with everyone, he needed to make sure she wasn't doing the same. It was hard to keep tabs on her an hour and a half away. There was a time when he would move mountains for her. Where he would do anything to make sure she was okay. Those days were gone. Camille no longer loved Stanley.

Since Stanley moved in with Matt, they saw each other a lot. She would spend most of the day visiting them while they played *Tomb Raider* or some other video game. She didn't mind it much. It gave her a break from her mother and Stanley, even though he was in the room paying her no attention.

Matt had a feeling something was up with her. Camille was even more withdrawn than before and it showed in her behavior. Even though he was Stanley's best friend since the choir, he loved Camille like a sister. However, there were even things she wouldn't dare tell him. There were times she would question where his loyalty would have been and didn't want to place him in a position to choose. They would, however, talk about everything else under the sun. She had become an avid fan of *World Wrestling Federation* and *Dragon Ball Z*, the Japanese amine cartoon, because of him. He had opened her to the world of the carefree nerd, and she welcomed it with open arms.

Camille actually didn't mind Matt being around at all. She knew that Stanley wouldn't hurt her with him around and she felt safe. Stanley was mostly preoccupied with trying to talk to other girls in Matt's building as if Camille didn't know. Camille was nice, but she wasn't dumb. It was a situation that she had accepted for the time being.

For a while, the three of them were inseparable. She would visit them or they would visit her. The basketball court was still a very daily routine on warmer winter days and the warm months. After a while, Stanley expressed to Camille that he thought Matt was jealous of him. Camille didn't understand how that could be since it was Matt that had the home and the family to live with in the first place. Stanley also believed that Matt was in love with Camille. He started keeping them from hanging out all the time. Camille wasn't sure if Stanley was right about that, but she knew if that is what he believed, they would be isolated once again. She did realize over the four years that Karen had a huge crush on Stanley. She didn't think too highly of her friend those days. It seemed as if she was just using her and trying to mirror whatever she was doing. After the choir was dismembered, she had removed herself from that friendship.

Matt was aware of the crush Karen had on Stanley. It was literally impossible to miss. There was one time a while back during the choir days, Karen had dared Stanley to do a sexual act for her. At the time, Camille was a virgin, and they acted like he did it, even though they actually didn't.

"Stanley, it's your turn. Truth or dare?" Karen looked at Stanley with a twinkle in her eye.

"Whatever! I ain't no punk. Dare!" Stanley said confidently. He wasn't sure what Karen had in mind, but he knew it was going to be dumb. It was always dumb.

"I dare you to put your finger in Camille's vagina!" Karen said proudly and giggling

"What the hell!? I am not going to do that! What the fuck is wrong with you, Karen? You see, it's always the quiet ones you have to look out for. Well I am not going to do it here with your nasty ass looking. I'll do it in the kitchen." Stanley was annoyed, and he knew Camille was embarrassed.

"I don't want to do that! Karen why the hell would you say that?" Camille was livid. Karen had taken this game and made her the brunt of the joke. Everyone in the room knew Camille was still a virgin.

"Damn, Karen! You nasty as shit. You are so dead ass wrong for that!" Claudette threw her two cents in. "The only reason why you dared them to do that is because Larry isn't here to finger you!"

Camille and Stanley went in to the kitchen. They stood there and looked at each other. No one was watching so they did nothing. No one could prove he did it or not. So, they just stood there. After a few moments, they walked out.

"Okay okay okay. That's done. Karen, your turn," Matt said looking at Karen. Camille was sitting with her head down still embarrassed. Matt had a feeling they didn't do anything in the kitchen, but he wasn't going to call them out on it. Especially not with Camille losing what little color she barely had left from being so flush.

"I choose dare!" Karen still reeling from what he had just made Stanley and Camille do.

Matt looked at Camille and smiled. Camille didn't understand the gesture until he spoke his next words. "Karen, I dare you to lick the window!" Everyone was pretty quiet for a while, and then the uproar of laughter set in and no one could control themselves.

"Lick the what? Lick the damn window?! What the hell! I don't want to do that! That's not funny. Stop laughing at me!" Karen was mad and Camille felt better.

"Go ahead, Karen. Get to it!" snapped Claudette. Karen got up and completed her dare by licking Camille's eighteenth floor apartment window. It was the funniest thing any one of them had ever seen.

Stanley kept speaking about who he didn't trust and why he didn't trust them. That was during the time where she didn't really believe what Stanley was saying to her anyway. How could he preach about trust after what he was doing to her! He had no right to any of it. She listened in silence. She would tune him out during his long ramblings and think about how she was going to escape her horrid living nightmare.

Chapter 6

Since the rape, Camille was scared. She was not feeling well and feared that Stanley had given her a disease. She made an appointment with her gynecologist. Luckily, she was due for a pap smear. To her surprise her test came back inconclusive. She didn't know what to do. All other sexually transmitted diseases had come back negative. This test was for cervical cancer. Camille was scared. What was she to do if she had it? Her mother had blatantly lied about the lump she found in her breast, but this was real. This was not some phantom charade to get sympathy. This was her life.

Camille suffered from terrible periods. She always had since she was thirteen. She would miss at least two days of school from her heavy flow and bad cramps every month. Her mother had taken her to countless doctors who all said her pain was an over exaggeration and the amount of flow that occurred each month was just because she was a *girl*. She had always thought something was wrong, but after a while she let it go.

She told Stanley and her mother about the test results. They both seemed unenthused about it. Camille had to see a specialist in

CYRENE RENEE

downtown Manhattan. She didn't bother to tell anyone else in the family. She didn't share with her friends either since they had all grown apart. At this point, Camille felt alone.

She arrived at the cold doctor's office and they gave her a gown. It was a small office with gray walls. The only bit of art work that was displayed were the framed posters of the female anatomy. The nurse didn't say much to her other than verifying her name and date of birth. After the confirmation, the nurse asked if she had anyone in the waiting room for her. Camille was alone.

The doctor informed her that this wasn't something she should go through alone, and at the end of the procedure, she needed not to travel alone. She would be uncomfortable, at a minimum, and wouldn't be able to administer the proper pain medication. Well none of this was going to happen. Camille lied and told them she had a ride coming to get her.

The procedure took a little over an hour. She was awake for the entire ordeal and wished she was put to sleep. She could see the cameras as they inserted them inside of her and projected her ovaries, uterus and cervix on the screen. The doctor started scraping and removing the bad cells. She didn't know what they were saying. Everything sounded as if it were a foreign language. After it was over, Camille felt terrible. Physically and mentally drained, the specialist told her that her cervix was 80% covered in the cells, and in about six months, had she had not come to get this done, she would have had full blown cancer. Nothing surprised her anymore.

She took her pain prescriptions and left the examination room without saying a word. "Excuse me. Where is your ride?" The nurse asked as she was about to walk out.

"Oh, my ride? They are waiting for me outside. There wasn't any parking in the neighborhood," she said lying to the nurse.

She tried to take the train home, but she lived too far and she couldn't get a seat. Less than half way home, she exited the Number 4 subway station after feeling dizzy. She hopped in a cab and gave her grandmother's address. She had no money, and she felt terrible, but she could not go home. When the cab arrived at the house, Camille rang the doorbell. Her grandmother could tell something was very wrong and paid the cab. Camille told her what happened and passed out on the sofa.

"I can't believe you let her do this by herself? What is wrong with you? If you could not have gone, someone would have gone with her. The poor thing almost passed out up the stairs. Why would you let her go alone? I would have never let you do anything like this alone?" Camille's grandmother was livid. She didn't know what her mother said on the other end of that phone call, but the phone was slammed down on her. She stayed with her grandmother for a few more days. She needed to be monitored and was in too much pain after the numbing shots that were given at the appointment had worn off.

Camille withdrew further into herself. She had always planned to go away to college, especially after everything had taken its drastic change. When she mentioned college to her mother, she laughed in her face as if it was the biggest joke of the year. "We ain't got no money for that! I am not wasting my time filling out those financial forms either!" She didn't understand how there was no money for school? Camille was the only child and only asked for the things she actually needed. She didn't ever have very expensive sneakers or clothes. She worked odd jobs doing hair and babysitting to make sure she had her own money for the small things she wanted. That was it. Camille tried to do it herself, but without her mom's financial information, it was impossible.

She went into the bathroom and cried. She cried for her heart. She cried for her body that was now not only abused, but disease stricken. She cried for her unknown future. It was then that she had a strong sense of worry. She moved the carefully placed can of air freshener. There she saw it for herself, and all her suspicions were correct. Four lines of thin white powder drawn out on the white porcelain toilet. The tears stopped. She wiped it off with a tissue.

Placing the can on the floor, she would just blame the cat for knocking it over. Whoever in the house that made the uproar would be the possessor for the powder. She waited. It was her mother that ran for hours trying to find the poor cat to beat her into oblivion for messing with her drugs. Even though she didn't say it.

"Mommy, why are looking for Dimples? What did she do?" Camille was just wondering what her mother could possibly come up with for an excuse.

"She is always messing with my shit. That was my shit!" Aleida was frantic.

"Mommy, what are you talking about? What stuff?" Camille played dumb convincingly. Normally, she wasn't a very good liar, but her mother was too preoccupied so she didn't have to give much effort.

"She bit my shoes again!" There was a pause as if she were thinking about what she was going to say. "Yeah, she bit my shoes. That damn cat thinks she is a damn dog. Always biting up the leather."

So that was it. That was what she came up with. *Poor cat. I am sorry. God forgive me.* After this new-found discovery, nothing surprised her anymore. She only shared the revelation with Stanley. He wasn't much, but he was all he had. After that, she stopped caring about school. Her grades began to slip to the point where she couldn't catch up. She didn't care. No one cared about her anymore. Why on earth should she care about anything for herself. Her boyfriend was abusive, her mother was a drug addict and she was sure her father knew about it. None of the teachers at the school cared. They just failed her. No one asked her what was wrong. She wished someone, anyone would have asked her what was wrong.

Stanley raped her one more time. She didn't quite remember it happening. As soon as the ordeal took place, she blocked it out of her mind. It wasn't until years later she had nightmares of him on top of her in her old bedroom. She was already lying down on her bed. She must have dozed off while watching TV. She woke up to find Stanley standing over her with his penis exposed.

"What the hell are you doing? My mother is home! Mommy!" Camille didn't know Aleida had let him in on her way out of the door. She didn't know Camille was sleeping and didn't bother to see if she was awake.

"Your mother left. We have the house to ourselves," Stanley said in the same tone as he had before on their last terrible encounter.

She knew the voice as soon as she heard it. Camille was scared. "Don't do this Stanley! Not again! I am on my period! Please don't!" It was too late. Stanley had ripped off her pants even though she was fighting him.

He pressed himself on top of her. "You know that you want this! Stop playing with me. This is *my* pussy! I take what I want and I don't give a damn about no bloody period! It makes it easier to fuck you. Last time I barely came since your ass was so dry! Now stop fucking fighting me and take this dick!" He struggled to open her legs and the wrestling was making him angrier.

Stanley had never spoken to her like this before. Eventually, she did lay there. Numb. She didn't move. She didn't moan. She didn't cry. She had forgotten it had happened while it was happening. She wanted to die.

That was the first-time Camille had ever thought about suicide. She had thought about drinking bleach but once it was in the glass she couldn't bring herself to drink it. She felt like a coward. The next attempt was the pills. She stared at all the bottles she had lined up. All the medications from her emergency room and doctors' appointments about her menstrual cycle. Again, she couldn't do it. She wasn't strong enough to take her life. She wasn't strong enough to live it either.

Chapter 7

"You're not going to graduate." Those words rang in her ears like piercing sirens. Her guidance counselor, Mrs. Brand, told her that with a stern look. Camille looked at her with no words and no emotion. She got up to leave. "Don't you have any questions for me?"

Camille retorted, "No, it's not like you had any questions for me in the four years I have been here." Camille left. She figured she would need her diploma at some point and enrolled in summer school and then night school. She might not graduate on time, but she would in fact graduate nonetheless. She was a bit happy she wouldn't be walking down the aisle in cap and gown. Although she would miss having that moment with her high school friends, she didn't want to give her mother the satisfaction of something she had nothing to do with. She was now living for herself. Stanley was in the same boat. He was more broken up about it than she was. She wasn't exactly sure why though. Stanley barely ever went to school, and other than math, his grades were terrible. Camille's mother didn't care and she was glad she didn't have to deal with it.

When she broke the news to her parents, only her father was disappointed. She had gone from being a straight A student to barely making it. Her mother wasn't too sad about it. They had planned this elaborate luncheon on the day of her graduation to act as if she did graduate. Camille thought the whole charade was comical, but like the good girl she was, she went along with it anyhow.

She remembered the night before her SAT exam when her mother purposely kept her up the entire night so that she wouldn't do well on the test. The test was on a Saturday morning and started at 8:00 a.m. sharp. Aleida kept her up until 5:00 a.m. and laughed in her face. "Now, you dumb bitch go take your little fucking test!" By the time Camille arrived, her eyes were blood shot from a lack of sleep. The administers for the test almost didn't allow her to take it. She didn't read any of the questions. She just took the #2 pencil and bubbled in anything. She was the first one done. When she did make it home, her mother was sleeping and had no recollection of the ordeal when she awakened. That is how it was for the sober. They were the only ones to remember long after the abuser had forgotten.

She had a new plan. Go. She walked home by herself at an unnatural slow pace for herself. Go. All she could think was what life had disintegrated to in the last few years. Go. Leave this place and everyone in it. Everyone that had ever said, "I love you, Camille." Go. Go as far away as she could away from everything and everyone. She would go and not look back, and when they called her, she would not answer. She would make a life for herself somehow. She didn't trust her boyfriend, her family, her parents, her friends or her church.

From time to time she would see the old pastors in the street. They were still taunting her even after a year later. She could hear them saying, "You are not God! You cannot judge us! You should never have left us!" At first the harassing bothered her, but over time, she didn't care if they spoke until their voices strained. It was old and they needed a new script. She needed Jesus, but they *really* needed Jesus. Camille felt sorry for them actually, and said a prayer for them. She would never step a foot back into their church again. All she had was God. God and her will to keep going no matter what. God and her future. She was no longer her past. She was not her mother. She was not Stanley's girlfriend. She was her own woman.

She never told anyone that Stanley had violated her. She never disclosed that her mother was a substance abuser. She never asked her father if he knew that her mother was on drugs. She never told her teachers when she rapidly started failing her classes. She never confided in her family about the real issues of her home life. She never told her friends why she would prefer to stay late for the talent shows she participated in instead of going home. She never told the pastors of the church how much they hurt her with their deception. She never told The Browns that she felt as though they used her and stripped her of her sacred God given gift. She vowed to hold it dear to her heart. It would be her secret, so that no one would take advantage of it again. She never told anyone how much she prayed that the Lord would spare her of this life. She never told anyone how much she wished for heaven. She never expressed how much she wanted the memories to go away over and over in her head. She just simply left. She left everything and everyone behind her.

CHASITY

Wherever I may go
I am loved
I am cherished
Even in the blackest of nights
Surrounded by clouds
Even in dark
My light
Must shine through
Even when
You
Fail to love me
The humanness of humanity
Prosperity
Calamity
I have seen it all
The beauties and despair
And at times I have to ask myself
Where is the love
I am reminded
Right here
My eyes
Reveal falsehoods
Of wicked shadows
And yearn for peace
I must remember the faith inside of me
I must tap into that place
My hidden secret
Because life is there
What seems tangible may not be fair
May not be enough
But please remember
Please remember that I am enough
That if I fail to hope

And cease to cope
With the ever-increasing heart beats
That pound fearfully in my chest
Grow in numb to the days that pass on to the next
Please remember
I am not just of this time
There are so many next lifetimes
Scenarios
While this sun that beams down
Creates suffocating strongholds
I fear no evil
Proudly I am a believer
Engulfed in beautiful flaws
Sometimes left to claw
Climbing out the pits of hell
Sometimes treating to shell
Isolating
Daydreaming of better days
Some days
It's so loud there
Most days
The screams of injustice
Bare the reflection of times
Gone by
We are asked to question
Where is the love
May I remember
It's right here
And although my people bleed
We too shall see
Love
I have to believe
This can't be done for vanity

That we matter
Don't cry for me
Hold me
And tell me everything will be okay
I refuse to allow you to call me other than my name
Yet I stand
Silent
In protest
Robotic
Stoic
Proud
I am not what you call me
I am my ancestors
Great grand grand grand
Who was shipped across distant lands
And yet they survived
So I know what runs through my veins
Brings strength
Stronger than your bullets
Kill me you couldn't
Because I am a walking legacy
And so are those that come after me

Hold me
And tell me everything will be okay
I refuse to allow you to call me other than my name
Yet I stand
Silent
In protest
Robotic
Stoic
Proud
I am not what you call me
I am my ancestors
Great grand grand grand
Who was shipped across distant lands
And yet they survived
So I know what runs through my veins
Brings strength
Stronger than your bullets
Kill me you couldn't
Because I am a walking legacy
And so are those that come after me

Chapter 1

Chasity could hear the echo between her ears from the Air Force Training Instructor Staff Sergeant Hillside, also known as TI. "Get off the bus now! Now! Now! Chasity had joined the Military. She was eighteen, and although she felt as though she was on her own for years, she was literally on her own now.

She was now in Texas at Lackland Air Force base. The first stop in the process of becoming an Airman. The plane landed in the middle of the night, and she was utterly exhausted. She had been traveling all day from New York City. It was as if they chose the longest routes and flights on purpose. They didn't land until well into the middle of the night, she assumed. They had no way to tell time. Now she and hundreds of other trainees were depending solely on the TI's for everything. Walking into the Air Force recruiting station one month prior, it all seemed like a blur. When she finally broke the news to her family about her decision, they were stunned. No one thought she would do such a thing. It isn't what the girls in the family did. It is something the men did to be men. All of her uncles had joined some form of military, and she would be the first woman. Maybe even the only woman. The pressure was on her to do great. She could hear the doubt in their voices. She could see the doubt in their eyes.

"Well, before you can join anything, you have to pass the ASVAB test." Her Uncle William said as a matter of fact.

"I have already passed my test," Chasity said confidently. The ASVAB is The Armed Services Vocational Aptitude Battery test that all military hopefuls have to take to qualify to join any of the sister branches. Chasity passed it with flying colors.

"Oh, you did? Well you need to pass the physical also," her uncle responded.

"Yes, I know I have already been cleared by the Military Entrance Processing Station (MEPS). I am physically capable to join. I have also received my job and what I will be doing in the Air Force. I am going to be Security Forces, and I leave May 3, 2000," Chasity stated confidently again.

Once her mind was made up, it was made up. The family was stunned, and she was at peace with her decision. She had heard the horror stories of Basic Military Training, but she was willing to adhere to it. It was time to make a life for herself. BMT couldn't have been so bad compared to what she had already gone through.

Chasity found herself in hot Texas with fifty-one other scared women. They lived in a large room split in half by a dividing wall. It was open ended on each side for exit and entry. Although it was filled with fifty-five beds and large lockers that stood taller than her for each trainee, there was an echo in the room as if no furniture was present. Most of the room was a drab shade of bluish gray, except for the walls, which were white. The beds were covered in blue wool blankets and white sheets. She would soon learn those blankets were the itchiest and most uncomfortable blankets she would ever touch. It was clean yet had no odor of cleaning products. It smelled like nothing.

This would be called home. There had already been an incident with one girl being sent home because she was pregnant. During the first week, another girl had broken her shaving razor, removed the blades and tried to slit her wrist. "What have I gotten myself into?" Chasity said to herself. She would pray every night to herself. It is what got her through the six weeks and four days. She was convinced her Training Instructor hated her guts. The TI hated everyone's guts, but especially hers. He wasn't a very large man. Only a couple inches taller than her. He was a very fit white man and highly intimidating. He called her not by her name, but simply "New York." He would taunt her in an effort to make her attitude show itself. Something New Yorkers are notoriously known for. He didn't break her. Not to his face at least. If she cried, she would excuse herself to the latrine and do it in private. She wrote herself a note and kept it in her sock, since if it was in her pocket it would be considered an unauthorized item.

Chasity,

I can do this. I have come this far and I am okay. I know that God loves me and will always be there for me. I have to make it. I will make it. I will graduate. I will be an Airman. There is nothing that can stop me, only myself. I am strong and loved. Even when I feel like I am alone, I know that angels are with me. I am protected. I belong here. I am stronger than I know. Lord, I ask you to show me my strength. No matter what I will be okay.

Psalm 27
The Lord is my light and my salvation; whom shall I fear?
The Lord is the strength of my life; of whom shall I be afraid?

Remember, I am never alone. Even in the darkest of moments. Those are the times my light can shine brighter. My light will shine brighter and it will keep me. God help me keep focused on my goals. Lord, guide me to be who you want me to be. May these words ring true on this journey. I have to keep going no matter what is placed on my path. I am going to make it. I must make it. I will not be defeated. Keep going…

Love, Chasity

113

She read this note sometimes six times a day. She never told anyone about the letter. She had included her favorite Bible verse of all time. She never had much to lean on other than her faith and right now she needed it more than ever. The Air Force was a different life. She was told when to wake up, how to dress, how to clean, what to eat, when to eat, when to exercise, how to wear her hair, individualism and teamwork. It was hard. There were days she didn't think she would make it. There were times she didn't think she could handle it. Her favorite days were Sundays. Those were the days they would clean and go to church. Church services during BMT were amazing. It was the time where she could release everything that she had bottled in all week. There you could see trainees crying during a sermon or song. The tears may have not had anything to do with the service at all or everything to do with it. No one knew and no one judged. Everyone just understood.

There was a sisterhood bond that developed over time. It was impossible to be great at everything. Chasity saw a fellow trainee having issues marching, so she would make sure she would march everywhere during the down time when the TI wasn't around. If a trainee was great at folding for inspection or making beds, she would go around helping and doing just that for the others. Everyone helped everyone while helping themselves.

One day SSgt Hillside had a surprise dorm inspection. The inspections always had the girls nervous. All they wanted to do was get it right to be left alone. Normally, Chasity always had something wrong with either her bed or toiletries. He found a strand of hair in her brush the last time she stopped using it. She kept her real brush in her laundry bag. That wasn't authorized, but it was effective.

"Gil, what do you have for me today?" He marched up to her quickly. Always starting with the uniform and making sure the boots were shiny. She had finally learned the trick to shining boots. Up until this point, they were black and dull. He was able to see his reflection in the steal toe tips now. Her Battle Dress Uniform (BDU) was properly creased at the arms and legs. Her hair was neatly brushed back into the 3 "bulk bun. He opened the wall locker to find all the uniforms were free of strings, tags and all facing the correct direction on the hangers. As he opened the drawers, the towels and wash clothes were folded perfectly in the "e" fold. The t-shirts were in six-inch squares. Moving on to her bed, the hospital folds were crisp and the pillow fold snapped back when he snatched it up. The floors had just been swept so there were no visible "dust bunnies." "So Gil, you have no demerits! Great for you! Do you think you are special Gil? Huh? Is that what you think? Well let me be the first person to tell you that you aren't!"

SSgt Hillside proceeded to throw all of her items around the large bay. Everything from her underwear to her towels. He flipped over her mattress. Chasity stood at attention in horror as all her hard work went down the drain. To make matters worse, as he continued the inspection, the items that he jolted throughout the room were considered unauthorized items for the other girls. Chasity felt horrible as the other girls got in trouble for the mess he made with her things. At the end, he ran over to Chasity. "See little Miss Perfectionist! Do you see what that got you?" All of his questions were rhetorical. She knew if she had answered she would have been in more trouble. She held her bearings and did not cry. Head and eyes remained straight forward. Her stubborn ways were reinforced that day. He stormed out the room.

"I am so sorry, Davis!" Chasity's bed was lying on her bunk mates. She was one of the ones that got written up.

"It wasn't your fault. He just hates us! I can't believe he did that to you." Davis was pretty shaken up by what just happened and it didn't even happen to her.

"That will be the last time I ever get a perfect score." Chasity walked around the bay and picked up her belongings apologizing along the way. After that she would find ways to purposely sabotage herself. "He will never do that to me again!"

Receiving mail was always a good time. It wasn't something to be missed. You wanted to be remembered and missed by family and friends. Not everyone acknowledged Chasity's absence, and she made note of that. People who she considered to be her best friends and sisters, since she was the only child, never wrote to her. She would always remember that. These were the same people that expected her to pay for everything or take care of them when they needed it. BMT taught her what mattered and who didn't.

"What the hell are you doing, Gil?" She could hear her TI screaming in her direction. Chasity was actually doing exactly what she was supposed to be doing. It was four weeks into training and the routine was embedded in the girl's head and heart. They were waiting to eat lunch and they needed to take that time to study for their weekly test. "Get your ass over here, Gil! Right now, Gil!"

There were a couple times during the last month when her TI treated her as a human being. The first was when she donated blood. She had volunteered only to get a break from him, actually. There she found out that she had a rare blood type, B negative. So rare that the Air Force was in demand for it. They ended up taking more blood from her than everyone else. They gave her extra cookies and juice, which was nice since she had neither in over a month, but it didn't help. She ended up getting a special letter from the blood bank that she would not be permitted to perform in any physical activities for 24 hours.

"Hey maggot, what's your blood type?" Staff Sergeant Hillside asked her curiously while reading the letter.

"Sir, Trainee Gil reports as ordered. I am B Negative Sir!" Chasity said in the correct format with her reporting statement.

"Oh hell! If I would have known that, I would have warned you! The clinic sucked you dry! They never have enough negative blood. Dammit, now you are no good to me. Fine. Sit your ass down before you pass out and I really have a problem on my hands. Goddammit!" SSgt Hillside was annoyed, but he was concerned. He was hard on the girls. He had to be, but if any of them got hurt on his watch, he was held accountable.

The second time she felt human was when somehow her eyes swelled up shut during morning exercises. She couldn't see at all. There were some bugs flying around on her path and she had no choice, but to run through it. Roughly five minutes later, she was unable to see anything. SSgt Hillside rushed her to the emergency. He was nervous and she was scared that she would be in trouble for missing a day of training. By the time he went back to the hospital, she was sitting in the same spot he left her in. Her eyes were still puffy, but she was able to see a little bit. The hospital had not fed her that day. SSgt Hillside went off on a nearby nurse. Celeste was starving, and he raided the vending machine with his own money to feed her. More cookies and more juice.

She had to keep a straight face, but she really wanted to tell him to shut up and leave her alone. "Proceeding Sir! Sir Trainee Gil reports as ordered." Chasity put her book in her portfolio and ran to the TI. She knew he was singling her out to mess with her. This was not one of those cookies and juice moments they had shared.

"March!" the Sergeant now put her on the spot. A place Chasity had always hated to be in. She prepared for what would be a 10-minute personal drill of facing movements. The hot Texas heat sweltered through her heavy uniform. With her hat resting on her brow, she prepared for a new battle. She was aware that the TI knew she was good at marching. She knew it was a matter of time before he tested her development. Any opportunity he found to make a fool of her he did just that. It was the first time he had singled her out or anyone out to do such a thing. "Forward March! Left face! Right face! About face! Halt! To the Rear! Change step…!" It just kept going and he just kept calling out commands.

She knew if she had messed up any of them he would finally stop. She also knew if she had messed up any of them she would get in trouble. Chasity decided to just get them right and suffer the repercussions. Her TI was always yelling at her for something. Today wouldn't make it any different. "Fall in!" He yelled at the top of his lungs. Chasity knew she did well, but sometimes doing well was what you didn't want to do at all. She waited as she returned to formation. "You see what this maggot just did? This is how you march. Good job maggot!" Maggots was the nickname their TI had for them. Chasity was happy, but dare not show it. She was finally making progress.

She passed. She was an Airman. She actually survived and she was proud of herself. No one could take this credit for her success. Not her family or friends. She was surprised at the fact her family came to Texas for her graduation. It was nice to have them here. Not all of the graduates had loved ones to wish them well. The training wasn't over. They had only passed phase one of the battle. The next would be the Security Forces Academy. She was determined to trade in her Air Force Cap for the coveted Beret. The beret is what the cops wore while the rest of the Air Force wore the standard uniform. She had a new goal and she will surpass it.

Her mother was nice to her during the graduation visit. It was nice to have her around without any animosity or hostility. Her Aunt Rebecca came also. She didn't have such a good time. She spent the majority of the trip too hot to enjoy anything. She wasn't a downer though. For the most part, her trying to find the nonexistent trees in Texas in the middle of June was rather comical. Her uncle, Ted, who had just retired from the Air Force, brought his family with him for the celebration. Her Aunt Joy and cousins, Michelle and Rodney, were part of the clan.

For the most part, everything worked out really well. Joy and Michelle did get in a big argument during the first night, though. It all started when Rebecca asked Michelle if she would join the Air Force too. If anyone was going to join the family you would have thought it was going to be her, since Ted had just retired.

"Why would I want to do a thing like that? There would be no way I would be caught dead joining anybody's military. I am going to be a dependent like mother!" Michelle responded in disgust. The whole table was quiet.

There was no way Joy was going to allow her daughter to disrespect her this way. Especially not in public in front of family. "Is that what you think of me? That I am just some dependent. Excuse me, young lady, but let me remind you that I have a job and I work every day. As a matter of fact, I make more than your father, so don't you dare talk about me as if I just sit around and do nothing."

Michelle was unfazed by what her mother had just told her. "Well I don't care. I am going to be a dependent. I am going to travel the world with my husband just like my family had done. The only reason why I even came to this graduation was to see what kind of men the Air Force was producing. I have seen some good-looking ones and one day I am going to get me one."

Everyone sat at the table in shock after Michelle's admission. Joy was entirely embarrassed, and Chasity sat there with her head down. She felt bad for her aunt and wanted to slap her cousin for being disrespectful. Michelle was going to college on her mother's dime and had no bills to pay other than her cell phone. Her tuition, clothes, car note, car insurance and room and board was all taken care of by her parents. Chasity would have jumped at the chance to have that kind of life. Instead, she had to fight and scrimp for everything she had.

Chapter 2

The academy was more strenuous than BMT. Her mind and body were being pushed to limits she had never seen before. *"I thought basic was hard!"* She proclaimed. She liked to keep her doubts to herself. She didn't want to show her weakness. Although, there were times when her emotions got the best of her. This is what the instructors wanted. Break you down and build you back up to what they wanted you to be. In some areas, it definitely worked. Chasity had already forgotten what her first name was. For the most part and the betterment of two months, all she heard was Gil, her last name. She was hardly ever called Chasity, and no one seemed to want to know it. It wasn't just her though. It was the same for everyone. Stuck in the same trainee boat. At least here they were considered Airmen and actually part of the Air Force. Even though it was hard, it had nothing on what she had just lived through, and she knew everything she was learning would somehow be needed to get through the rest of her life.

The little things mattered. Attention to detail was the way of life. She had even forgotten how she originally folded towels and shirts. 6-inch squares for shirts. Always 6-inch squares and e-fold for towels. It must be e-fold. She had no idea how she did it before the Air Force.

Some things she just had to brain dump just to get by. She struggled with running. She hated that she had a weakness and it was a weakness everyone was aware of. Every other day she went to the medical unit to get her calves evaluated. Running was such a major part of training.

Despite the 100-degree heat the Airmen had to run everywhere. Every step felt like burning blisters in her calf muscles. She was determined to go through it. Even the instructors were worried. Chasity, however, refused to let it get her down and kept going. She made sure if that was going to be her weakness it will be her only one. She would run through the pain even when her body was telling her stop. Even when her body was pleading with her to stop.

Like most of the girls in Basic Training, Celeste had not had a period. They weren't sure why. The doctors were saying stress, but the rumors were that there was something in the funny tasting Gatorade, they were forced to drink. The girl's menstrual cycles mysteriously stopped and the guys said they could no longer get an erection. For most trainees, they feared their hormones were being altered with some of the shots that were mandated. When her cycle did come down, it was like a Mack truck had hit her in a head-on collision. She was in the middle of jumping jacks and that was it. As her hand clapped over her head and she came crashing down. She had seen other girls in her flight go through similar occurrences in the past week.

The medic ran up to her "Are you okay?" Staff Sergeant Hillside was nervous. He had seen this before with an Airman the day before.

"No, no," Chasity said gasping for air. "It's my stomach. Something is wrong. It hurts." Like the previous girls, he picked her up and brought her to the medic truck. He took her to the hospital, and it was confirmed her cycle had returned with a vengeance. She had always suffered from bad cramps, but nothing like this ever. She was permitted to stay in her dorm room for the rest of the day, however, the next day she needed to return to training. And on the next day, it happened to another two girls. They were dropping like flies.

121

Her determination paid off. Even when her mother doubted she would make it after getting a call from the hospital about her condition. If Chasity just spent thirty minutes a day at the hospital, she was okay. Anything longer than that would impede on her training and would put her in jeopardy of getting kicked out. That was not an option. She would make it. She figured out the formula that would help her get through it.

The instructors trained the Airmen for war. Battle tactics and survival drills had the Airmen thinking attack was eminent. They ate, breathed, slept, and tested on written exams. There were times when the heat would be so overwhelming that trainees would pass out in the middle of the woods. Team work. It was then that the Airmen would have to pick up their fellow comrade and get them to the road. Get them to the medics. Get them to safety. Turn around and complete the training. It was excruciating. Shooting range days were hard. If you didn't pass, you didn't continue. No one wanted to repeat anything. Not everyone would make it. Some people that performed well with physical exercise may not test well and fail the written exams. Everyone had a weakness. The training was designed to expose the weaknesses and you, the individual, had to find a way to overcome it. The team as a group had to figure out how to help you. It was all methodically detailed. Adapt and overcome. That was the motto. That was the way of life.

She passed. Again, she passed with pure will and determination. She invited no one to her graduation. No one got her there this time. No one cheered her on this time. It was all His will be done. It was all God. It was all the sheer stubbornness that had fueled her each and every day. If she wanted it, she got it. If she wanted to do it, she did. Whatever "it" she needed to conquer, she overcame. "It" was anything. Her family. Her own doubts. Her physical issues with her calf. It was strained, but she was walking. It was strained, but she kept running. It was strained, but she kept going. The instructors were impressed. Her beret had been earned.

Chapter 3

When she arrived at her first duty station, Langley Air Force Base, she was nervous. She was on her own before, but that was different. The training environment had been so controlled. Everything was handed to the Airmen there. This was different. Turning nineteen in her third week at the academy, she was eight hours from her family and working full time day and night for the Air Force. The Air Force owned her in a sense. The government will have its way with her as it saw fit.

She was still in processing when she met Jason. She remembered seeing him during BMT. It was during the time the trainees were first introduced to war games and tent life. For some, that would be the last time they would experience it. With her being Security Forces, that would be the first of many. She remembered he was not a good leader. Then, she wasn't impressed by any means. However, in this new setting, he seemed cool. He was even funny. She looked at him with different eyes.

Chasity didn't know many people arriving to Langley. Really, she only knew the people she was recently in training with. Naturally they gravitated to each other. They would all hang out during their down time. Langley was nothing like Texas. The dorm rooms were private depending on your rank, and they only shared bathrooms. Chasity was an E-2, an Airman 1st Class, so she had a room to herself. The privacy was welcoming. Especially being an only child. She had learned to share because of family and the number of cousins she had. Her family was rather large. Her grandmother and grandfather had eight children total. It was her immediate family that was small. She liked the peace she had when she was to herself, but she had her own lessons on sharing throughout the years.

By the time Chasity had completed in-processing and started working her shifts with her flight, she and Jason were already in a relationship. They gravitated to each other instantly. He, too, was nineteen, and this was his first time away from home. Maybe that was it. The fear of the unknown and being alone. He spent a lot of time in her dorm room. Jason was of a lower rank and he had a roommate. Even though his roommate wasn't a bother, he would rather spend his time with his girlfriend. Chasity didn't mind. She could use the company, and she liked taking care of people. Making sure they were okay and they had what they needed.

They made the most of her schedule. She worked six days straight with three days off and a 24-hour break in between to break up the day and night shifts. He worked a normal Monday through Friday since he worked in the Communications Squadron with computers all day. It worked for them. They made it work. When they were together, they had a good time. It wasn't perfect, but they had each other. It was both of their first times being away from home and they were no longer in the care of their parents.

Jason had to deal with some backlash over dating a cop. His friends would make fun of him, and Chasity could tell that it bothered him. "So, man, if you hear a strange noise do you send Chasity or do you go check it out? What do you do attack with? Your keyboard?" The jokes kept coming and he kept getting frustrated. There was nothing she could do. It wasn't her fault she was military police. She, in essence, had a more "hard core" job than he did. She fought crime and he pushed paper. It was just her profession. It didn't change that he was still the man in the relationship. They argued about this often. This annoyed Chasity. She hated all forms of conflict, especially about something neither one had any control over. Simply put, Jason's ego was bruised not by her, but by outside influences that he allowed to do so.

Briefly they broke up over the jokes and expressed frustrations that Jason had. Chasity started noticing changes after he got his car that she helped him pay for. It was $5,000 in total, but all he had was $4,000. She gave him $1,000 to make up the difference. Chasity loved him and wanted to help him out in any way that she could. Jason started spending more and more time at the different clubs with his friends in Virginia Beach. She didn't mind it so much, but she had a feeling since most of his friends were single, he was flirting with other girls. It all came to a halt when Jason decided he was going to move in with friends and move out of the dormitory. With Chasity not driving, it would be hard to see him at his new place. He had two roommates, Carla and Woody.

Chasity never liked Carla and for good reason. Carla was always flirting with Jason even when they were together. "Why the hell would you move in with her of all people knowing how I feel about it?" Chasity had to pause and breathe. This is not how she wanted to spend her evening, but when Jason rolled up smiling brightly flashing his new apartment keys she had enough. "So, you just did it? You just ran off and moved in with them and didn't even talk to me about it first. Wow!"

"I don't have to run to you and tell you everything that I do! Who are you?" Chasity was floored at this admission. They broke up on the spot. Her friend, Kyle, could hear the yelling on the other side of the door. She didn't know it, but Kyle had stuck around to make sure the yelling didn't progress to anything more. When Jason stormed out of Chasity's dorm room Kyle was right there waiting for him.

"Everything alright in there?" Kyle asked sternly. He and Chasity were good friends, and he didn't appreciate Jason yelling at her in that manner.

"I don't think it's any of your business, actually!" Jason was pissed off and now taking his frustrations out on him.

Kyle told Jason, "Well, it is my business. And what you are not going to do is yell at her like you're her damn father! If y'all are beefing, then take your ass home and cool off. Do you understand that?" He wasn't a fan of Jason, but supported Chasity in anything that she wanted. He had run into Jason at a few of the clubs he frequented and didn't like what he saw, which normally was Jason getting other girls numbers. From what he could hear from the argument, Jason had messed up again. He loved his friend and was tired of her coming to him with their issues. Kyle and Chasity worked the same flight and shift. Normally people in the same flight were close knit. After spending hours upon hours on posts together, people tend to be more like best friends. He found out a lot about Chasity and only wanted to see her happy. Jason was not making her happy. Jason ran down the stairs of her third floor dormitory and sped off in his used blue Honda Civic.

Kyle stepped into her room. "Hey C, are you okay? I can't stand that dude."

"Yes, I am ok. Jason moved in with Carla without even letting me know beforehand. He knows I can't stand that chick." Chasity was exhausted. They were on their 24-hour break preparing for their midnight shift the next night. The goal was to stay up all night to get the body acclimated to the change. She normally still fell asleep around 2:00 am no matter how hard she tried. She was never a "night owl".

"Well I never liked that dude anyway. I think you can do better. There is something about him I just don't trust," Kyle said looking at his dear friend with caring eyes. To him, Chasity was the prettiest girl on base. He loved his friend. He wasn't in the position however to approach her in a romantic way. Kyle had a reputation of being a male whore, and Chasity was well aware of that. She didn't judge him for his escapades.

They stayed up talking for the better part of the night. He refused to leave her and stood up his date for the evening. "Don't you have plans tonight?" Chasity could have sworn she heard him bragging to the other flight members about getting with some girl from the supply squadron.

"Oh, yeah I do, but you are way more important than any hoe," he said laughing.

Chasity playfully punched him in the arm. "See that is why people can't take you seriously. You have *hoes* all over the base. She is thinking she could be the next Mrs. Kyle. I am sure of it."

Looking directly in Chasity's eyes, "I would only need one woman to take me seriously and *then* I am sure I would drop that name and make her Mrs. Anything she wanted to be." Chasity caught his gaze and smiled.

The next few weeks were nice. Kyle and Chasity spent a lot of their time at work together and off duty time as well. His *dates* were less frequent. He loved spending time with Chasity so much that he started to fall for her. "You know what C, you are really easy to love. I mean just damn. I never met a girl like you before."

Chasity sat there astonished. She could probably count on her one hand when she was rendered speechless. This was one of the times. "What do you mean? I am easy to love?" She had to question him. Up until this point in her life, she was made to feel like *loved* would be the hardest most distant thing for her to be.

"You just are. The way you are… so relaxed and so unique. At the same time, you are smart and call people out on their shit. At your core, you are the sweetest person ever. If anyone could ever fully get there, they would be the happiest man on earth. You have the ability to make a man feel like he is the only one that counts. Most often girls these days make dudes feel like an add on." Kyle spoke openly and sincerely. "When you do for people, you do it with nothing but a pure heart. Unlike many who do it to get shit in return. That is so dope to me. The fact that you are beautiful is just the added bonus to it all."

Chasity wasn't used to the compliments. Jason wasn't one to give her them for the most part. If she took the time to get ready and dolled up for him, he would just look at her and walk out the door. This was different. This was new and she liked it. It was as if he was almost talking to her in poetry. She was never one for superficial anything, but when a man stops and takes the time to tell you words straight from his heart, it was a lady's job to stop and listen and give him her undivided attention. That is exactly what she did. She didn't expect it, but she welcomed it. Kyle leaned over and kissed her so gently she could feel his love. He may not have said the words, "I love you," but he *showed* her and that mattered just as much. The only thing worth more than that is the confession with the action. Chasity kissed him back.

By now, Chasity and Kyle knew very intimate details about each other. When Kyle brought up her and Jason's previous sex life, she got quiet and admitted some things that she had never told anyone before. "What the hell do you mean he doesn't like going down on you? What the hell?!" Kyle was floored and annoyed. "That is foreplay. That is *needed*. Damn man. He ain't putting it down, huh?"

"I guess that is why your girls stalk you and always come back for more, huh? Because you give them head?" Chasity joked. She was the only one that could be so unfiltered, so honest and yet non-judgmental at the same time.

"Listen, ain't no shame in my game. I like eating the *cookies*. A man needs it for proper nourishment. Besides, if I don't do it, then someone could swoop right on in and do it for me." He looked at her again. "Hey C, do you think that you would ever give a guy like me a chance?"

The question was out of the blue and caught Chasity by surprise. "I would if you weren't running around doing what you do. I see what the other girls see. I think you are handsome, have a great body, flash a nice smile and all that superficial stuff. I also see you have a good heart and are protecting, caring, understanding and honest. Honesty is hard to come by these days. Your personality is great and you crack me up with your antics!"

It was this time she left him speechless when she kissed him. They were alone in his dorm room. "I am sure you have had a lot of girls in this position, huh?"

"None that I ever cared about. None that I ever wanted as much as I want you…" He kissed her again. "You may never be mine, but today I am going to give you something that ole boy won't and if you are ever with him again, you will think of me." Kyle was only 21 years old. He was not in the position to settle down. He knew Chasity would never take him seriously, but he wanted her that day and any other day she would allow him to do so.

Easing her pants down slowly and then taking off her panties, Kyle started to lick Chasity in the area that had been neglected for almost a year. She had forgotten how good it felt to be tasted. Jason made it seem as though the whole ordeal was repulsive. He had done it once and never again. She was having doubts about herself up until Kyle devoured her for hours. She had never climaxed before orally until that day. He licked and licked and licked her until her moans turned into screams. The more she moaned the more he flicked his tongue. He noticed she became unhinged when he flicked his tongue on her clitoris. That had been severely neglected with the added bonus of her not being a fan of masturbation. He drank every drop that she poured for him gladly.

He loved her sweetness on his tongue. He could perform this new ritual for her every day if she would let him. The more she reached out for him the more he became addicted. She was his weakness. Right there in his room in between her thighs it wasn't lust. It was love. It was giving back to her all the love she had given him and not even noticing. It was returning every smile, every giggle, every time she *listened* to him and gave him a hug after he admitted something hurtful.

He knew Chasity was a giver and he wanted to give her ecstasy ten times over. He didn't want intercourse. He just wanted her to be pleased.

Chasity had never been so aroused in her life. Up until then, she had not had very good oral sex performed on her. Between her first boyfriend and Jason, it was as if she was some scientific experiment gone wrong with more error than trials. She didn't know just how important it would be for her until Kyle. He had his technique down pat. He was the first one in her life who knew what he was doing and took the time to do it. He seemed to enjoy it just as much as she did. Maybe even more. After he was done, he held her while she went to sleep. He wanted nothing in return. She had given him enough from his point of view.

The days after that, nothing changed with them for the most part. He was grateful that he was able to give her a little something to remember him by. She knew it was not going to lead into an exclusive thing. They were still friends. Friends without limits who had shared the most intimate details of themselves with each other. Kyle kept on with his dates, and Jason started fishing around again. They had gone on a couple dates and actually he admitted he was wrong for how he went about things. Chasity looked at Kyle, but knew he wasn't ready for a relationship. They remained friends even when she and Jason got back together.

"So, has ole dude eaten your cookies yet?" Kyle was curious, but he was sure he already knew the answer to that.

Chasity laughed, "You are always talking about somebody's cookies. And to answer your question, no, he hasn't, and I don't bring it up anymore."

"Well my opinion, but that dude is dumb because I know what you got down there and that is something that *needs* to be *adored*." He was serious, but he chuckled.

Chapter 4

Chasity was still sleeping in preparation for her swing shift. It was only 9:00 a.m. and she didn't have to get to work until 12:00 p.m. She heard a banging at the door. Jason burst into the room. "You need to get up now! You need to call home!" Chasity was confused. Why was Jason in her room so early? He should have been at work. Why would she need to call home? Home is fine. New York is fine.

The date was September 11, 2001. It was the day everything changed for everyone. Jason turned on the TV. It was just then Chasity saw a plane crash into the World Trade Center. "Jason, what is this about? Why are you showing me a movie?" Chasity was still groggy and didn't have a clue as to what was going on.

"This is no movie, C. This is real. We are being attacked. The news is saying terrorist." Jason rattled off the words so fast she could barely understand what he had just said. She sat in horror. She sat in silence.

9/11 was one of those times in life where you knew exactly what you were doing, who you were with, and where you were in full detail. Some things you just don't forget. Some things are so embedded in your heart that they replay over and over at the slightest thought of that time period. This was one of those devastating times.

Chasity grabbed her phone and tried to call her mother. None of the signals worked. She could hear her instructor's voice. "We will train you for war as every other Security Force member has been trained before you. As we were all trained!" War? The country was at war. She was at war. Her brothers and sisters were at war. At this very moment. There is no turning back. She gathered her thoughts and sprang into action.

"Where are you going, C? What are you doing?" Jason panicked. She had been so quiet and now she was moving so fast he couldn't keep up.

"I have to go to work," Chasity replied calmly and grabbed her uniform, helmet, chemical warfare bag, bullet proof vest and flak vest. By the time Jason could say another word, Chasity was in full battle gear.

Chasity had yet to get her driving license. Jason took her to her Squadron. They drove in silence. The base was silent. Everyone that didn't need to be on base was evacuated. There were all kinds of reports. There were more planes. More planes were crashing. A plane had made it to the Capitol. A plane made it to the Pentagon. People were being murdered. We were being attacked. "I promise to protect and defend..." Chasity had repeated an oath that every other military member had sworn and she was helpless. What could she do? How was her family? Were they okay? Could she get there? Her thoughts were interrupted as the car came to a halt. "I'll be in my room. Call me when you have a chance. I need to know you are okay," Jason said in a concerning tone. Chasity had stopped speaking. She couldn't find any words to say anything. She was devastated and it showed in her face. She had lost her words.

Training had prepared her for war. It didn't prepare her for this. Her life up until this point had prepared her for this. She had to dig down in her instincts and dig up that faith. She had to dig into that strength. A place she didn't have to go often. This strength took concentration. She had to grow in her pain once more. *"My family…"* She had family members and good friends that worked inside, next door and around the corner from the Trade Center. She had a cousin who had joined the New York Police Department a year before she joined the Air Force. They were more like brother and sister than cousins. They were raised together. According to the media, all NYPD emergency personnel were dispatched to what is now been labeled *"Ground Zero."*

As she exited Jason's car, he gave her a hug and she walked out without saying a word. It was a mad house. People were running and donning gear. The heavy weapons were being issued. Not just the M-16A2 rifles and the normal 9mm hand guns. SF members were carrying machine guns and loading them on the High Mobility Purpose Vehicles (HMMWV). It was unlike anything she had ever seen in her life. It was something she never wanted to see again.

"All SF members from New York and surrounding Tri-State areas please report to the guard mount room ASAP!" the commander's secretary announced. Everyone grew quiet again. This attack hurt everyone, but for the New Yorkers it hit their core.

"We are aware of the devastating situation in NY. We are sending an emergency team there as we speak. None of you will be permitted to be on the emergency team. It is too emotional for you all at this time. We are also aware that you all are not able to reach your family members. Please continue to try to reach your family. The phone lines have all been crossed and we have not had proper contact with anyone in NY. Please give my secretary a list of numbers and contacts for us to try to call. If any of us finds any information about your family's whereabouts, we will let you know ASAP! The country is in mourning and we know this is hitting home for you all. By right we should not be arming you with weapons, but due to the nature of the situation, we have to post you. We have decided that your special group will not be permitted to be posted alone. All of you will be with a minimum of a four-person fire team. We are in fact in Force Condition Delta. The base has been cleared out of all civilians and contractors. If you all see anyone that does not live on this base, I don't care who it is, you will detain them. Our thoughts and prayers are with your families and we will do everything we can with what we have to ensure they are safe. God bless us all. You are all dismissed." The Colonel finished his speech. They could all tell it was not easy for him to get through, but as the commanding officer of over 500 Airmen, it was his duty. The rest of the unit received a less detailed speech with the addition of making sure everyone takes care of everyone. He reiterated that they were all family.

"Chasity, are you okay?" Colonel Disk asked her. He could tell out of everyone in the room, she was the most stone cold faced there. Her normal pleasant demeanor was gone. He was genuinely worried about her.

"No, sir. I am not." Those were the first words Chasity had spoken in about two hours.

"Your cousin, he's NYPD, isn't he? I remember you telling me about him." Col Disk was very personable. He wanted to know everything he could about his Airmen. A grand rarity amongst leadership.

"Yes, he is. From what I heard on the radio, all emergency personnel in NYC is considered missing." Chasity spoke with her voice as even as a straight line.

"What is your family's number? I will call them myself. I will sit here until I reach someone." Col Disk was genuine and he cared. He didn't lie to Chasity. He finally got a hold of her mother the next day. It was confirmed that her cousin David was missing. Chasity's heart sunk when she heard the news.

David was not deemed safe for another three days. Her other family members and friends were safe too. One of her aunts was stuck in a building that was going to collapse because of the amount of debris from the nearby dismantled buildings. The weight was too much for the surrounding buildings and businesses. Her other aunt who worked nearby had to walk from Manhattan to The Bronx. The subway and bus systems were all shut down throughout the city. As for her friend that worked inside the Trade Center, he got up late for work that day and never made it in.

Chasity was working over sixteen hours a day, and it was a tireless effort from all involved. She knew it was a matter of time before she would get the call to go overseas. Her family dreaded that call. The teams started going out about a month after. The base had opened up to more workers, but there were very strict rules. Due to the high demand of cops needed, the other units had to backfill and augment while the SF members got ready to deploy. Jason was chosen to be an augmentee. He finally understood what Chasity was actually doing in her daily and night job. He had complained that her job was easy. This was until he had to do it himself. He had nothing left to do but apologize.

Chasity spent most of her days trying not to think about 9/11, which was impossible since it now consumed everyone's life. That devastating event single handedly changed how all military bases conducted day to day operations. ID checks were in effect regardless of status and rank 100% of the time. There were more random anti-terrorism defense measures being performed throughout the base. Training was being changed at the Security Force Academy to combat more domestic threats to government assets and civilians. Everything had turned upside-down.

Chapter 5

The grueling hours, the Southern heat, the doom that the attacks had just begun, the reports from the news, the insurmountable amount of intelligence that was coming in. It was a lot. On some days, it was too much to bear. She was trained for this. Seven hours into her shift on the main gate into the base, the duty phone rang.

"Golf 1 A1C Gil speaking." Chasity answered the phone. She was the highest rank on the gate at the time overseeing the operations and augmentees.

"A1C Gil you are officially relieved of duty. You are to report to supply with all of your gear packed and ready to go. Go to the armory and turn in your weapon." The desk Sergeant rattled off her instructions and hung up the phone. She had no time to answer any questions. Just then a patrol car came driving by her flight chief. She loaded up her work gear and he took her to her dorm room. She was to grab her things and be at supply within two hours.

"Hi, Mommy." Chasity figured she would break the news to her mother first.

"Chasity, why are you calling me during the day? I know you are at work and phones aren't allowed. What is going on?" Laura knew something was wrong as soon as she heard her daughter's voice. Chasity was a strict-by-the-rules type of person and she would not be calling her. Chasity wasn't expecting her mother to catch on so quickly, but then again it was her mother.

"I am leaving." Chasity blurted the words out without any hesitation.

"Leaving to go where?" Laura was not happy and she wanted answers Chasity didn't have.

"I don't know. I have to report in to supply with my bags and gear to be checked. I guess I leave in the morning at 0600 hours." Laura was quiet. Too quiet for Chasity's liking. "Mommy, are you there? Did you hear me?" Just then Laura started to cry.

Chasity's father snatched the phone from her. "Chasity, you don't worry about anything back here. You do what you have to do and come home safely. I will take care of your mother. Don't worry. Now get your stuff together and call when you can. We love you."

Chasity made one more phone call. It probably should have been her first phone call about the deployment. Her grandmother, Mary. She started it the same way she started the conversation with her mother, but only her grandmother had a different reaction. "Young lady, I am proud of you. I am so proud of you and you make my heart smile. I want you to be safe and don't you dare worry about anything back home. We will be just fine and waiting for you to come home just as safe as the day you are to leave. If I were younger, I would go right along with you and we would do this together, but I am always with you. I love you." That was it. That was all Chasity needed to get herself together. "I was *trained* to do this."

She called Jason and he left work immediately to help her get ready. His shift was almost over and word had gotten around the unit that Chasity had been put on one of the "Teams to *nowhere.*" They got the name because the ones departing didn't know where they were going until they landed. They were sure it was to a desolate bare base.

One of those bases where there were only tents, no hardened facilities, potable water, toilets and other essentials.

When she arrived to supply, she counted 12 men and then herself as the only woman. She had no idea how she had gotten on this team not only being the only female but one of the only women that didn't volunteer in the first place. They simply replied, "You volunteered when you raised your right hand." After the bag check, they were told to report at 0400 for the 0600 departure. This would be another hurry-up-and-wait scenario. She didn't really have any friends on the team, but she figured sooner rather than later everyone would learn everything there was to know about each other.

Chasity had more reasons to be alarmed. After she made her phone calls, she ran to the hospital to get cleared by her doctor to deploy. Nothing that was supposed to happen in normal circumstances was being administered. Chasity, at this point, had her period for more than two months straight without any breaks. She was severely anemic. Her doctor had prescribed iron pills to control her levels.

"Am I going to be cleared to deploy, Sir?" Chasity asked the doctor nervously. She wasn't sure how she was going to leave under these circumstances. She was always fatigued due to the amount of blood she lost every day.

"Yes, I am clearing you. You will be fine. Here is a one-year prescription for your medications. I added more pain medication also. I assume you will be uncomfortable for most of your trip."

"Uncomfortable? I am not uncomfortable! I am bleeding and I have been bleeding for over 60 days and you are sending me to a bare base without proper hygiene and medical staff?" Chasity was upset and for good reason.

"Well I guess you better stock up on enough pads for a year then, huh?" the doctor said in a cold-hearted tone. He didn't care and handed her back her folder with her cleared paperwork. Chasity was devastated and told no one about the appointment other than Jason.

0300 came quick. Jason had stayed with her and took her to the meeting point. They hugged for a long while. "You call me as soon as you land… Wherever that is and whenever you can." Jason gave her a kiss and pulled away.

"I don't know when that might be. We are hearing different things, but one thing is that there are no phones where our final destination is, but I might be able to call while we are in transit." Chasity had no clue what she was getting herself into and doubted she would be able to comply with Jason's request.

"Just do what you can and let me know. Get me an address and I can send you whatever you need when you get there." Jason drove away. Chasity's heart sank as she noticed everyone was saying goodbye to their families and friends. One of the other squad members obviously thinking aloud, "Where the hell are we going?"

As they got to the C117 it was cold. The plane was noisy and everyone was too rattled to listen to any safety briefing. They were all giving individual hearing protection and wrapped up in their poncho lining. At first it was uncomfortable but they all managed to drift off to sleep. Their first stop was Portugal. It was beautiful. This had been the first time for many of the members of the team to leave North America. Chasity noticed it was a cow on the flight line. That would have never been permitted on Langley. It wasn't cold there. The temperature was just right. She noticed the roofs of the houses looked like a sea of half broken terracotta pots. *I would like to come back here one day*, Chasity thought. She was quiet for most of the trip. The other members were quiet as well. She did manage to make a quick call to Jason, her mother and grandmother while she was there.

The next destination had landed her in Kuwait. Kuwait was hot. It was the hottest place she had ever been in her life. She was delighted to hear that too was not their final destination. They stayed there in the terminal for over 10 hours. She didn't mind. She didn't want to explore anything about that country.

The next stop on the trip was Oman. Oman was another desert. It was hot, but the temperament was calm there. She had hoped they would stay there but they had too many cops and no work for them to do. They stayed there for a week. Finally, they reached Qatar. Qatar seemed hotter than Kuwait. It was a bare base like Oman, but with even less facilities. They were delighted to hear that they had just installed the shower tents. "At least we can wash!" she joked with Joey one of the members from her Squad.

"Yeah C, the little things aren't so little anymore." Joey responded with a half-smile. Joey was a year younger than Chasity. Those words meant so much.

She wasn't able to call home at this part of the trip. She did send letters. Unfortunately, the mail was very slow and it would be at least a week before they would receive it. "I just want my family to know I am okay."

They started working as soon as they got there. Within a day of landing she had her new flight and shift all worked out. She didn't know anyone, which could work out to be a good thing. She ended up getting posted with a guy named Jason. "You have the same name as my boyfriend back home so I will just call you J for short!" They became best friends' in Qatar. They had the same work schedule and days off. The guys she came with pretty much ignored her for the most part so she sought friendship with other people from other bases. There weren't too many girls there either, as you could imagine.

One day, Chasity was singing to herself. She didn't realize she was audible. She had her headphones on a little too loudly and couldn't hear anyone else other than Jill Scott. She was listening to her favorite song from her debut album *Who is Jill Scott*.

"You love me, especially different, every time. You keep me, on my feet, happily, excited, by, your cologne, your hands, your smile, your intelligence. You woo me, you court me, you tease me, you please me. You school me, give me some things to think about, ignite me, you invite me, you co-write me, you love me, you like me, you incite me to chorus…"

140

Chasity sang the lyrics and J took it all in. He had never heard anything more peaceful and more calming. *He Loves Me* was everything to Chasity and now it would be everything to him. He didn't realize how memorized he was until she caught herself and stopped singing.

"Oh, I am so sorry I get carried away sometimes!" Chasity was completely embarrassed. She didn't like to sing in front of people anymore. That was a hidden talent not to be shared with just anyone, which made her question why she did it in the first place. She was more comfortable with J than she wanted to admit.

"No, no please don't apologize! That was amazing. That was beautiful. I need to get that CD A.S.A.P!" J spent the next 5 minutes reassuring her that it was okay. "In fact, I would like it if you would sing to me more often. Your voice is my new favorite place." It was then she learned intimacy was not limited to any physical capacity.

She gazed at him and smiled. She really didn't know what to say. Other than playing at karaoke and being silly she never really did sing seriously anymore. Not until that day and that time. She agreed to give him his peace. Chasity sang to J every day that she could. He loved when they were posted together alone while on duty. It was filled with nothing but songs and poetry.

The team from Langley had been in Qatar a little over a month. They were called for a secret intelligence briefing. They didn't understand why until they got to the Intel tent. "You all have gotten orders to forward deploy to another base within the country." The team was stunned. No one had any answers as to why. They were to leave in two days. Chasity and the others quickly wrote letters to their families letting them know they will be departing to yet another unknown location.

When they arrived to the new base they were the only Airmen there. Period. Chasity was now the only woman on the base. They didn't stay long. Just long enough to set up the Tactical Automated Security Equipment (TASS). That is when Chasity realized how and why she was put on the team. Chasity and Joey were recent graduates of the training program. They only stayed in that location a week. They never had an address so they just left. There was no one to tell and no way to tell them of their new destination.

The team landed in Spain. There they stayed for five days awaiting their next destination. "Hi Mommy! I am okay!" Chasity said in a tired but cheerful voice.

"Where are you? You sound much closer than you had been before." Laura was alarmed but happy. It appeared Chasity was finally out of harm's way.

"We just landed in Spain. We will be here for a few days while we wait for our next destination." Chasity had heard rumors they were going to one of the "Stans" but wasn't sure, and surely, she would not worry her mother for no reason without having had a firm answer. "I am not quite sure where we are headed Mommy, but if I can call when I get there, I will."

The US troops were headed to the mountains of different "Stans" in search of terrorists. That was one place she didn't want to go either. She was going to cause even more ruckus than needed before she had all the details.

Spain like Portugal was beautiful. She was loving Europe at the moment. It was making all of this jumping around worthwhile. They needed new gear. They had always been sent to warm climates and this time they would be flown to the complete opposite. The men in Spain flirted heavily with her. She was starting to see a trend in the European countries and she appreciated all of it. They had nothing for colder weather. An emergency order and authorization to get cold weather garments, boots, gloves and all the essentials were immediately approved.

They left in the middle of the night. They had to fly at night apparently due to the dangers of landing during daylight. It was freezing. Chasity had felt New York City cold and even Canada cold, but she had never felt Uzbekistan cold. The frigid wind seemed to cut through her uniform as if she didn't have anything on. The members exited the C117 and laid prone forming a 360-degree security of the plane. The crew was small. To include the 13-man team of SF, it totaled around 20 people. There were four women in all. Chasity, two other white women and one other black woman.

Once the plane was secure and had taken off, it was time to convoy up to the where-they-would-call-home for the next 30 days. It was hard to describe it as a convoy since it only consisted of two local vans. As they arrived to their destination the sun was beginning to rise and they could see exactly what the country looked like. The streets were empty because of the early hour. They drove into a large gate and walked into the house. That is when they all realized they would not be staying on a base. They would be staying in a community. The neighbors started peering and forming their surveillance as soon as the Americans walked into the small compound. They were greeted by two Russian soldiers who knew hardly any English. "What in the world is this place?" Chasity thought to herself.

All of the other cops claimed the basement. Since she was the only female cop, she stayed in a large room with the other three women. After about two days, the four women turned into three. Apparently on the flight line the local people were not very welcoming to the other black female.

One of them shouted "Girl Nigga" to her and she pointed her weapon at them. To combat an international incident and due to the sensitive nature of the event, the sergeant was shipped out the very next day. That is when Chasity began to understand the nature of this particular destination.

Chasity hated Uzbekistan. The only people who were nice to her in the entire country were the translator and the two Russian soldiers. The soldiers called her "Beauty" and in the most broken English she had ever heard they warned her to be careful. She would soon figure out what they meant by their warning.

Her next shift at the flight line she was greeted with the same men that had taunted the other woman. For hours she heard "Girl

Nigga, Girl Nigga!" Chasity held her bearings unlike the other woman and took the abuse. Finally, one of the Uzbek soldiers that shared the flight line with the Americans and the French, ran the guys away. Chasity was grateful for their kindness, but the taunting continued every single day she stood her post. The flight line was hardly considered that and very hard to secure the area so locals had ample time and space to shout their derogatory slurs against her.

By the next time the men returned they were throwing their money at her trying to get the men she was working with to sell her for prostitution. She felt helpless and violated standing at attention holding her military bearing. The racial taunt did not cease. It was the first time she had been called a "Nigga" to her face and she was stuck to endure it in a third world country.

She wished she were back in Qatar with J. She would have never wished for him to be in Uzbekistan with her to witness her constant turmoil. There was no way to write him or anyone else from their previous deployed location. In some cases, it was easier if people were overseas at the same time to communicate, but without an address, reliable phones and email it made it impossible. There was no contact with family and friends back home either. She was stuck in a real-life hell.

Since the Americans were not on a military installation like most deployments they had to go to the market like everyone else. Another duty for the SF members was to go and provide protection at the market for the finance officers buying the food. Theft was high in Uzbekistan and it was well assumed the American's had money. The value of a dollar was worth way more than the value of their denarii.

The first trip for Chasity at the market was seemingly uneventful. The market was outside. It was just a blocked off section of the road where people would sell goods, food and other items. Fresh cut meat hung from hooks, beans and rice were in large bags to be scooped and measured, fruit were left out to be picked and sorted, different kinds of premade salad was left out in the elements to be chosen and bought. The market area was big and crowded.

People stared at her as if she was a visible walking ghost. They would not speak to her or help her. After the issues, she had on the flight line, she didn't think she would get much help anyway. However, the second trip to the market didn't go so smoothly. The children had run up to her and started to pull her glove back on her hand. "Why are they doing this?" she asked the translator.

With down cast eyes, she replied "They want to see if your color will come off. They think that you are dirty. Most of these people have never seen your kind before." The response from the translator jolted through Chasity.

By the third and final trip to the market Chasity was officially scarred. She didn't feel so comfortable after the second market trip so she opted to carry an additional 9mm concealed in her coat, as well as a knife. As soon as she exited the van, the stares began. Eyes followed her all through the aisles and it began to lightly snow. The locals started throwing food at her. Rice and beans were being spewed in her direction. All of a sudden she heard the translator scream to her "Run! Run! Run! You must go to the van! Leave now!" Chasity without hesitation left without a single reply. She made it to the van and it took off. The driver knew exactly what to do. Those waiting in the van covered her with a blanket and she rode the way back to the compound on the vehicle floor.

Chasity's heart was pounding. She was out of breath. She only ran in life and death situations and she assumed this was one of those times. She had only been in the country for 2 weeks. The entire country hated her. Chasity had become a social outcast from an entire country. To make matters worse, some of the guys that vowed to treat her like a little sister were looking at her as if she was just another woman. Her team leader Master Sergeant Kris had tried to get her drunk a number of times even though she was only 20 years old. It was so bad that she would have to curse him out and tell him she would report him. He would simply say, "Report me to whom?" He was using every trick he could think of to try to sleep with her.

She was alone. She was alone now in a country that she hated and a country that hated her. She was no longer permitted to go to the market and soon after, she wasn't allowed to work on the flight line either. Chasity was confined to the compound. There were no phones. There was no mail. There was no family. There was nothing but despair. She fell into a deep depression. She would sleep with her weapons wrapped around her at night. She didn't feel safe because she knew she wasn't safe. She trusted no one.

Finally, they got the orders to leave immediately within one hour. There was no hurry up and wait this trip. As the next 13-man squad exited the plane the team from Langley loaded up. There was no "out" brief. There was no conversation. The next thing they knew, they landed in Germany. By then Chasity had withdrawn to herself and her team didn't seem to mind. The first night in Germany was terrible. Her team lead tried, again, to get her drunk. It was so bad the bartender was warning her not to drink the drink he said was cranberry juice. On the next stop her immediate supervisor had trapped her in a corner trying to accost her. Joey and another team member, Jake, had to pry him off of Chasity. She was crying uncontrollably. They rushed her in the cab. Her offender went to grab her and Jake punched him in the face.

After those incidences, Chasity spoke to no one. She ate by herself and stayed on base alone while the others explored Germany. She hated everything about that country. At this point, she just wanted to go home. She knew if she called home now she would burst into tears and didn't want to alarm her family. It was time to go home. Team Langley would finally, be able to go home. Chasity breathed a sigh of relief. In five short months she had traveled to destinations she had never thought to dream of, met people she would have never known, been called a nigga to her face, tried to be bought for prostitution and experienced team members' abuse. None of that mattered. It was time to go home.

Chapter 6

It took about a year for Chasity to get adjusted to being at home. When she returned from the first deployment she was not the same person she was when she had left. It was noticeable at first. She never spoke of what happened overseas, but there were rumors. Soon her team lead was removed from her unit altogether and she never saw him again. That was a comforting fact. She was awarded the Air Force Commendation Medal for her trouble. A small token of thanks for nearly losing your life and sanity. She was still bleeding. She had bled every day of her horrendous deployment. The doctors did nothing for her. She finally was able to change her primary care provider and her new doctor had placed her on birth control to try to combat the irregular cycle.

She was used to the phone call. It was déjà vu. "Hi mommy…" It was as if she could hit record and play the whole conversation over again. It was time for Chasity to go on another deployment. Another team to nowhere. This time was a bit different. There were rumors that the US was heading to war with Iraq and needed troops on the ground before anything was to start up. This was another volunteer deployment that she, once again, didn't volunteer for.

This time she had a week to prepare. Jason who had stuck by her for the first trip, was still by her side for the second. Although seemingly a little distant this go around. Chasity figured it was her nerves. If she survived the first one, she would survive the second. She was now 21 and had too much life ahead of her. At least this time she had time to complete her Will.

They left right before Valentine's Day and found themselves landing in Saudi Arabia. It was hot during the day and freezing at night. That particular base would not be their final destination, but, at this point, Chasity knew the drill well. This time around she was not the only female on the 13-man team. This made it easier. She didn't know Jane very well but they were slotted to live with each other for 6 months to a year. She knew by the end all they would have was each other. Jane had just gotten married the day before they left. Her honeymoon would be spent in the desert with her husband another cop in VA. Jane was crazy, but she was funny. As long as she remembered to take her medication, everything would be okay. Chasity never found out why Jane was on meds. She didn't want to pry either.

Once they made it to their final destination for the time being, it was all surreal. It was completely bare. Most of the cops on the team looked to her, Chasity, for guidance since she had just come from a bare base. Her friend Thomas was on a previous team to nowhere but he ended up in a different destination and had not experienced this before. She was closer to the people on this team than she had been on the last. That was reassuring. She had gone through the academy with two of the members. They were more like family than teammates. She was already off to a better start this go around. However, it didn't remove the danger.

The sirens blared throughout the base. The war had begun. That was their notice. There were no phones or email at their location. Chasity heard the sirens and jumped out of the vehicle she was posted in on the flight line. She donned her new chemical suit as she was trained to do and performed a good seal on her gas mask. Now it was time to wait. Wait for an explosion, a chemical attack something. Wait for anything. Wait for everything. The sweat dripped from every crevice of her body. The heat was excruciating with the extra layer of equipment. "I could *die* today." That was her realization. When most 21-year-olds were somewhere getting drunk she was sitting on a flight line sealed in chemical equipment praying that if today is the day of her death that her family knew she loved them.

She knew they would know. Like she always did since Basic Training she kept a note for herself for encouragement and a note to her family just in case she didn't make it home the way she left. The all clear siren beamed over the base. It would be safe to assume that she would live to see another day. How many days that would be? Well that isn't a question she had the right to ask.

Chasity prayed often. She didn't have much time to go to church, but when she did, she met a friend named Tony, another cop from another base who had a lot in common with her. This deployment was just all around better than the last, if not for the comradery alone. Chasity's team worked 30 days before they had their first day off. They were the first team to make it to the base and the first team to get orders out.

The war in Iraq was raging on. It was taking longer than the first Gulf War had ever been. That one was barely a week. Chasity remembered because she was just in the 4th grade during it. She remembered sending letters to the troops down rage. Now she was the Airman receiving letters from the elementary school students. "Langley is going to Baghdad." Those words rang in Chasity's ears like the first siren from the scud missile attack to the base. The Air Force was now sending her to the heart of the war. The US had just taken over Sodom International Airport and renamed it Baghdad International Airport. When the news broke out about Langley's orders, the other teams were quiet. Everyone was getting sent to a safe destination. Well as safe as you can be with your country at war.

As the plane loaded up, she could hear OutKast's song *Bombs over Baghdad* screeching through the airwaves. Everyone stopped and looked at each other. They waved and boarded the plane. It was the worst flight any of them had ever taken. Because of the threat the C130 had to take extra precautions and fly under the radar. The plane was still taken fire occasionally which means turbulence was eminent. So many people started to throw up. There was no room for some to sit and others had to find a place to put on gear and equipment. The plane reeked of the odor of warm vomit. It was the longest 2-hour flight any of them had ever had.

As soon as they landed, the Iraqi welcoming committee greeted them with a mortar attack to the flight line. All of the service men and women dropped to the hot pavement. The steam from the ground drifted to their faces. The hot tarmac seeped through their uniforms. They had nowhere to go. Eventually the explosions ceased.

Chasity knew they would be put to work as soon as they landed. What she wasn't expecting was to pitch a tent before she had to go to work. The women didn't have a place to sleep. The tents could fit ten people comfortably. In most cases 15 to 20 were crammed due to space issues. It was hot. It was dusty and, like the other desert countries, it had a stench unlike anything she was able to describe. She never understood the smell, and Iraq, like Oman, Qatar, Kuwait and Saudi Arabia, had a foul smell in the air. It was impossible to escape. After a while people would get used to it. It was a sign that they had been there too long. Six hours later Iraq smelled normal. It was Iraq, it was May of 2003 and it was hot. Chasity was used to the heat. It was that kind of hallucinating heat that made you believe you can see the waving in the air.

For the most part, the team stuck together and made the most of the base. There, Chasity was exposed to more than she had ever been. Even more than Uzbekistan. She was exposed to death. They got attacked every single day. The members grew numb to the sound of exploding concrete. *If I can hear it, then I am still alive.* That is what Chasity told herself as she rolled over and went back to sleep.

On one normally hot day Chasity was pulled from her post to run a c-wire detail outside of the wire for the base. She hated going out there but she didn't have a choice. The Sergeant from another base requested her assistance. Her immediate supervisor was not around. She hopped in The HMMWV with the Sergeant and an Airman, she had never met. HMMWVs are big and clunky yet they have little room inside which could leave people crammed. There was not comfortable at all, but essentially, they were the safest way to travel besides an actual tank in that environment. As most desert vehicles this one was tan to help camouflage and blend in with the surroundings. When they arrived, they hopped out and she put on her specialized c-wire gloves. The gloves were heavy and hot. Thick staples were throughout the gloves to further protect your hands. She kept them on her at all times.

Just as the detail was about to finish out of the corner of her eyes she saw a car speeding in the direction of the base. This wasn't too uncommon. The airport was holding various prisoners. Everyone from curfew violators to terrorist. She would see them being hauled in the back of cattle trucks with potato sacks over their faces so they couldn't tell anyone else the layout of the airport. The car parked in front of the last entry to the base. At that moment, everyone in the vicinity ducked for cover. Somehow it had sped past a number of truck searching checkpoints on the way to the base. There were always multiple search pits to check for an array of explosives that could be hidden on the vehicles. This was at a time where suicide bombing was being used as a defensive tactic.

Chasity's weapon of choice for the day was her favorite, a M203 grenade launcher. She liked it because of the fact that she had two weapons in one. She had already had a round in the M16 chamber, a mandatory practice for everyone who worked outside the wire at that particular time. Crouching behind the barrier, she could hear the Marine give the commands for the area. At this point, it wasn't about being a separate service. They were all American. They were all military. "203 load grenade." Chasity removed a grenade from her vest and loaded it in her barrel. She waited. She breathed slow and steady. She was able to see three people in the front seat of the vehicle.

"Father, protect me. Father, forgive me," she said a silent prayer.

"203 gunner prepare to fire." She heard the Marine's command and she was prepared. She was trained for this. "Just come home *safely*." She remembered the words of her grandmother. It was one of the last things she said when she hung up the phone. "God *forgive* me," Chasity prayed again. There were times when her religion and her duties collided and today she prepared to sin.

"203 *hold!*" The Marine commanded. The instructions were short and to the point. This wasn't the time for extra syllables and fluff. The quickest way to let the troops know what to do, how to do it and when to do it. This was a life or death situation. At this point it seemed as though death was the only option. Death for her or death for the three passengers in the vehicle. And all she heard was the Marine. All of a sudden, as her finger was on the trigger to release the grenade, the car slowly backed up. "203 prepare rifle," the Marine commanded. At this point, the car was too close for the grenade and was in range of her M16-A2. She followed the car looking through her weapons sites. The car turned around and drove away.

Chasity, up until this moment, was merely highly trained to protect and defend, but today that training was tested and she knew without a shadow of a doubt she could kill. It was a startling discovery. It was a side of her she had never seen. She wasn't quite sure what to make of the whole ordeal. Just then she realized that the Airman that had ridden with them had a panic attack. He had freaked out crying and screaming right next to her and she had no idea. The Noncommissioned Officer in Charge, better known as the NCOIC, of them was trying to calm him down. Chasity was amazed that she was able to block everything out.

They arrived to the Air Force tent area. "You really didn't hear that knuckle head go off back there, did you?" the NCOIC broke the silence.

"No, I didn't. I only heard the commanding Marine's voice," Chasity said in a solemn tone.

"Well young lady, what you did back there was one of the most heroic things I have ever seen anyone do. You were prepared to save all of our lives no matter the cost. No matter what was going on around you. You were so focused. Thank you!" The Sergeant thanked her as she stared out the window.

She didn't know what to make of what he said to her. All she could think of was the honest truth "I am just doing what we are all trained to do. I just want us to get home safely. All of us."

The Sergeant looked at her and said, "I would go to war with you any day. I know that you are going out of here in one piece." She didn't reply to that. She may get out in one piece, but would she return the same? She wasn't sure if that was a compliment or not.

By the time they exited the vehicle, word had spread like wild fire of the incident. Her supervisor ran up to her and asked if she was okay. She just walked away without saying a word. He was back briefed of the details by the NCOIC. At that moment, no member of Langley's team was allowed to go anywhere off their original post without notification of their supervisor. Chasity turned in her weapon early that day. She wanted to cry but she couldn't. She didn't know what she was crying for. "Father, forgive me."

Chasity's supervisor Staff Sergeant Alton was in charge of the team. Even though he was not their team lead. Master Sergeant Clayton was actually the Squad leader. After finding out the team would be forward deploying to Iraq, he wanted nothing do with his Airmen. "I can't believe I am going into the *shit* with you two," MSgt Clayton said pointing at Celeste and Jane. Clayton was one of those people who didn't believe women should be in the military. It was a sad and unfortunate discovery found out half way through the grueling deployment. After his rant, the team members lost respect for him and wanted nothing to do with him at all. When something went wrong or right, they went straight to SSgt Alton.

It was hard for Jane and Chasity to deal with the realization of knowing that there were still, after all this time, soldiers who were against women being in their career field and that some didn't feel they were worthy of that beret. The beret they all wore and earned. That day when Chasity walked away quietly MSgt Clayton ran after her to get the story. She kept walking as if he didn't exist. Regardless of his feelings of her or anyone like him, she was going to be the reason everyone would have survived that day. Without hesitation, Chasity was prepared to do exactly what it took to make it home, even if that meant taking another life.

The next few weeks were a blur. The attacks at the airport occurred every day. If the base went without an explosion for more than 5 hours, people panicked. Chasity couldn't however get used to the number of wounded soldiers and marines that would flow through her check point. It was gut wrenching. She would never forget the looks on their faces as they held their fellow comrade with their blood mixed with his. Unable to tell one from the other. The gruesome details of those days would haunt her nights. The countless body bags that were air lifted from the medical tent also doubled as the morgue. She spent her 22nd birthday in Iraq. It was one to remember for all the wrong reasons.

Chasity always loved fireworks. Granted her birthday was on the nations coveted 4th of July. Not only was she an Independence Day baby, she was a veteran. Not just an average veteran, but now a veteran of a foreign war. She was posted on the flight line that night. The closest thing to fireworks she would see or hoped to see was the random trip flares that were going off around the base.

Over the radio, she could hear the sound of chaos and the screaming for her to leave the area of her post. She floored the gas pedal of her HMMWV and left her area. Just then explosions were going off behind her. The mortar attacks were at her post that night. She had moved her vehicle right on time. Had she not, she didn't think she would have survived or at a minimum severely injured. Chasity was just trying to make it home.

The stress mounted on the team. It was hard. Every single day was hard. Every single day was hot. One of the members had a nervous breakdown. Trevor could no longer take the stress of being in a war zone and so far from home. He was posted on a 4-man fire team around the flight line. During their break, he calmly un-mounted his M60 machine gun, laid prone on the hot desert ground and proceeded to aim his weapon at the command tent. "Do not aim at anything you don't intend to shoot!" We all knew the rules for our weapons. It had been engrained in our heads and hearts. Trevor had every intention of shooting his target. It struck everyone to the core. It was almost unbearable, the terrible realization of leaving Virginia with a 13-man team and only returning with twelve. They took care of him the best they could. He was assigned to the medical tent. The same medical tent that doubled as the morgue. How was that fit for an unstable individual? Around the clock they would sign him out as if he were a piece of equipment. He couldn't take hearing the screams from the soldiers being operated on. We all heard the cries. We all saw the blood. He was shipped to Germany for observation. The team was disheartened as well as relieved. He didn't need to be there. He didn't need to see that.

After the departure of Trevor, the team hit an all-time low. The smiles that kept them going dissipated as sweat evaporated from the 125-degree heat. With the amount of protective gear warn it could feel an upwards of 135 degrees. Langley was the first team ordered to return to home station. They had been gone the longest in Baghdad. After the incident with Trevor, leadership feared it might set a precedent.

There was a minor incident that further troubled Chasity. While doing a patrol in what the compound called "Tent City" where the Airmen would live, eat, sleep and mostly work. There had been a breech in the c-wire by a woman in the Army. Chasity was shaken by this. Her leadership really wanted to treat her as a criminal. "Search her," the onsite supervisor said.

"Why? I don't understand? Why am I searching her? She's an American. We wear the same uniform. She is not a criminal! She is just hungry. She didn't breach us for violence. She had nothing to eat!" Chasity was upset and the supervisor was unfazed.

After the search, the two ladies spoke softly in the tent. The woman was about the same age as Chasity. Sitting on opposite ends in the tiny space. Chasity asked, "What's your name?" The soldier replied, "Private Cole." She was in her physical training gear and not her Desert Dress Uniform, the DCU.

"Why did you do it? Why did you steal? You could have just asked for food." It broke Chasity's heart to have this conversation. Here they were in the middle of Iraq and they were not only fighting to survive the war from hostiles, but they were fighting for the basic needs to keep them going.

"I was just so hungry. I hadn't eaten in days. Everyone here knows that the Air Force has food and supplies. I was just hungry. I didn't mean anything by it." The soldier put her head down in embarrassment. It was at that moment she knew she had chosen the better branch of service to enlist into.

"I notice something majorly different about the two branches. You see with the Air Force deploys, even when we don't have much, all the units and career fields bring our resources together. Whether it is food, tents, water or other supplies. The Army, I noticed, kept things for themselves. If one Battalion has tents and the other doesn't you all don't share. If one has food and the other has water, you don't combine your resources it seems. When we deploy, we build up until we can't. Until we are literally kicked out of the country. We are constantly building a base even if it is temporary and consistently increasing the standard of living. I drove by an Army compound and the tents were not complete. The hot desert air and dust were blowing. I will never understand that about you all. If anything, I would say that is what makes us different. If you are hungry, ask. If you are thirsty, ask. Do not steal. Please." Just then Chasity gave the woman her breakfast for that morning. It was okay that she skip a meal. They were only rationed three Meals Ready to Eat a day. She knew she could count on her team to share their MRE with her. It was just for one day. It wouldn't kill her.

Cole was grateful. She ripped open the MRE and at that moment Chasity knew she was telling the truth. It had been days since her last meal. Chasity handed her a bottle of water. Another necessity that was scarce for some soldiers. In fact, she had been sharing her water since the time she landed. It seemed to be a precious resource that was hard to come by. With the sweltering heat, it was impossible to live without it. Joey's words chimed in her head "The little things just aren't *little* anymore." She gave Cole a hug and she cried. Not a dramatic cry. Just a soft whimper.

"We are going home finally!" Chasity thought to herself. She was exhausted. What he had experienced in Baghdad was unlike anything she had ever experienced in her life. It was like living in a movie that she was trapped in and couldn't escape. For weeks, she had nightmares of seeing blood. Blood of the fellow military members who voluntarily put their lives on the line to protect and defend the United States of America. She would never forget. She couldn't forget. Iraq had taught her so much about herself and her own perseverance. The plane took off. "Father, *forgive* me," she silently prayed one last time.

CILICIA

I loved you
I loved you on the conditional basis
That you
Would love me too
And even when
You showed lack of affection
Dismal attention
Character defamation
I still
Loved you past the prime
Past the time
I should have
Gotten rid of your presence
From my present
Long before
I learned to love
Correctly
Effectively
Subjectively
I will not submit to you
How dare you throw
The bible and its rules
As if I have not read
As if not engrained in my spine
As I
Erectly stood up with no curves in mine
I told you no
I told you to go
Back to the place
Where earth meets fire
To the depths and core of inner seasons
You gave me every reason
You gave me no choice

To voice to you what your ego
Couldn't handle
Well I am not your ego stroker
And you are not my choke holder
I have broken free
From the clenches of your fist
The screams
I love you means nothing
It's a figment dream you sold me
And I naively bought
Your fragrance is stench
Your touch is jagged
As if walking on broken glass
I gladly did
That was the path
That led down the roads away from you
With blooded feet
And whipped hands
I trailed that way from you
I ran away from you
So the conditional love
I speak of
Has fallen away from you
Because you rejected
My reflection
Placed in the tiniest
Of gifts
My very own coco covered porcelain doll
You cannot break her as if she were me
As if she were nothing
Spirits please I beg please
Guide me
For the shared pieces of broken glass

Is just my heart
That I too took part
In shattering
Now forced to run
With all of this under my feet
I'll come back for it some other day
But right now
This very instance I must go
And leave it all behind
I must go
And hide
I must pray
I must decide
That the lies I have told
Big and bold
In notes that I wrote
Mean something
I matter
I do
I believe it to be true
And now
I am free of you
I am free of me
Believing lies
Believing your hostility
Was love in the first place
And maybe if Daddy didn't lie
All those times
And maybe if I would have fought just a bit harder
Surrounded by golden sun kissed painted walls
And screamed
Just one more time LET GO OF ME

You would have never occurred
Because I would have seen your snare
From miles away
Understanding
Wolves in sheep's clothing
Your smile
Your grimace
And my karma
As I run for my life
Trampling on my deadened heart
That no one really cared for
I accept the lessons learned

Chapter 1

"New York is just a regular city, just like any other city. I don't know what is so special about it," Jeremey stated.

"Only people who have never been there would say something like that. Jeremey. I am really tired of you talking about my city, so I arranged for us to go to New York for a 5-day trip. We will be staying in a hotel in the heart of the city. After the five days are up, *then* we will see if it is just like any old city," Cilicia teased.

The vacation was all set and Jeremey even though he had talked a bunch of mess to Cilicia. He was originally from Indiana and later moved to Florida when he was about 9 years old. His argument was that he was from a "Ville." Evansville and Jacksonville were both "big cities." Cilicia at that point had not gone to either one and still didn't know how he could come up with that conclusion.

"Aren't we driving?" Jeremey asked. He wasn't up for driving the eight hours, but how else would they get there?

"Nope, we are taking the train. I have two Amtrak tickets with our names on it. There is no reason to drive, if we are staying in the city. Besides, I don't feel like dealing with the hassle of trying to find some place to park it," Cilicia responded casually.

"Okay so I guess you have everything all set up, huh? All I have to do is show up," Jeremey laughed. Cilicia ignored him and kept packing.

"Are we going to visit your family while we are there? I have only met your dad, mom and cousin." Jeremey was full of questions.

"Yes, we are going to visit but we are not staying with them. They are all in the Bronx. We are staying in Manhattan." Cilicia was hoping this was it for the questions, although she knew that there would be a million more before they even made it to the station.

Two days later they were off. The train was spacious and relaxing. Cilicia had made some snacks for the trip so they would be good along the way. "Now we are in Jersey, the next stop will be Penn Station. When we get there, stay close to me. It will be crowded. You will get pushed and shoved. It's okay. They don't mean it. People are just busy trying to get to where they are going. New Yorkers get a bad rap but we are good people. We are just focused, that's all," that was his disclaimer. She knew he wouldn't pay attention to what she said at first, but he will need them. Just wait on it.

"Are you really giving me instructions?" Jeremey laughed hard. He thought she was over reacting. Clearly everything would be fine.

"Okay, we are here. Keep your bags close and stay ever closer to me. I walk fast when I am home and I need you to keep up," Cilicia said as she exited the train. They rode the escalator to reveal the massive sea of people walking briskly in all directions. She looked at Jeremey to see the shock in his eyes. Now she was the one laughing "Come on!"

"Wow I have never seen so many people in one spot in my life! I wish I could see Madison Square Garden!" Jeremey couldn't hide his excitement.

"Oh, that's an easy one. Turn around and look up," Cilicia said giggling. "The station is actually under Madison Square Garden." Jeremey was speechless and just stood there looking up. He didn't even realize Cilicia had stopped and purchased two WNBA tickets. It was the only event going on during their stay. It was the end of the New York Liberty season and this was their final game.

They walked passed Macy's and got a cab. They made it to the hotel and checked in. The room was on the 15th floor. "I have never stayed this high up before!" Jeremey exclaimed.

"I figured that so I had the receptionist place us on a higher floor. How are you liking your New York experience?" Cilicia said with a warm smile giving Jeremey a hug.

"I love it! Okay, I have been here for 30 minutes and I can say this is nothing like any 'Ville' that I have ever lived in," Jeremey finally admitted.

Cilicia is not the "I told you so" type of person, but that would have been the perfect time for it. They decided to walk up and down Broadway. "I want to see a play. I have never seen one before and it looks like we are staying right where they all are playing. I can get tickets for it! Let's see a play!" Jeremey said walking up to one of the ticket booths.

Cilicia knew about him wanting to see a play from before they left Virginia. He had made such a big deal about it, he ran out and brought himself a brand-new suit for the trip. He even had her buy a new outfit for it.

"We are going to see Aida! Tony Braxton is in it! You love her. Wow this is like seeing a play and a concert all for the price of one. Do you think your mom wants to go? I can get her a ticket too." And that is exactly what Jeremey did. The play was in a couple days, but first things first, she had to surprise him with his ticket to the WNBA game.

"Thanks! So now that we have that all taken care of, we need to get ready for the event tonight." Cilicia didn't tell him what the surprise was until they arrived at the Garden. It was such a good night. Jeremey was so happy he kissed her right there on the spot. She was always pretty good about keeping him happy, but this was over the top. It didn't matter that the Liberty had lost to the Los Angeles Sparks. They had gotten so many free things that night, since it was the final game. The free t-shirt was just an extra token of just how memorable the trip would be.

Jeremey was having a great time looking like a tourist. He was taking pictures of buildings and walking around with his head up the entire time. Cilicia let him have his fun as she stayed on the lookout for potential threats. He was just taking it all in and she loved every minute of it. They didn't have time to take a bus tour so they did some sightseeing on their own. It was turning out to be a wonderful trip.

The night of the play Jeremey was extremely nervous. Cilicia didn't understand why? They arrived at the theater and her mom, Carol, and Aunt Darlene met them there. The play was amazing! The theater was beautiful. It looked as if they had walked in to the midcentury with the walls dipped in gold and grand chandelier of crystals. Jeremey was so happy and her family really enjoyed it also. Tony Braxton gave a superb performance which lead to a standing ovation.

For Cilicia, this was not her first Broadway play. Darlene had taken her to her first play for her 16th birthday. She surprised her with tickets to see Rent. It was the perfect "Sweet 16" gift! Her mother had promised her a huge birthday party to celebrate on a glass bottom boat. Needless to say, the party never happened. Not only did the party not happen she didn't even have a birthday cake. Cilicia ended up going to the bodega on the corner and buying a Little Debbie Cupcake and singing happy birthday to herself with a single candle. If it weren't for Darlene, she wouldn't have had any good memories about the supposedly "Sweet 16" for the rest of the month. Cilicia was singing to herself "500,025,600 minutes…," a piece from a song called Seasons of Love. That number was in the running for replacing her already favorite number four.

168

Chapter 2

After the play, Darlene and Carol said their goodbyes and parted ways making their way back to the Bronx. Jeremey and Cilicia stayed in Manhattan. She would always tell him about her high school prom. It was held in the beautiful Marriot Marque in Time Square. There was a revolving room that overlooked the city. If you sat in one spot, you could see all of New York in a one hour turn. During the prom, it was where the cocktail reception was held.

They got off of the elevator to meet the hostess. The venue was broken up into three parts. The restaurant, dance club and lounge. The couple wasn't hungry so they opted for the lounge. Jeremey was in awe of the view. The entire ordeal was breathtaking.

"Are you having a good time?" Cilicia asked Jeremey. Up until this point she was sure he was, but now he was fidgeting and appearing to be uneasy. *Maybe he doesn't like the lounge*, doubting herself.

"Uhhh yeah, I am having a great time," Jeremey said nervously. The waitress came and took their drink order interrupting his statement, which appeared to be a relief for him.

I wonder what he is up to. Cilicia said to herself. Jeremey was normally the life of any room. He was always comfortable and would be his own entertainment if he had to be. He had a very outgoing personality, which balanced Cilicia's somewhat quiet demeanor.

The waitress came over and gave them their drinks. Even though they were both twenty-two, Cilicia did not drink alcohol. She ordered her favorite virgin strawberry daiquiri. Jeremey, aware of this, didn't like to drink alcohol around her, so he ordered a sprite.

The two sipped their drinks in silence. The next thing Cilicia knew, Jeremey had gotten up from his chair and was down on one knee. It was right then that her heart stopped. She was in such shock that she had no clue what he was saying although his lips were moving. The tears ran down her face and she felt her head shake in a "yes" movement.

Cilicia wasn't one to like to be the center of attention. Even though she was happy, she was a bit embarrassed when everyone in the lounge cheered for the newly engaged couple. She would have preferred it be done in private. In fact, she always told him her dream proposal would be done on a simple picnic in a secluded area. Although this was not her dream, to say the least, she was still delighted in every which way. She was a hopeful bride.

The next day they went by subway to the Bronx for a family barbecue. Everyone was so happy to see the couple and for her to show off her diamond ring. It wasn't elaborate, which she was thankful for. Cilicia was a rather simple woman with elegant taste. Gaudy was not her thing and definitely not her style.

The rest of the trip was the equivalent to a fairytale dream. They went to another play by Billy Joel called, *I'm Moving Out*. This was more of a dance based play. The piano appeared to be hovering over the stage the entire time. The performances were excellent.

"So how did you like New York?" Cilicia asked as they boarded their Amtrak train to return home.

"It was great! I don't know if I could live there with all those people, but I think it might just be my favorite place to visit. We never got a chance to do that carriage ride. Now we have something to look forward to when we visit again. Not to mention, we are engaged!" Jeremey had been planning the proposal unbeknownst to Cilicia for a few months. He had asked her mother and her father for her hand in marriage. That was why Carol and Darlene met them at the play, to wish him luck and give him their love.

Darlene was the one that let Jeremey know about Cilicia's love for the arts. That is why he was so adamant about seeing the play. He wanted to make sure Cilicia was doing something she loved to do. There were so many times where she had gone out of her way for him and making things special. Even though it wasn't very customary, Cilicia would buy him roses and leave it on the windshield of his car during her lunch breaks and little love cards. She was naturally romantic at heart.

Jeremey, in that way, was the opposite. He didn't give her many compliments even when a part of him knew he should have. He was, in a sense, making up for the lack of romance he had given to her over the last three years that they dated. He was going to be a better man to her and it started on that warm September night in New York City.

"I don't want a big wedding, Jeremey. I don't want a big fuss. Something small would be fine." Cilicia was never one of those little girls that dreamed of the huge wedding with 300 guests. If they did have one, it would be no more than 100 people. "If you want, we could have something for just the two of us and then later on have a reception." Jeremey liked the idea and they planned to get married on their anniversary later that month.

Chapter 3

The wedding date was all set, September 26, 2003. They would go to the court house and get it done. He liked the idea of the small wedding and a reception later. None of their family lived in VA, so it would just be them. He wasn't very close to his family and he was perfectly fine with all of it. In fact, Jeremey didn't even tell his parents, Harry and Patrice, the wedding date. When Cilicia found that out, she was livid and called them herself to tell them. Patrice was not very warm to Cilicia in their first meeting, but they should have at least known their son was getting married.

Jeremey didn't have a great relationship with his father. He actually had a better relationship with Cilicia's dad. She thought that was a bit weird, but didn't harp on it. Not every family was the same and this was something she would learn to accept. Cilicia would often have to argue with Jeremey to call his parents to say "hello" just because it was Tuesday. This behavior didn't surprise her about him not telling them of their upcoming nuptials. It did annoy her though.

Things got really awkward when Patrice sent Cilicia a wedding gift. It was a long white nightgown. Cilicia never wore the gift. She simply said thank you and shoved it in the back of her drawer. It reminded her of something someone would wear on their wedding night in the 1950s. It wasn't remotely pretty and it gave her the sense that his mother believed they were virgins, which they weren't.

Even though they were just going to the justice of the peace, Cilicia went to David's Bridal and got her a wedding dress on sale for $100. It was a simple ivory gown with spaghetti straps and small crystal buttons down the side throughout the length of the gown. She decided to make a simple bouquet. A bride needs a bouquet even if her wedding was simple, small or wasn't a wedding at all.

Everything was set and then disaster set in. A hurricane was coming in a direct hit of Hampton, Virginia where they lived. They were forced to evacuate. It was a week before the wedding and they were packing up their cars heading to Delaware to stay with friends. Cilicia couldn't believe this was happening. Since the engagement, Jeremey had not been the nicest to her. She figured he was stressed about the wedding preparation and moving into their new apartment.

After Hurricane Isabel raged through Hampton Roads, it was deemed safe to return. Everything was in shambles. The streets were still flooded, the power was out in most of the city, there was no gas for cars, there was hardly any food in the grocery stores, and people were displaced. It was madness. The young couple was in the middle of moving from the town house they rented with roommates and their apartment. The townhouse had all of their furniture, but had no electricity. The new apartment had electricity but no furniture. They opted to stay in the new apartment and sleep on the floor with blankets. At least it had lights.

The wedding day had come and nothing had changed with the city. They had a 2:00 p.m. appointment with the judge to get married. Everything was a mess and unorganized. Cilicia hated when things were unorganized. It didn't help that Jeremey had an attitude the entire day. She did manage to find some ivory tea roses from Costco earlier that day. She made a small bouquet with them and placed a few in her hair.

"Pull over right now! Right damn now!" Cilicia screamed. Normally she was able to keep calm in mostly every situation, but this was not the day for that. "Do you even want to get married? All month you have been pissed off at the world like I did something to you. I haven't done a thing to you. I went out and bought this gown! It took me two hours to find a store with only half-wilted flowers to make this bouquet! I laid out your suit and I ask you to get your shoes. I have no idea where you put anything. You are in dirty sneakers! I have remained calm and tried to be supportive. You didn't even want to tell your parents about this! Why not?! Are you ashamed of me or something?"

"I just have a lot on my mind. Forget it. Let's just get this thing over with! Get back in the car now!" Jeremey yelled back.

"Get this thing over with? Get this thing over with?" Cilicia couldn't understand what she was hearing. It was his idea to have the wedding this month. She wanted to wait. Now it was a get-it-over-with scenario. *Maybe I shouldn't marry him*, saying to herself. "You haven't even said I looked beautiful. This is our wedding day and we are screaming at each other." Cilicia at this point couldn't hold back the tears. She didn't cry hard or loud but just streaming tears.

"Just get in the car," Jeremey opened the door and sat there without saying another word.

"Is this how it is going to be Jeremey?" Cilicia asked and he never responded.

They got married in a messy office at the court house. The whole thing happened so quickly it barely felt like anything. The exchange of "I do" only took three minutes. There wasn't much to celebrate. The city was still in ruin and most of the restaurants were still without power.

"Looks like the only thing open is Bennigans." Jeremey pulled in the packed parking lot. Cilicia didn't really like the food there, but the options were dismal and there was no place to go. They ate their food quietly and went home. After all that had happened, the marriage was not consummated that night. They both just went to sleep on the stacked blankets piled on the floor.

So, this is what marriage is all about, huh? That was her last thought before drifting to sleep.

Chapter 4

The temperament of their marriage didn't change. She desperately wanted it to, but it seemed she couldn't do anything right to please him. She worked, cooked, cleaned, baked, and wore sexy clothes in the house and entertained when he wanted to, even if she didn't feel like it. Jeremey couldn't cook at all. She didn't mind it though. She liked cooking and serving her husband. It was something she saw her grandmother do for her grandfather and her mother do for her father.

It wasn't enough. He complained about things she didn't know was an issue. "Are you going to wear that out? You know you are a wife now?" Jeremey said to her with an attitude.

"What is wrong with what I have on? I have always worn this outfit. It's what I have. These are my clothes. When did you have a problem with MY clothes?" Cilicia was annoyed. The only time he noticed what she wore these days was when she had on something he didn't approve of. It was never for a compliment.

"Well if I don't say anything, then you look fine. If I do, then you need to change!" Jeremey was yelling at her. Cilicia wasn't one to be stepped on and belittled. She was by no means going to allow him to dictate and talk to her any way he pleased. The only time he spoke to her was to start an argument.

"What is wrong with you? I have on a skirt barely above my knees and a tank top. What is wrong with this? I am not showing anything risqué or being disrespectful. What is your problem now?" Cilicia shot back. These arguments were daily and straining to her. She was the type of person who hated conflict but she refused to be judged every day by what she wore.

Cilicia was stressed. It didn't help that Jeremey had hurt his knee playing basketball. He went up for a layup and came down hard. When he landed, he couldn't get back up. He had torn the ACL and other ligaments around his knee. After his surgery, he was on bed rest. Cilicia's only break from the home was going to work. At the time, she was working a grueling fourteen hours a day. With him not being able to work, walk or cook, she would go to work and come home, make his meal, serve him, do all the chores then prepare breakfast and lunch for him for the next day. She even moved the microwave in the bedroom for him. His medical ice bucket needed to be filled daily. She would fill that up as soon as she got home from work and the last thing she did before she left at 3:00 am.

"I am bored sitting here all day! All you do is work and cook. I don't even think you want to take care of me! Do you? Do you? Yeah! I bet you don't!" Jeremey picked a new argument with Cilicia every day. These days she wouldn't respond as much. She figured he was just stressed from his injury and staying home all day. "I am not the homebody! You are! I need to get out of this damn apartment! Are you even listening to me? Do you even care?"

"If I didn't care I wouldn't come home to you to take care of you after working these long hours. Wait… I live here! You are my husband and I am doing the best I can! Matter of fact, if I am not doing such a good job, why don't you call Shauna to take care of you?!?" Cilicia yelled back.

Shauna. Shauna was the woman she found out about just two weeks after getting married to Jeremey. Cilicia logged on to their computer to check her email. For some reason, her password wasn't working and an alternate email kept popping up. She wasn't knowledgeable with computers at all. All she knew how to do was log onto her yahoo account and even that wasn't working. "What the hell am I doing wrong now?" Cilicia said frustrated. It was her day off and Jeremey was at work. He was the computer wizard but she couldn't call him, since he worked in a secure area most of the time with no cell phones allowed.

"I am going to get this thing to work!" It was now 30 minutes later and Cilicia was completely frustrated with herself. She tried her password one last time. She started to click through the screen and nothing looked like her mail, however, it was of someone's mail.

Ever since your girl went away on business you have been with me the whole time. We are together so much. I really like you. What's up with that? What do you want to do?

Shauna

"Wait, what? Who was this Shauna person?" She had heard her name before in passing, but she had never met her formally.

I know we have been spending a lot of time together and I really like it. I really like you. I want you.

Jeremey

Cilicia's heart sunk into her chest so deeply that she it appeared she would never feel it the same way again. "He was cheating on me!" With this new revelation, Cilicia was hurt, confused and angry. It took a lot to get her angry. Right now, she was wishing she had left Jeremey behind with Hurricane Isabel. She quickly dialed his number. He picked up on the third ring.

"What's up I am at work this better be important." This was the normal way Jeremey answered the phone for her when he was at work.

"Ever since your girl has been away on business…" Cilicia read verbatim what was on her computer screen. She even stated his response. "Jeremey who the hell is Shauna?" Before Jeremey could respond Cilicia hung up the phone. The next thing she knew Jeremey was standing in the living room. They didn't live very far from where he worked and she figured he was on the way as soon as she started reading the message.

"What the hell are you doing in my email?" That was the first thing Jeremey could come up with out of his mouth. Cilicia figured out why her password didn't work. Jeremey had never properly logged off, so when she tried to put her password in, it didn't take and remained in his account. She wasn't even purposely snooping, but this was obviously something she needed to know.

"I don't know how the hell your email was up, but when I went to log on, my account wasn't coming up. When I clicked on the name, this shit came up and I want to know who the hell is Shauna? Are you having an affair with her? What the hell is, *I like you too*? What the hell are you doing Jeremey? Why ask me to marry you, if this is what you are going to do?" Cilicia spent a lot of her time now yelling back at Jeremey.

"No I am not with her and no I am not going to be with her and whatever!" Jeremey was annoyed and didn't feel like dealing with any of it.

"What the hell is whatever!?!" Cilicia was angry but she refused to cry. *Never let them see you cry.* The words of her father crept up from the back of her mind. He never wanted his daughter to be seen as weak. Especially to a man. She chose her battles very carefully and this one she was willing to fight for.

"Get over it," Jeremey said in a menacing tone. He would have this conversation with her no further and nothing she said, at this point, mattered.

"Get over it? What the hell do you mean get *over* it!?" Cilicia had enough of him, and if she could have, would have gotten a divorce that very moment, but she didn't. She didn't want to look like a failure. They had only been married for two weeks and this was the first of many devastating blows. *Get over it.* Those words would ring between her ears for months to come.

"Do you even want to take care of me? What the hell are you bringing up that bitch for? I told you to get over it and I am not talking about no damn Shauna to you!" Jeremey lay in their bed with only the light from the TV glaring back at them. Cilicia exited the room and went to the living room where she slept. She secretly cried herself to sleep.

Chapter 5

*M*y *marriage is a sham.* Cilicia didn't do as her husband told her to do to get over the Shauna situation. She was taking care of a husband that showed her no love, yet he expected her to be submissive to him. She told no one. She withdrew into herself and fell into depression. The holidays were approaching and she wasn't looking forward to them at all. She loved this time of year but all she wanted to do was cry.

Day in and day out she avoided the arguments that Jeremey sparked. This tactic only fueled him from trying to upset her in different ways. It was as if he wanted to see her live in misery. The happy, care free guy she once fell in love with only showed that side of himself in front of other people. She was never one to fake a face so Cilicia was sick of trying to hide her misery. Most often times she was perceived to be in some ill mood that Jeremey played on to his benefit.

Thanksgiving was here and she was determined to have a good first holiday while married. That was until he got an out of the blue phone call from his parents that they will be popping up on them the next day. Cilicia was annoyed. She had already gone grocery shopping and now needed to go back to the store to pick up more plates, glasses and silverware. She was trying her best to have a special holiday. She knew how it was going to be ruined.

Jeremey was still on bed rest and she was cooking. His parents insisted on having him meet them and take them to their hotel. Cilicia was pissed, but kept her mouth shut. They were late. Not by a little bit but very late. This further annoyed Cilicia. She had told Jeremey that she wanted them back by no later than 1:00 pm for dinner. They did not arrive at the apartment until 4:00 pm. Jeremey was on very good behavior when his parents arrived. He didn't want Cilicia to let them know how he was acting and how he was treating her. He was unusually quiet.

As Patrice walked in the door before she even said hello or acknowledged Cilicia, she made an announcement in crude tone. "I am on a diet."

Cilicia, already bothered, stated back, "Well not today. I don't have anything on the stove that is healthy, so your diet will take a pause." Jeremey noticed Cilicia didn't miss a beat and hoped their exchanges would be kept to a minimum.

"You cooked all this?" Harry said seemingly trying to keep the peace. "I am thoroughly impressed!"

"Yes. Well, I added to the menu last minute. I didn't know you guys were coming in. When did you decide to drive from Florida to Virginia?" Cilicia really wanted to know this answer. Her parents would have never popped up on them last minute unless for emergency.

"Oh, we just figured we'd drop on in and see you guys," Harry said cheerfully. However, Cilicia was feeling anything but cheerful.

"Can I have seconds please?" Patrice gave Cilicia the plate while she was still eating. Cilicia thought this was pretty rude, but she got up and took the plate.

"What would you like?" Cilicia had a full spread of turkey, ham, sweet potatoes, backed Mac and cheese, collard greens, corn on the cob, cornbread stuffing, fresh cranberry sauce, gravy, dinner rolls and for dessert a chocolate strawberry walnut cake.

"I would like a little of everything again please. Although, I am used to having green bean casserole. Did you not think to make that?" Patrice jabbed a little and she could tell from Cilicia's face that question annoyed her.

"Well no. I pretty much made what Jeremey and I liked to eat. I hadn't a clue we would be having extra guests. There was not time to ask what anyone else wanted you know." And that was it. Cilicia was annoyed and Jeremey knew it. It's not like he has made things easy for her the last few months. He sat at the table eerily quiet.

Patrice was the last one done with her dinner due to the second helping. "That was really good Cilicia." When Patrice put down her fork, she picked up her cell phone that was lying on the table. "Girl she *actually can* cook. You know that was the only reason we came all the way over here in the first place." There was a pause. Cilicia assumed whomever she was talking to was responding back. "Yeah I don't know why. When I call, they are always eating out. She had me nervous. I can't have my baby eating any ole thing you know?"

That was it. Cilicia was annoyed. The whole conversation had her pissed and she was very much ready for them to return to their hotel room. She had done her best to plan a pleasant Thanksgiving dinner. She was even happy she had the day off to do so. Jeremey sat there still silent. He knew that Cilicia was tired and angry. He knew that his mother was being rude and wrong. He knew that his father was oblivious to anything going on and just wanted to go to sleep.

"Well, if you all call us, it's during Friday nights. I don't cook on Fridays. It something that I got from my mom. I cook six days a week. I deserve a break too. It's not like you ever taught Jeremey to cook to help out or anything. So, I deemed that my day to exit the kitchen. It's normally our date night." Cilicia spoke as casually as she could. Jeremey couldn't boil water. She was raised to cook and clean by her family. She didn't mind doing it, but she wasn't going to have someone come in and disrespect her at her dinner table in her own house where she helps pay the bills.

"Oh, I have never heard of that before. A wife not cooking on Friday's. Interesting." Patrice not touching the fact that she didn't teach Jeremey how to cook. By rite, she set him up for failure long before Cilicia got into the picture.

The first time Cilicia had met Harry and Patrice was right after they got engaged. She had never met them beforehand. They had come to visit Jeremey in Virginia since he lived there. During the couple days during the first visit Patrice was not very hospitable to Cilicia and there was nothing she could really do about it. She questioned Jeremey asking if he thought his mother liked her and the best answer he could come up with was, "I don't know."

Cilicia got up to clean the kitchen. She was exhausted and still no one had bothered to ask her if she needed any help. It was going on 7:00 pm and Jeremey's bucket of ice needed to be replaced, the food needed to be put away, the dishes needed to be cleaned and she still had to get up at 3:00 am to get ready for work. She got done with everything around 8:30 pm. "Well I am about to get ready to go to bed. I have to get up in the morning."

"Oh, I am sure you can stay up with us a little longer. It's still early and we would like to talk to you," Patrice butted in.

"Actually, I don't have the extra time. I have to be up by 3:00 am and I still need to take my shower and get ready for work tomorrow." Cilicia was not in the mood for the back and forth and wasn't going to do it.

"Yeah Ma, she has to get up early. Good night honey," Jeremey said. Cilicia looked at him as if he had four heads sharing six pairs of eyes. *When the hell did he start being nice to me?* she pondered. He obviously read her thoughts because he immediately put his head down.

"Good night." Cilicia had enough and exited the living room without looking back. It was one of the worst Thanksgivings in her life and she was exhausted. She found refuge in knowing she would be working fourteen hours the next day. That would be less time she would have to spend at home and with them. All of them.

After work Cilicia came home to find them all in the living room. "Hello," she said as she walked straight to her bedroom and closed the door. Jeremey knew she was pissed already. Cilicia didn't miss anything and he was sure she saw the huge bucket of Kentucky Fried Chicken on the dining table.

"So, whose idea was it to buy KFC? Surely everyone is aware that Thanksgiving was yesterday and there are a ton of leftovers in the fridge." Cilicia didn't care about her tone at that moment. What the hell was she supposed to do with all those leftovers? "I guess I can take plates tomorrow to work for the people who didn't have a good meal for the holiday." She devised her own plan even though she didn't feel she should have to. "Yes, that will work. It will make them happy and I would not have wasted my time and money on all this damn *food.*"

"Oh, we decided we didn't want that." Patrice again. Her voice was really getting to Cilicia. It was only day two of their visit and twenty minutes of her being home. It had already been too long.

They sat down again at the table. Jeremey was still quiet but Cilicia was about to change all of that. "What did you all do today? I see a lot of shopping bags from the outlet mall in the living room."

"Oh yes, we did a little shopping today. It was such a beautiful day also. Too bad you missed it and you had to work, hon," Patrice said slyly.

"Yeah it was a nice day. So, you all found the mall to go shopping? Did you use MapQuest for the directions?" Cilicia wanted to get to the bottom of how they got there in the first place. "Jeremey, how did your parents get to Williamsburg? You know it's about a thirty-minute drive."

"Uhhh... I took them," Jeremey hesitated. He knew up until this point he had made himself out to be helpless and now here he was driving an hour plus, walking around with crutches and toting his parents all around VA.

"Oh honey, remember you need to elevate that leg. You must follow the doctor's orders. We need to get you well," Patrice interjected.

"Your mother is right." Jeremey looked at Cilicia as if she was the crazy one. Had she actually agreed with his mom? "You should have your leg elevated and resting just like the doctor ordered. Although I am sure that was impossible to do, since you were driving back and forth today and walking around. You did say you took your parents, right?"

At that point the family was quiet and Cilicia had just scored a major shut the hell up in her house point against Patrice. Before then, Patrice had made reference to Cilicia not caring for her son properly, alluding to her working the majority of the time. Jeremey must have been complaining to his mother. Cilicia thought the whole ordeal was comical, especially since it was her that made him call her once a month anyway.

"So, I was talking with Jeremey today and I asked him about what he thought of you all having a formal wedding in Indiana during the family reunion. I think it would be a great idea. We can plan the whole thing for you. You wouldn't have to lift a finger. All you would have to do is show up!" Patrice was beside herself with this one.

"Oh really?" Cilicia paused to look at Jeremey who was now shoveling coleslaw into his mouth. Jeremey hates coleslaw. "Well he brought that up to me last week. We decided that isn't in our best interest. As a matter of fact, I was in the room when he told you that we wouldn't be doing that."

"Oh, he did mention something about that, but I figured we should sit down and talk about it again. Like I said before, it would be a great idea."

Cilicia looked at Jeremey. He was still shoveling that damn coleslaw in his mouth. "Well like we told you before, we won't be doing that. My family is in NY. They are not going to be traveling to Indiana. If we decide to have anything formal it will be right here in

VA to be convenient to everyone, but we do thank you for the offer." *And* checkmate. Cilicia had not only won the battle but the war.

It was just then Patrice tossed her plate of food to the middle of the table, having an adult temper tantrum. Cilicia was completely disgusted at her behavior and excused herself. Jeremey hobbled behind her to the bedroom. "Are you okay?" he asked.

"What the hell do you mean am I okay?" Cilicia said, trying not to raise her voice over a whisper. "Your mother has been hitting me with bullshit ever since she got here and you haven't said a damn thing in my defense. Funny because you have much to say when they are not here."

"Aren't you going to clean up?" Jeremey asked, ignoring everything she said, as always.

"Clean up? I will not clean up paper plates of damn KFC when we could have and should have had leftovers. Hell no! You know what? Since you want to run all around here and you aren't playing helpless, clean it up your damn self!" That was it. That was all Cilicia had to say. She went to bed. There was no good night.

Two days later, his parents went back to Florida. She was so happy for the peace. What little peace she had anyway. There was still Jeremey left to deal with. Cilicia was raised to be respectful, but to not let another woman come in and run her house. She could specifically hear her mother's advice or warning "Don't you let another woman come in your house and tell you what to do. Not even me. That is your house. You are the backbone of that house. I don't care who it is." She had taken heed to that warning. Jeremey had been quiet during his parent's stay. He even left her alone a few days after his family's departure. But in time, things were back to their miserable normal.

Chapter 6

The holidays were over and Cilicia was happy Christmas was a bit quieter. There was still drama but not his family's drama and that was all that mattered. Jeremey was off of his crutches and just wore a knee brace. Cilicia was happy he was able to return to work. It gave him something to do other than yell at her.

New Year's Eve turned out to be pretty bad also. They had all went out to a club with their friends only to have Jeremey's friend Andre and girlfriend Tina get into a major fight in the club. They all ended up running out before security came to defuse the situation. They dropped him off reluctantly at his apartment.

To their astonishment, he had come back knocking on their door at 5:00 am. The fight apparently raged on without any interruption from anyone else. Tina had hit him with an iron on his side. When Andre lifted his shirt, it was black and blue. Jeremey tried to get him to go to the hospital. They were sure something was cracked or broken. Andre just wanted to sleep.

"I can't believe my friend is in an abusive relationship," Jeremey said to Cilicia while Andre was sleeping on the sofa. Andre stayed with them for three days before he went home. Tina kept calling him accusing him of staying with another woman. When Tina threatened to go over to Cilicia's house, that is when she stepped in to let Tina know that wasn't about to happen. Tina didn't come over ever again.

After Jeremey saw all the drama with his friend's relationship, he started treating Cilicia better. They were enjoying each other's company more and more and it was finally nice. Cilicia's parents were going to visit soon and they were excited about it. Jeremey really liked Cilicia's dad Rick and her mother was funny.

The visit between the two parents was night and day. The only special treatment they received was Rick wanting his daily newspaper which Jeremey happily got for him. Cilicia always spoiled her father's sweet tooth so she made him brownies.

It was Valentine's Day and the two couples had tickets to go to the Virginia Beach House of Comedy for a show. It was amazing. They had a great time laughing with each other at the comedians. This was a spot Jeremey and Cilicia frequented. She liked going to clubs, but she didn't like the alcohol. Normally, by midnight, everyone was drunk but her, which left her annoyed.

That night, for the first time in their relationship, they had sex without a condom. It may have been customary for other married couples to not use condoms, but Cilicia wasn't sure that Jeremey wanted kids. He would always change the subject when it was brought up. He was finally being kind to her again and the last thing she wanted to do was ignite the flame again. Not to mention the dooming cloud of Shauna that still hung around.

It was the first time in a long time that Jeremey actually made love to his wife. In recent times, there had been no tenderness or romance. That night he actually took his time and kissed her. Touching her tenderly and passionately. Something magical was happening between them that she had never experienced before with anyone. It was the first time she had made love to anyone.

About four weeks later Cilicia wasn't feeling the same. Something about her had changed. To make sure she was feeling the right thing, she had taken a pregnancy test. With her grandmother on speaker phone in the bathroom Cilicia peed on her little stick. "Honey bun, what does it say? What does it say?" Mildred rushed the words so fast, she could barely get them out clearly.

"The box says I have to wait two minutes grandma. Cilicia was nervous. She really didn't know what to do. What if she was pregnant? "Grandma, what if I am pregnant?"

"Well, dear heart, you're a married woman. You two will just raise this baby in the love he or she was created with," Mildred said in a sweet voice. Her grandmother always had a sweet voice. They spoke just about every single day. They were best friends and right now Cilicia had her grandmother as close as she could to her in the bathroom while she waited for the two minutes to pass.

"Oh, Grandma, it says *pregnant*!" Cilicia started crying. She wasn't sure why she was crying, but she was crying. Was she happy? Sad? Regretful? It was only that one time they had ever had sex without a condom. It would be their first and last actually.

"Dear heart, why are you crying? Are you okay?" Mildred knew her granddaughter enough to know something was wrong.

"I just feel like I am going to be doing this all by myself, Grandma. I don't know if I can do it." Cilicia had feelings all the time. Ever since she could remember her intuition would warn her of different things in her life. Guiding her and leading her along the way.

"Well there is no reason for you to doubt yourself now. You have overcome every bit of everything you have ever faced in your life. If you weren't ready for it. God would not have allowed it to happen," Mildred said comforting her best friend. It saddened her that Cilicia felt this way. She could tell by the sound of her voice that something has been wrong for some time. She didn't want her granddaughter to feel alone. Not at a time like this. "Well honey bun, it's time for you to go tell your husband the news. I love you."

"I love you too, Grandma." Cilicia hung up the phone. She walked out to Jeremey sitting on the sofa watching TV. "I have something to show you," she stood blocking his view. Jeremey was annoyed because his program wasn't over. "Here." She handed him the pregnancy test.

At first, he sat there with a blank expression and then worry crept over his face. He looked at her, "Are you pregnant?" Cilicia shook her head yes. "How? It was only that one time?"

"Jeremey, it only takes one time." Cilicia was crushed. She knew he wasn't going to be happy about it.

"Is this the only test you have taken? Go to the store and get more. Get like eight of them. Get different brands too!" Jeremey panicked.

Cilicia reluctantly went to Walgreens and got eight more tests. She went back home and passed every last one with flying colors. Jeremey still didn't want to believe it. She was sure he wasn't happy about it, but he would fake it in front of anyone else. *I am going to be doing this alone.* The thought echoed over and over again.

Chapter 7

It took a couple of weeks to warm up to the idea of the pregnancy. When Jeremey first found out, he was distant and quiet. Soon, he was talking to her and even smiling about it. "Maybe it won't be so bad after all." Cilicia couldn't help to think and be optimistic. The angst of doubt drifted away and she was comfortable with the idea of her being a mother.

A few other people had other things to say however. Latoya, the wife of Dereon, one of Jeremey's friends, said the most insensitive thing to an expecting mother. "I just can't picture you being a mother to anyone." Cilicia wanted to throw her out of her house. Instead she just simply walked out of the living room and laid down. She had not been feeling very well. Her doctor was telling her it was just because she was in her first trimester, but her body was telling her something was wrong.

She had been back and forth to the emergency room three times in one week. Jeremey was nervous. Cilicia had extreme morning sickness. She threw up on average 30 times a day. This was not normal behavior. This was not shaping to be a normal pregnancy at all. "I don't know what is wrong with me. Is my baby okay? Is my baby alright?"

Cilicia asked the doctor. He had just taken another sonogram to be sure.

"Yes, your baby is doing fine. You, however, are not. You have been throwing up so much your blood pressure has spiked and then, at times, it drops dangerously low," Doctor Smyer said with much concern. "I am going to put you on bed rest for a week. Maybe you just need rest."

Cilicia went home and laid down as the doctor ordered. Now it was time for Jeremey to take care of everything. Jeremey still couldn't cook, but that was not the issue, since Cilicia couldn't eat. The only thing that mostly stayed down was ravioli from a can. She ate it for breakfast, lunch and dinner. She ate it so much she would cry at the smell of it. Jeremey would buy it by the caseloads from Wal-Mart.

"Jeremey! Jeremey! Ahhhhhhhhhhhhhhh! Jeremey!" Cilicia was screaming for him from the bedroom. She was in so much pain she could not walk. "Jeremey help!" She didn't know what was wrong but she had never felt pain like this before. "What is happening to me?"

Jeremey ran to her and looked at his wife balled up gripping her pillow for dear life. He tried to get her to stand but she just screamed even louder. He ran, put his shoes on, grabbed the keys and picked her up. She shrieked in pain "Oh God! Ahhhhhhhh! Owwwww!" she screamed every time Jeremey moved. Cilicia cried and cried as he sped down the road to the emergency room. He didn't have time to call anyone. He had to get his wife help. Something was wrong and they needed answers. Jeremey and Cilicia was scared.

When they arrived, she was placed on a stretcher. The technicians could not examine her. They could not touch her. They could not treat her. She was immediately admitted and given morphine for her excruciating pain. Cilicia needed to sleep. She cried so hard her eyes were swelling shut. Her blood pressure was very high and she was in distress. The baby, thankfully, was fine.

"We are going to run some tests on you. We need a lot of blood from you and you will not go home until you are properly diagnosed." A specialist was speaking who was not her doctor.

"Where is Dr. Smyer? He normally treats me. Who are you?" Cilicia was alarmed. Where was her doctor and who was this man in her room with her? She wished her family were closer so they could be there with her. Jeremey was at work and she was at the hospital alone.

"Dr. Smyer is no longer your doctor. He doesn't seem fit to treat you properly. I am a specialist that handles high risk pregnancies. My name is Dr. Folks. You are considered high risk Ma'am."

"He isn't fit to treat me? I am a high risk? High risk for what exactly? Death? My baby is fine. It is me who isn't from what I was told." Cilicia was under pain medication, but she still had her wits about her.

"Ma'am we are going to do all we can to figure out what the problem is. We are going to monitor you for as long as we need to and you will get the proper care you need. Please get some rest. We will be running the tests starting today and we need you to have the energy to do so." Dr. Folks exited the room leaving just her and the nurse.

"Don't you worry you are in good hands. Now get some rest Cilicia." The nurse then excited the room and against all that she wanted to do, Cilicia fell asleep.

Chapter 8

Cilicia spent most of her time in the hospital alone. She had very little visitors and she was learning just who her friends were. She came to the conclusion that she no longer had many. To her detriment, her friends were Jeremey's friends. She had wrapped her life around his and intertwined herself within him. She was beginning to lose her identity. Since she had gotten sicker, he was growing distant again. She didn't think the yelling would start up again anytime soon, but he was spending less time at home.

Dr. Folks entered her room interrupting her rambling thoughts. "It seems that we have figured out what the issue is. You have fibroid tumors. It appears since you have been pregnant the tumors are dying off. The baby is taking the tumors supply of nutrients and blood supply. This is why you are in so much pain. This is why we are unable to touch and examine you."

"Wait, tumors? Did I hear you correctly?" Cilicia had to question this diagnosis. She had never heard of such a thing. "How long have I had these… things? Are they cancerous? What do you mean dying off?"

"Most fibroids are benign which means they are not cancerous. We will give you medication to stabilize your pain. You have been here for seven days. I feel you would be more comfortable at home in your own environment. You won't get the adequate rest you need to keep going if you stay here. We are obligated to take vitals frequently and we will disturb your sleep thus creating more stress for you. The key to your treatment is lack of stress. You will be placed on bed rest for three additional months. You are not permitted to do much and you are not allowed to drive. The spiking in your blood pressure is not stable. I don't feel comfortable with you behind the wheel. I am really sorry to tell you this. I know it is a lot to take in, but we must keep you as healthy as we can to keep your baby healthy."

Cilicia wanted to cry, but she knew that it wouldn't do any good. It could possibly do more damage than not. She was free to go home, but she couldn't drive. Besides, her car was at home. Jeremey was still at work, but didn't get off until 4:00 pm. It was only 11:00 am. She was stuck. She tried to get up to take a shower and could barely move. She feared she would fall clutching the IV stand. She pressed and buzzed for the nurse for help. "Oh no! You can't be out of bed alone, Ma'am. You might hurt yourself." The nurse ran to her completely concerned about her wellbeing.

Cilicia had gone from a healthy and active 22-year-old woman to a very ill woman who needed to be monitored almost twenty-four hours a day. "Lord please help me." All she had at this moment were her prayers. The nurse helped her to the shower. The warm water felt good on her body. She wasn't quite showing yet. She had always been slim. She started to wonder what she would look like with a huge belly. "What if I don't make it to labor?" These harmful thoughts crept into her head like poison seeping through her veins. She was scared with every reason to be.

Jeremey picked her up from the hospital wheeling her out in the wheel chair. "What will it be like now?" Everything fell on Jeremey to do and he wasn't handling the stress very well. It was not like when he had torn his ACL. It was difficult, but she managed. She could physically see him stressing out about everything and there was nothing she could do to help. Some might say this is karma. She would say it was torture for her. She hated not being able to do her part and pull her weight around the house. She also wanted him to take her frustrations out of her. At least, before, he couldn't complain that she was lazy. Laziness was something that she felt was not in her DNA. What she wanted to do she would get done, but not right now. And not for the next six and a half months that she has to be pregnant.

Chapter 9

Cilicia felt miserable. During her months of bed rest, she still had weekly appointments to see Dr. Folks. He was monitoring her, the baby and now the tumors closely. The tumors were decreasing in size, but she was still not well.

"You are still very sickly Cilicia. If we can get you to five months pregnant we can save your baby," Dr. Folks said to her and Jeremey during one of their appointments.

Cilicia took in what he had just said to her. Analyzing everything from his tone to the choice of words he spoke. "You said that you can save my baby if I can make it to five months? What about me?"

"Well honestly, your baby is healthy. It is you who is having the problems. I have theory that your baby's blood may be compatible to yours, but since you are B negative your blood is not compatible to your baby's. You are still early on in your pregnancy. If you want, and I wouldn't suggest this if I didn't feel like—" Dr. Folks was immediately cut off by Cilicia.

"Don't you dare say what you are about to say. How dare you? You say you can save my baby, well then save my baby!" Cilicia was visibly upset. Her doctor was about to give her the option to abort.

Jeremey was confused and didn't understand the conversation. Dr. Folks departed. "What was that about?" Cilicia explained to him what the doctor was suggesting. "Then we need to do that! What? Why wouldn't you at least discuss this with me first before making a decision?" he said angrily at her. A tone she was very much aware of.

"Because this is my body! If I die on this table right now for this baby, then so help me, that is what I am going to do! It will not be you or anyone else that can change my mind!" Cilicia was yelling. She wasn't supposed to be yelling. She wasn't supposed to be stressed.

Just then Jeremey responded "What makes you think that I am going to want to have anything to do with that thing, if it kills you?"

"Thing? Thing? This is our baby! Are you crazy?" It was at that moment Cilicia became a protective mother. There was no backing down. A new nerve has been struck. One that she had never dealt with before. Normally if he was to yell at her, she would ignore him, but this was different.

Jeremey looked at Cilicia and realized he had lost this fight. He stormed out of the room. He felt as if Cilicia had taken him out of the process. He didn't like her gaining control of the situation and didn't know how to handle it. Cilicia didn't care at that point. She refused to back down from this. No one, including any doctor or her husband, was going to hurt her baby. She couldn't help to think about that moment in the bathroom when she found out she was pregnant. "I am going to be doing this by myself."

Cilicia focused her attention on looking out the window. It was now her normal thing to do since she had been on bedrest. The only time she was able to venture out of their two-bedroom apartment was for appointments. She liked to look at the people go by living their life and going about their day. Life had completely changed for her and it was once again the little things that matter the most. *My baby is healthy.*

I might not be, but my baby will be okay. I will make it to five months, she told herself.

Her favorite thing to see out the window is someone exercising. She would use that time to secretly cheer for them on their athletic journey. They always looked like they were in the zone and she loved it! Everyone has a goal and she hoped they would meet theirs. Jeremey had not said a word to her since their argument in the hospital. Even in her fragile condition she figured things would go back to the way it was. It was a risk she was willing to make.

After that whole episode at the appointment, Jeremey solicited help from his friends to take her to the appointments. Cilicia was not comfortable with this. She knew his coworkers, but she would have rather just taken herself. In fact, against doctor's orders, she had taken herself a couple times. Her appointments increased with more specialists. She had an episode of heart palpitations and irregular beats. Jeremey had to take her to the emergency room because she wasn't breathing properly. They kept her a couple days for observation then sent her home with a heart monitor.

She wasn't feeling any better, but she had so far defied all odds and had not only made it to five months, but she made it to seven months pregnant.

They had found a three-bedroom apartment to move to. Jeremey was stressing with packing. Cilicia was very limited still being on heavy medical restrictions, but his uncaring attitude lead her to do more than what she was supposed to do. Even with the Zofran nausea medication she was on, morning sickness still affected her daily. It went from on average thirty times a day to six times a day. That was a major relief to her even though she was in her third trimester throwing up. Her nutritionist put her on a strict diet. Everything she ate had to be cold or nearly frozen. She learned that she would still feel nauseated, but less likely to perform the act which helped her gain a bit of weight for her and the baby.

Cilicia's parents visited whenever they could or when she was having inpatient hospital stays. They were very worried about her. Sometimes driving all night Friday just to spend Saturday with her, which was simply watching her rest. Then driving back to New York Sunday morning. It was an eight-hour commute for her father since her mother couldn't drive. Patrice didn't bother to call Cilicia at all during her pregnancy. This fueled Cilicia's anger and built up animosity towards Patrice. At this point, she wanted nothing to do with her on any level. She no longer fussed at Jeremey to call his parents anymore and he didn't.

Chapter 10

"Mommy, I know we are planning the baby shower but we are going to have to cancel it." Cilicia called her mother and told her the doctor would not clear her to travel. She had made it to her eighth month and he didn't want to add any pressure on her. "He won't lift the bed rest for me. We have to cancel everything." Cilicia was extremely sad. She desperately wanted to see her family. Jeremey hardly talked to her at all these days and she was lonely. Her mother told her not to worry. The family ended up sending their gifts right to the new apartment.

Move in day for the new place was a mess. Jeremey had yelled at her for not helping enough. To the point when one of his friends had to tell him to relax and remind him that Cilicia was not well. Dereon was one of the many friends solicited to take her to her doctor's appointments which normally left Cilicia embarrassed. She knew they didn't want to do it and she was never given the option not to accept. She was told.

She went to pick up a box she had no business lifting. "Wait a minute now. You can't be doing any of that young lady," her dear friend Jermaine said with a light laugh. He could see the tension with

Jeremey and was worried about his friend. He took the box from her and smiled. "I got this. Whenever you feel like lifting, just tap me on the shoulder, okay?" This made Cilicia feel a little better. "Matter of fact, I will take you to the apartment. There is no reason for you to be around here with all this mess. You can do something like unpack the light stuff." She nodded her head in agreement. She liked that idea. She was still able to be a little useful.

Jermaine and Cilicia had been friends for years. She had met him a while back on business and lost touch. It happened that Jeremey was in a training course with Jermaine's girlfriend Tyesha. When Jeremey and Tyesha had their award ceremony Jermaine and Cilicia was there. Tyesha and Jeremey was surprised they had already known each other. The couples were instant friends. When Cilicia called Jermaine to help he jumped at the chance to help his friend. Especially with her being so sick. He had also bore witness to some of the treatment she endured with Jeremey.

Cilicia doing her normal staring out the window on the way to her new apartment. The couple was moving to York Town Virginia about twenty minutes down the road from where they lived now. The apartments were bigger and cheaper. She liked the peace and quiet of it all. "Hey you. What are you looking at?" Jermaine asked her interrupting her thoughts.

"Oh, I am sorry. I didn't mean to ignore you. I normally just peak my head out of the window during car rides. I don't get out much, you know? Not since the baby and all," Cilicia said in a low tone. She didn't want to talk at all really and she wasn't a very good liar.

"No worries, I am just making sure you are okay. You were doing way too much back there. You needed to get out and get some fresh air." Also, meaning she needed to get out and have a break from Jeremey. Everyone that helped them move could feel his tension. They all figured that he was just stressed out with everything going on.

Nesting. Cilicia started nesting as soon as the last box was brought in to the apartment. She couldn't help herself. She knew she needed to rest but there were boxes everywhere. Nesting, explained to her by her doctor, was the point where the body literally begins to prepare for birth. Not just in a physical sense, but mentally and emotionally. Everything needed to be in its place. Everything needed to be right. Everything needed to be unpacked. Cilicia did the best she could while Jeremey was at work and nowhere around to fuss at her constantly. Either she wasn't doing enough or she was doing too much. There was something always to complain about.

Cilicia was prepared for her baby to be born. She made it to the ninth month and she was so very happy. A far cry from the five months Dr. Folks had originally given her. She was as healthy as she was going to be and it was time to push. Cilicia was in labor at this point for seven hours. She had refused all medication for pain management. She was determined to do this on her own. She earned the right to do it.

"Push!" Everyone in the labor and delivery room waited in anticipation for this child. Cilicia decided she didn't want to know the sex of the baby during the pregnancy which really pissed off Patrice. Patrice even requested that the doctor call her personally and tell her. Cilicia simply ignored that request. Patrice had waited until one week before the delivery to call Cilicia and ask her if she was okay.

"I am okay now, yes. The last nine months, not so much." Cilicia was annoyed and she still needed to try to open this box of gifts sent from her family.

"Yes, Jeremey told us that you weren't feeling very well," Harry chimed in. Whenever anyone talked to them on the phone it was always on speaker. Cilicia never understood that.

"It really wasn't that I was not feeling well, it was more like the doctors didn't know if I would survive," Cilicia was not going to allow them to downplay her pain.

"Oh yes, we heard about that too. So, you still don't know the sex of the baby? We really want to know! Oh, and Jeremey mentioned that you decided that he will only be permitted in the delivery room. We really want to be there for the birth," Patrice said.

"Oh no one will know the sex of the baby until I give birth. I personally don't care about if my baby is a boy or a girl as long as he or she is healthy. When you have gone through what we have been through nothing else matters. As for the delivery room. Yes, only Jeremey is allowed. He has been the only one to help me through this process. Most people I didn't even hear from the entire time," Cilicia said, taking the time to throw a light jab at his parents. "So, I decided I don't want anyone else in the room. Besides I will already be stressed and I don't want to deal with anyone else." In hindsight, she barely wanted to deal with Jeremey. The last thing she wanted to deal with was his parents who have been MIA also.

"Puuuusssssshhhhhhh!" Jeremey told Cilicia.

Cilicia was doing the best she could. This labor was the hardest thing she had ever done. Up until about seven centimeters dilated she was throwing up with every contraction. Dr. Folks feared it could spike her blood pressure and put her in danger. He talked her into taking her nausea medication. Reluctantly, she agreed. Shortly after in the middle of eight centimeters dilated, Cilicia passed out.

Jeremey panicked and called for the nurse. Dr. Folks ran in and smiled. "Oh, she's okay. She is just tired. I have seen your wife near death for nine months. Her body is getting the rest it needs for the final part of labor. Trust me when she wakes up, there will be a baby to greet us. Push the button when she wakes okay?"

"I see the head! You are doing so good! Breathe. Breathe." Dr. Folks was coaching her. "Push through the burn! The shoulders! Just push through it!"

"You're a *beast*!" Jeremey was yelling that to her during the entire labor. By the time she started to push, she had believed him and that notion that she was appearing to be some kind of monster had set in. It actually made her cry. She knew he didn't mean any malice by it, but the last thing she wanted to be called was *that*!

"Please sir, stop calling her that! She is upset and she really needs to focus right now. We are almost done and now she is off track. Cilicia, listen to me. Push... Breathe... Push!" Dr. Folks had to say something. He had been listening to Jeremey call her a beast ever since the contractions were roaring in like waves crashing on a pier during a storm. He was getting on his nerves and obviously, Cilicia's too, with her break down.

Cilicia had never been in so much pain in her entire life. She gave one last tremendous push. The cries of a bouncing baby girl filled the room. She was exhausted and even happier. "My God! You did it! You did it Cilicia. Congrats!" Dr. Folks was just as relieved as the couple. Jeremey seemed really happy too. The nurses cheered.

For the first time in nine months Cilicia felt okay. She felt as if nothing had just happened. She held her baby girl for the first time and the nurse snapped the picture. There was no more pain. They took the baby to clean her up and give her the blood work. Cilicia went to the bathroom, took her shower and called her mother. "Mommy! I had a girl!"

"Wow! This is the most energy I had heard in your voice in months. Oh my God! I am a grandmother! I will be there tomorrow. I already bought my train ticket. See you soon. Get some rest. I have to call the rest of the family!" Samantha hung up full of excitement.

Chapter 11

Cilicia was pissed. Samantha had just made it to Virginia and everything had been arranged. She had everything set for her mother before she gave birth. Samantha was going to stay with them the first week to help Cilicia get settled. As she held baby Ayanna for the first time, Jeremey got a call from his parents saying they were one hour away. "What do you mean they are one hour away?"

Jeremey knew his wife was not going to like this one bit and it was nothing he could do about it. His parents, once again, were popping up on them. When they arrived Patrice still didn't give Cilicia a warm welcome. She was upset because the room she had prepared for her mother was now going to his parents and Samantha would be forced to sleep on the sofa.

After about four days, his parents went back to Florida and Samantha moved into the room she was originally supposed to have. It was nice having her mother there to help her get situated. It was also nice to be around someone other than Jeremey 24/7. The bliss of being a new mom came to a screeching halt when she received a call from her cousin Jazmine. "C something is wrong with grandma! I don't know C! She's not breathing! The paramedics are here! Oh my God! It's not looking good!"

Wait. What is her cousin saying to her? She couldn't comprehend it. She couldn't understand any of it. "Jazz please slow down! What are you saying?" Cilicia needed her to talk slower. Say different words. Speak anything other than what she was saying.

"C, I am so sorry. Grandma died," Jazmine said hysterically crying. Jazmine and her family lived in Illinois. Grandma had been living there for a few years with them. Cilicia hung up the phone. Once again, she was numb. Her grandmother had died. Her best friend was gone. She looked down at her baby. Ayanna was only seven days old. Her own grandmother's birthday was November 13th just three days after Ayanna's. Mildred had just turned eighty-five when she died.

"Jeremey, bring Mommy back! She has to come back!" Cilicia called Jeremey frantically. Jeremey was on his way to take Samantha to Amtrak to go back to New York.

"What are you talking about? Your mother is on the train already. She just boarded. Why are you crying? What's going on?" Jeremey could hear the trembling.

"Grandma! She died! My grandmother died!" Cilicia started screaming on the other end of the phone. Jeremey sped home to his wife and his daughter. She was holding Ayanna crying uncontrollably. He placed them all in his lap and held her through her tears. There was no consoling her. He knew this was a blow that would be detrimental to her. All Cilicia does is talk about her grandmother.

Jeremey called Dr. Folks to get cleared to travel with Ayanna being so young and before her two-week appointment. He reluctantly said yes knowing full well there was no way to say no. They had to drive. With the baby being so young they had to limit the amount of people they were around due to germs.

The funeral drew people from all over. Even family from St. Thomas, where her grandmother was originally from, came to the viewing. It was a beautiful service. Cilicia sat there numb with tears streaming down her face. Jeremey held Ayanna for her. Jazmine grabbed her hand and held it as she cried. There wasn't much Cilicia wanted to do. She stayed to herself. For the most part, she had to for Ayanna's sake.

It was like a little piece of her died that day and a large piece of her was reborn. She had never known to be happy and sad at the time. Until now, she had thought it would be impossible to feel both emotions at the same time. However, she was doing it. It was her reality.

It took some getting used to not calling her grandmother every day. She wanted to share with her the little things that Ayanna was doing, but she was no longer a phone call away. Now she was an angel that would guide her and her little love for the rest of their lives. Cilicia was now a house wife and full time mom.

Chapter 12

Life got harder. Jeremey was spending more and more time out of the house. He was coming home later and later. At first, they would fight about it and then Cilicia just stopped. She focused her attention on being a good mother to Ayanna, cooking and cleaning. She hardly went anywhere. When she did, Jeremey would make her call every five minutes. Even if it was something as menial as grocery shopping.

He was even more controlling now that he was under his income. She didn't like it but she thought she could live with it. The screaming and yelling he did at her increased. The insults increased. Jeremey was miserable and now so was Cilicia. The only time he would show his true colors was around Tyesha and Jermaine. Cilicia wasn't sure why he felt so comfortable around them to do so. He didn't act like his normal self around any of his other friends. Even though it was embarrassing, it was comforting to know that she wasn't insane and she wasn't lying.

Cilicia started looking for a job when Ayanna was just three months old. The original plan was for her to remain at home until Ayanna was of school age, but the way Jeremey was acting, she needed her own money. He loved this control he had over her too much and she secretly feared him. She could never show it. She would never show it, but she was scared of Jeremey and no longer knew what he was capable of.

There were a few nights that really terrified her. She was in the shower in the master bathroom. Jeremey was in the living room with Ayanna. All of a sudden, she heard screaming. She jumped out the shower soap all over her and wrapped herself in a towel. She ran into the living room only to find Jeremey screaming at Ayanna at the top of his lungs. "I said stop that damn crying right now!"

"Who the hell are you yelling at?" Cilicia asked now yelling at Jeremey.

"She won't shut up! I will make her shut up!" Jeremey hollered back.

"I don't know who the hell you think you are talking to, but I'll be damned if you yell at a three-month-old!" Cilicia was furious.

"How about I just yell at you then? How about I tell you to shut the hell up?" Jeremey now placing his focus on her.

"I don't give a damn what you say to me, but you better not ever in your damn life speak to her that way again!" Cilicia shouted back. She walked over to him soaking wet and took her baby, who was still crying. She grabbed her baby rocking chair and dragged it to the bathroom with her and closed the door behind her. She calmed Ayanna down and placed her in her chair getting back in the shower to rinse the soap off.

Things like that happened often. Cilicia grew very over protective of Ayanna while she was in the care of Jeremey. She wasn't sure just what he was capable of and didn't want to tempt him do something crazy. "I think this man has lost his mind! Jermaine please come by! Can you talk to him? I know it's late. I am sorry. I am not home. Ayanna and I left. I need to know it's safe for us to go back. I am so sorry but I don't know who else to call." It was one in the morning.

"I'll be right over C. Don't worry I will call you when I get there." Jermaine threw on some clothes and grabbed his keys. He had just got done talking to Jeremey. It was now 2:30 am. "C, where are you? I will meet you there." He met her in Wal-Mart's parking lot. It was only three miles from their home. She had chosen this to be her spot because it was well lit, well populated, video cameras and stayed opened twenty-four hours.

"I think he is crazy C. The stuff he was telling me. I don't know. I told him to go see a therapist. He says he is mad at you. You were just pregnant and he thought you and him would have to lose weight together. Since he put on so many pounds with his knee, but you bounced back without doing any work. You woke up and you were just your normal you. Now when you do go out all you get are compliments. People think Ayanna is your little sister. He is so jealous of you. No one notices him anymore. It's always about the baby. When friends come over its just to see the baby. He says he is tired of the baby. He is tired of you. I told him most men would kill for their wives to go back down to their pre-baby body in a month after birth. I told him he needed to appreciate you. There is always dinner for him and breakfast if he wants. Ayanna is a good baby and doesn't bother anyone. I told him that you clean and do anything that he needs you to do without asking twice. Yet he still hates his life. It's like he hates you. I am scared for you C."

Jermaine kept talking and Cilicia kept listening taking it all in with her baby peacefully sleeping in the back seat. *Why did he marry me?* she wondered. So, Jeremey was jealous of what some men pray for. There was nothing she could do about the way she looked. She had been small all her life. Jeremey had intruded a few times during the day with his friends for lunch. He never let her know he was on his way. She normally walked around in booty shorts and a small tank top. It always made her feel uncomfortable for his friends to look at her in that way.

Cilicia hugged Jermaine and headed home. She figured there would be a little peace for her. Ayanna would be up in a couple hours and want her bottle. She was tired and her eyes were bloodshot. She opted to sleep on the sofa. She would spend many nights on the sofa after that day. Jeremey and Cilicia had no sex life. It was normally okay, but now when he did lay on top of her that is all it was. He laying on top of her for no more than fifty seconds and that was it. She even timed it one night. It was horrible. He never kissed her or touched her tenderly. There was no reason to waste her time anymore with him or intimacy.

Valentine's Day had recently passed and it was the worse one she had ever spent. She knew that things were bad between them, but the magnitude of the issues showed its ugly head. Cilicia loved all holidays. She was a natural doer. Holidays were a way for her to really show people what they meant to her, even if they hadn't been the best to her. She had decorated the apartment with pink and purple balloons with hearts on them. It was hard enough to get a babysitter and everyone she knew would be out spending it with their loves. She planned a date night in for them.

After the decorations were up, she made homemade lasagna. She put rose petals on their glass coke bottle top dining table. A wedding gift from her parents that Jeremey had picked out. She even put Hershey's kisses in the shape of a heart on their bed. Everything was set and ready for him. He got off work at 4:30 pm and he was due home at 5:00 pm.

5:00 pm came and went. Cilicia didn't know what was keeping him. She tried to call and it was going directly to voicemail. There was no way he was working late. 6:00 pm passed and she was getting worried. Constantly looking off the balcony waiting for him to show up. By 7:00 pm, dinner was ice cold and she was upset. Her dress had creases in them from sitting so long in the same spot. The curls she had in her hair went flat.

Jeremey arrived at 8:30 pm. She was determined to have a good night. She had put so much work and effort into the evening that nothing was going to spoil it. Not even her hurt feelings. "Oh, wow you decorated. Right. Happy Valentine's day," he said as he handed over a Wal-Mart shopping bag filled with bagged candy that she didn't like and his deodorant. "The store was packed. Everybody was in there. I forgot all about today and figured I would get you something."

"I take it this is yours?" Cilicia handed him the deodorant. "Thanks for the candy. Are you hungry? I made dinner."

"Yes! I am starving! Thanks!" Jeremey sat at the table and noticed the petals and the heart shaped candle. He didn't say anything about it. They ate in silence. When he opened the bedroom door, he saw the candy on the bed shaped in a heart. He walked over to his side of the bed and lifted up the comforter by the corners and pushed them all to her side of the bed. He got in and went to bed.

Cilicia watched in horror. It was as if this was not happening to her. About fifty chocolate kisses were wedged on her side of the bed. She took off her dress, threw on one of his huge unflattering t-shirts and grabbed her pillow. Back on the sofa she will go. The next night Jeremey had a lot of energy. He opted to go out to the club with his friends going away party who was moving to Texas. Only he had forgotten that he used that excuse last Saturday. It didn't help that he got home at 4:00 am. There isn't a club in Hampton Roads that stays open that late especially on a Thursday night. Jeremey was sloppy and Cilicia stopped caring.

His late nights increased dramatically. He was hardly home and when he did come home all he wanted to do was fight. He would walk in at 3:00 am and wake up Ayanna claiming that he missed her and hadn't seen her all day. Cilicia would argue that maybe if he came home at a decent hour he would have time to see his daughter. He didn't care. He would disturb her sleep and give her to Cilicia to put to bed while he passed out from his night of whatever he did with whomever. Now that his friend had moved away, his latest alibi was karaoke.

Cilicia couldn't blame all of their issues on Jeremey. She played her part in the demise of the marriage. She stopped fighting for him. She stopped fighting him. In her heart, she knew he was cheating on her and she did nothing about it. She didn't know who it was or if she knew them, but there was definitely another woman. It was sad, but she just stopped caring. As long as he wasn't bothering her. As long as he wasn't bothering Ayanna. She didn't imagine her marriage being this way, but thinking back to their wedding day she had ignored that huge red flag.

Easter was a mess. His parents decided to pop up on them once again. The difference was this time they really had nothing to do with each other. Jeremey's treatment towards his wife and daughter were very noticeable. For the most part he ignored everyone. Cilicia had overheard a conversation between Patrice and Jeremey. They didn't know she heard it. They happened to have their little pow-wow in Ayanna's nursery. The same nursery that housed the 24-hour baby monitor.

"Jeremey, it doesn't matter if you like her or not, just take her out. You guys don't talk. I know you don't want to be here, but you might as well do something," Patrice told her son.

"Take her out where? She never goes anywhere. She is always with the baby. When I go out, I go out alone. I don't want to be seen in public with her. She knows this. I told her the other day when she wanted to go out for my birthday." Jeremy was being honest with his mother and that is exactly what he told Cilicia on his birthday when she offered to take him out for a steak dinner.

"Just do it and get it over with. I will watch Ayanna. Maybe that is why she doesn't go out. Because there is no one she trusts to watch the baby. You don't like her fine. You don't have to." Patrice won the battle. Jeremey walked to Cilicia and told her they were going out to eat. Unbeknownst to them, Cilicia was not thrilled for more reasons than one.

"Can I take your order please?" The waitress asked the couple.

"I'll have the baked chicken with the loaded backed potato." Jeremey handed the waitress his menu.

"And for you ma'am; are you ready to order?" The waitress thought it was odd she had never opened her menu.

"I will have just a water. I do not want any food. I refuse to eat with a man who would have to get talked into taking his wife out by his mother." She hands the menu to the waitress. Cilicia continued and turned her attention to Jeremey. "See I heard your little conversation with mommy dearest over there. You never thought one second that I could hear everything you two said about me when you know good and well Ayanna has a baby monitor in the room. I could hear everything." Cilicia stood up to leave. "As a matter of fact, I will be in the car. There is no way I will sit with a person who has told me and now his mother he doesn't want to be seen with me in public." Cilicia walked out without looking back. Jeremey got his food to go and drove home quietly.

Easter Sunday was just as bad. Before his parent decided to plan their spontaneous trip, Cilicia had arranged to have a dinner party. The best thing about the whole thing was she would be cooking all day. If she was cooking, she wasn't pay attention to anyone else other than her daughter. She was in tunnel vision and found solace at her stove. She ignored everyone. The guests arrived and she was able to relax a bit. After everyone had left she retreated into herself once again. The weekend was finally over and all she wanted to be was alone with her baby for a while.

Chapter 13

Jermaine, Tyesha, Jeremey, Cilicia and Ayanna went out to a hibachi grill. Jeremey was getting ready to go away on business for a couple months. Cilicia was thinking that maybe that's what they needed. A break. She hoped the evening would have gone great. She was looking forward to having a bit of girl talk with Tyesha.

When they arrived, Jeremey seemed easy going which helped Cilicia relax a bit. She leaned over to whisper something to Tyesha and she started laughing.

"What are you whispering about?" Jeremey asked. She couldn't quite figure out his tone but he didn't seem upset with her.

"Oh, it was nothing. Tyesha had asked me a question and she couldn't hear me so I just said it in her ear," Cilicia casually answered.

"Okay, so what was the question and what was your answer?" Jeremey was getting frustrated and was trying to sound calm. Jermaine was noticing the change also. The table started to tense.

"Well this was a private conversation between Tyesha and me." Cilicia was getting annoyed and was not going to interrupt her conversation with Tyesha. Tyesha had actually asked her if she had any feminine products with her because she had left them at home. It wasn't something that Cilicia was going to blurt out at in a crowded restaurant.

"Was it about me?" Jeremey still questioned, visibly upset.

"I am sorry Jeremey, but not everything is about you. This was between Ty and me. It had nothing to do with you." Cilicia was getting angry.

That is when Jeremey filled a straw with water holding it with his finger and releasing the fluid on her thigh. "There will be more of that when you get home. Don't play with me" He now had a menacing tone.

Tyesha got scared. "Cilicia, are you okay? Is everything okay?"

"Yes, yes I am okay. It will be fine," Cilicia said with her head down. She was so embarrassed. If Jeremey felt she was misbehaving in any way, he would fill up a big gulp cup from 7/11 and pour it on her head. She excused herself to the bathroom. On the way, Tyesha followed her and Jermaine sent her a text. As it seems the evening would not be a good one after all.

Because of the incident with the water, Tyesha and Jermaine decided to head back with the married couple and hang out. They really just wanted to make sure Cilicia was okay. The couples walked in and Cilicia put the sleeping Ayanna in her crib. She lay on the floor watching TV while the three of them were on the sofa.

"I have an idea," Jeremey broke the silence. "Why don't we swap spouses?" he asked laughing.

"Dude, what the hell are you talking about?" Jermaine was offended and now he was even more upset. He had been upset since the straw incident and did his best to hide it but now he was just angry. "What do you mean swap spouses? How do you just disrespect your wife like that dude? That's not cool man. That's not cool at all."

"I don't like that, Jeremey. Don't say things like that," Tyesha interrupted. "Cilicia, are you okay? You should come home with us for a while." Tyesha was angry also.

"Ummm. I am okay. It's okay he was just playing, *right Jeremey?*" Cilicia wished at that moment the ground would have opened up and swallowed her entirely. The couple left shortly after. Cilicia didn't want them to go, but she didn't want them to stay either. She hated her life.

Tyesha whispered to her "You call me anytime. Jermaine will come over there and make sure you are okay." Cilicia nodded her head slightly to not give any inkling of what Tyesha had said.

As Jeremey prepared for his trip, Cilicia was feeling relieved. She needed him to go. No one in the family at this point had any clue about what was going on other than Samantha. Cilicia had confided in her mother. She felt lost without her grandmother. Samantha had told her to get a diary of everything that Jeremey was doing and what he was saying. Hide it good in the apartment and if anything happened to her they would find the diary. That is exactly what she did. She hid the diary under the washing machine. The only person who knew of it was Jermaine.

There were a number of times where Jermaine came in the middle of the night for one reason or another. The disturbances between Jeremey and Cilicia didn't subside. As time went on, they seemed to have been getting worse. Jermaine no longer had to ask her where she was parked at 3:00 am. Being well aware she was sitting in her spot right behind the Wal-Mart three miles down the street. He too was glad for Jeremey's pending departure. The worry for his dear friend mounted with each passing night. Keeping both their phones nearby in case of the phone call. Tyesha felt even more uncomfortable about the situation after the mentioning of swapping partners. Did that mean that Jeremey was into her? She wanted nothing to do with him.

Ayanna stopped sleeping throughout the night because of Jeremey waking her up to play. Cilicia finally had her on a sleep schedule for a while, but at six months old their baby would wake up like clockwork at 2:00 am expecting Daddy to be there. At this point, that was the only time he saw her. When most families were having their quality time in the evening hours, Jeremey flipped it to where only havoc occurred in the middle of the night after his escapades

Chapter 14

Jeremey was gone and still managed to make Cilicia's life even more so a living hell. When he was not at work, he would make her keep him on speaker phone all day and all night so he could hear what she was doing in the apartment. He also told her she was only allowed to answer the house phone for him, his mother or her mother. Cilicia thought it was insane. His controlling had gotten too creative since he was not able to keep eyes on her day and night.

Cilicia thought it was fitting to change the answering machine to something more fitting to the guidelines of her new rules.

"Hi you have reached Cilicia. If you are not my mother, my mother-in-law or my husband, please contact me on my cell phone. I am no longer allowed to use this phone other than for those purposes per Jeremey's instructions. Sorry and have a great day. Leave a message at the Beep!"

She had finally let go of the shame of her abusive marriage and felt comfortable letting everyone know that it wasn't a good situation for her and her daughter. She was tired of keeping up the false appearances. A lot of the time it was easy because her family was so far away, but they could hear it in her voice during conversations that something was wrong. The imperfection was not accepted and it was time to fix it or get the hell out. In either case, it was time for a change and the time for secrets had come to an end.

Ring, Ring, Ring. Cilicia let the phone go to voicemail on purpose. It was Jeremey calling for his daily checkup. "Goddammit, Cilicia. Answer the damn phone! I know you are in there! You better pick up the damn phone right now!" She stood there and listened to the message. Right then her cell phone rang.

"Hello." Cilicia answered in a cheerful voice

"You take off that damn message. I am not playing with you. What the hell is your problem?" Jeremey as usual was pissed and yelling.

"Why should I change the message? It's what you told me. I am just letting everyone else know that as well. I don't want anyone to worry about me, if I don't answer the phone." Cilicia was very cheerful. Too cheerful. "As a matter of fact, my aunt is calling now, but she's not on the list!"

Cilicia hung up on him. He called her back over and over and she ignored him. More and more of her family called to listen to the voicemail. They left message after message. Jeremey was still calling and he was pissed.

The next day she got a call from the complex that Jeremey was trying to get the lights cut off in the apartment but because it was all utilities included, he wasn't able to. After that was the cable. He had reduced the package to the bare minimum. His reasoning was that she didn't deserve all those channels. Following the cable was removing her from the car insurance. Geico had called to tell her that news. She simply told them that it was a mistake and she was to be kept on the policy.

Jeremey left a voicemail, "Bitch, you still haven't changed that damn message? That's why you are going to be sitting in the dark soon! How dare you disrespect me! I am the one that makes the rules around here. Love, honor and obey Bitch! Did you hear that? *Obey?* You will obey!" She looked at the message and saved it. There would be several just like them. If a family member didn't believe her, she would simply put the landline and cell phone on speaker. They were free to hear his words for themselves. She was tired of keeping quiet about her living situation. She was exhausted trying to keep up false appearances of him being a loving father and husband. They had no family pictures, because they weren't a family. Just some broken people who came together making a mess of things.

Jeremey and Cilicia was on a Sprint family plan under her name. They had combined the bills after they got married. Since he was removing her from everything she called the phone company and got his phone taken off. Jeremey didn't know what was going on. The representative had placed a special access number on the account that he couldn't get to. He ended up having to get a whole new number and account under his name. It took three days for him to get it all straightened out. That was three days of peace for Cilicia.

"What the hell did you do to my number?" Jeremey was furious. Cilicia was somehow beating him at his own game.

"Well actually it's *my* number and I figured since you wanted to cut things off that I wouldn't be able to afford two lines anymore. I needed to remove yours from my account. No hard feelings. It's just the way things are now." Cilicia hung up and went to tend to Ayanna.

She was well aware of how ruthless he could be. He had gone through her search history and got mad that she was looking for a job a few months back. He then placed a bug on her laptop and she had to call Dell tech support to get it off. Jermaine confirmed that something had been placed on it. He was currently in school for computer technology. The same field Jeremey worked in. It was that moment Cilicia vowed to learn more about computers, passwords and how to lock things down from him.

Cilicia working would give her independence from Jeremey. With him as the bread winner, he felt he had control of everything and she was just simply there with no place to go. It made her *need* him and gave power he had never had before. He only shared a few stories about his home life with his parents in Florida, but from what she noticed in his actions Jeremey had turned out to be just like his father. The one person he despised. Harry also controlled Patrice and deemed himself dictator over their home. Cilicia remembered after Easter, Harry called her apologizing for Jeremey's actions toward her and Ayanna. "I noticed how my son treats you and my granddaughter and I am calling you to personally apologize."

Cilicia who sat silent on the phone for a while didn't want to disturb his speech. "I wasn't the greatest example to Jeremey and he didn't see me start to treat his mother right. I didn't start that until after he had moved out of the house. I know it's hard right now, but my son doesn't know how to be a good husband and father because of me."

"I thank you for the apology," acknowledging the gesture Cilicia still sensed he had more to say. He really should have ended it there.

"But even though he doesn't treat you right you have to wait for him to do better. For as long as it takes. You are his wife and you are to be *submissive* to him no matter what. Eventually, he will too learn the right way," Harry continued.

"So, what you are saying to me is I am to wait a possible twenty plus years for Jeremey to learn, grow and be a good man to me? I am sorry, but I won't sit around for decades in hopes for a person to start treating me right and my daughter." Cilicia was not going to allow him or anyone else to talk her into staying in an abusive relationship. "We deserve much better. Jeremey is on the path for that day to never come and I can assure you if he doesn't get his act together soon, this marriage will never see that day."

Harry was annoyed. This was not going according to plan. Cilicia was to take his advice and adhere to it. "Well then maybe you should read your Bible. It clearly tells you, the wife, to be submissive to your husband."

"Oh, I am very well aware of what the Bible says on this matter. Thank you very much." Cilicia was not going to back down from him

224

or anyone else. It wasn't her nature to do so. "I am also aware that husbands are to love their wives *first*. Now if you would excuse me, I have a hungry baby to feed. Have a nice day." That was the end of the conversation. She knew Patrice was on speaker phone the entire time, however, she didn't contribute to the conversation.

Wow, another message? I am getting more and more popular these days, she said to herself listening to yet another voicemail. This one was from Latoya. Latoya was a wiz at computers also. She had actually placed a password screener on her computer so no matter what site her husband went to she would have access to his account. She had tried to talk Cilicia into doing the same thing. Cilicia didn't care that much for all of that and thought Latoya was crazy for going through the hassle. She would hear Dereon come over and complain about how his wife knew about everything and he didn't know how. Cilicia would giggle to herself and go about her business as usual. Latoya was under the assumption that Dereon was cheating on her.

At first Latoya was considered a friend, but she quickly realized she could not be trusted. It was Latoya who Cilicia told that she was looking for a job. She didn't say anything more than that. It wasn't a secret because Jeremey already knew. The next thing she knew she got an email from Jeremey stating that Latoya told him her plan to get a job, clean out all of *his* money and ultimately leave him. It was impossible for her to clean him out of anything since they had always had separate accounts. *Wow so this chick is telling lies on me now? Fuck her!* That was the end of the friendship. Even though Cilicia never told Dereon or Jeremey how his wife knew his email account and black planet passwords. When Latoya would call her, she would simply ignore her. She had no use for people like her in her life. For all she knew, she was just trying to get more information to create against Cilicia.

Cilicia had no time to be sad, angry or anything. She had to stay focused and get herself in a position to take care of her and her baby.

She reached out to her mother for help, but her parents turned their back on her.

"You have a good man don't mess this up," is what Samantha told her. Cilicia had heard from Darlene that Samantha was speaking to Jeremey every night. She wasn't sure what lies her mother could be filling his head with. Whatever it was, it was bad. At this point, Cilicia had expressed to her mother and to Jeremey that she thought it best they separate. Jeremey didn't believe her. Samantha was filling his head with lies and he trusted what he was being told. It had been a while since Samantha and Cilicia would be at different ends of the spectrum but their past was bubbling up and showing itself.

Cilicia found herself a part time job doing security work. It paid $15.00 an hour. It was a good start and she would save every penny she had earned. She had found a home daycare center for Ayanna through one of Jeremey's coworkers, Clark. Clark's wife ran the daycare and had room for an additional child. It was all set. She had even joined the Air Force Reserves. As a soon-to-be single mother, she didn't want to be a full-time Airman. She needed the freedom to take care of her daughter. Jeremey was again furious and showed every bit of it.

"You did what? I hope you die! I hope they send you to war and the only thing Ayanna has to remember you by is a flag," was Jeremey's reaction. Nothing he said to her mattered anymore. She was done. She didn't even take the time to respond to him. He was due to come home soon and she was sure all hell was going to break loose in the process. She was ready.

Chapter 15

Jeremey was coming home today. He had been gone for four months. His trip had gotten extended which gave Cilicia more time to prepare. There was a knock at the door. It was him. There was a look in his eyes that she had never seen on him before. However, she had seen the look before on others. They were going to fight.

Cilicia still had on her work clothes. She changed out of her professional attire in exchange for her sneakers, jeans and a t-shirt. Her long dark hair was placed in a tight bun. She looked at herself in the mirror for a long time. She was ready. She had no fear. 'Father, protect me. Protect Ayanna. *Amen.*"

"We need to talk," Jeremey said as she entered the room looking like another person.

"Okay talk." Cilicia was short with her words. She didn't care what he had to say.

"Why is all your stuff in the other room? I was told you wanted to work things out?" Jeremey quizzed.

"Well whatever my mother told you was a lie. I told her and you that after you wished me dead for joining the Reserves, I didn't want to be with you anymore. Any man that can wish death on his wife doesn't deserve a wife." Cilicia's voice was completely even. There was no emotion.

"Oh, so that is what you think, huh? Well fine I can be honest too. I don't want anything to do with you. I don't want anything to do with her." Jeremey was pointing at Ayanna who was in Cilicia's arms. "Matter of fact, I don't care if I never see you two again. Fuck you and fuck her!"

"Oh, I am fine with that. We will leave and that will be that." Cilicia got up hoping this would be the end.

Jeremey got up too. "Where the hell do you think you are going?" He tried to push her down. Cilicia didn't budge.

"I am leaving like you said. So now just let me go!" Even though Jeremey had pushed her, she didn't fight back. Her focus was now to leave. In her car, she had already stashed $300.00 cash, both her and Ayanna's birth certificates, social security cards, savings bonds, her car title, Will and an overnight bag with clothes.

Jeremey pushed her again. Now trying to pry Ayanna out of her arms. That was it. That was the trigger. Jeremey, being stronger than Cilicia, was able to do so with little struggle. Cilicia was fighting back now with all her might to keep her baby with her. "If you say fuck us both, why are you trying to keep her?" Jeremey never answered. Instead he turned the corner and went into the nursery. The rest for Cilicia was a blur. Jeremey did the unthinkable and tossed the 10-month old baby in the air and into her crib. As he turned around Cilicia punched him in the face. Jeremey was stunned. He was not expecting that from the once calm Cilicia. She was fighting even harder to get to the crib. Ayanna shrieked. Her cry was so piercing. Cilicia had never heard anything like that before.

Cilicia then jumped on Jeremey's back and put him in a headlock. She brought him to the floor and they rumbled to the floor in the small nursery. "Stop! Stop!" Jeremey yelled, but it was too late. Cilicia had backed out and he had opened the flood gates of her rage. He dragged her out of the room. "I am going to kill you!" When Cilicia heard him threaten her life, she made a mad dash to the kitchen. Jeremey knew she was trying to get a knife. He tried to grab her from behind, but she hit him with the back of her fist. She was fighting for her life. She was fighting for her baby's life.

Jeremey then tried to drag her out of the apartment. She jumped up and was parallel to the wall and the door. She put her feet up used all her strength to propel back, broke free and hit him again. Finally, he dragged her out of the house, leaving her banging on the door. "Get the fuck out you crazy Bitch!" She called Lisa, another friend of hers that she had befriended through a coworker of his. Lisa was on her way and then she called the York Town Country Sheriffs.

The first cop arrived. "Ma'am do you need medical attention?" She had no idea why he was asking her this. Cilicia was unaware of her own bruises.

"No, I am fine. My baby is on the third floor. Her father and I just had a fight. I need to get my baby. I think she is hurt. He threw her in her crib. Do you hear her crying? Do you hear my baby crying?" Cilicia pleaded.

The cop ran up the stairs. "Open up it's the police! Sir we know you are in there! Open this door now!"

Jeremey opened the door laughing. "Are you serious? You called the cops on me? You did, huh. Wow!" Everything was a joke to him. He was talking to one cop and the other was talking to her. Ayanna was being checked by the paramedics who said she was okay. They really wanted to check Cilicia. The officers told him to vacate the premises, and a no contact order was placed against him. Lisa talked Cilicia into going to the hospital.

Cilicia had no idea that she was so badly beaten up. Jeremey wasn't in the best of shape either. She had bruises on her neck, arms, and legs and a bruised rib. She took the next day off of work and kept Ayanna home from daycare. She did notify Stacy, Clark's wife, of the assault and the no contact order.

"You need to come home!" Samantha demanded. She had heard the story from Jeremey. Whatever version he told she was sure she was made out to be the villain and didn't care.

"No, I tried that, remember and you told me I was married to a good man. I think I am going to stay in VA and figure this mess out myself. A mess that you helped create, feeding him lies!" Cilicia hung up on her mother.

Darlene found out about what happened. To get to the bottom of things, she took a flight out to VA. Cilicia had told her aunt everything that happened including the second altercation when he was allowed to come back into the house. That night the pushing began again. He had threatened to throw her off of the third-floor balcony. Cilicia got away from him and barricaded herself in Ayanna's room. She hid her cell phone under her bed along with a change of clothes just in case something had occurred. If another incident were to happen she knew she had to get to Ayanna's room. Cilicia didn't know if Jeremey was allowed back in the home. She was resting on the couch and he was standing over her watching her sleep.

She could hear through the door that he was punching holes in the walls. Cilicia got scared and called the police again. By the time they got there, all of her belongings were thrown around the apartment. Everything was a mess. They left that night and moved into a hotel. Cilicia was officially homeless and had no place to go. Darlene was floored at the developments. What ticked her off was Jeremey had gotten a hold of Cilicia's phone book and called different people in the family. Darlene was one of the people he called. That conversation ended with Darlene cursing out Jeremey, as did every other conversation with him during that time.

Jeremey didn't know Darlene was in town helping her move her things from one hotel to the next. He actually didn't know where his wife and child were and didn't seem to care. When Jeremey called Cilicia threatening her for the tenth time since she was removed from the home, Darlene snatched the phone and cursed him out again.

Jeremey got nervous when he realized she wasn't alone and hung up the phone immediately.

Darlene's visit was much needed and very much appreciated. Cilicia couldn't depend on her parents and most of the people in the family treated her as out of sight out of mind. Cilicia had called her parents before Jeremey had returned home asking if she could move back to New York. She had a feeling that things were going to get worse for them and feared her and Ayanna's safety. "Mommy can I please come home? I have no place to go and I am scared for our lives. Jeremey is crazy and I don't want to have anything to do with him."

"No, you can't." Samantha liked Jeremey, which explained her not so secret nightly conversations with him. He had always made her laugh. Even though she was aware of the issues, she wanted her daughter to stay with him. It was better for her to be with him than to be alone. It was better to have a husband even if that husband was not treating her right. People treated you *different* when a husband was mentioned and Samantha wanted her daughter to have that status no matter what. "You married him! This is all your fault. Now you deal with it. You have a good man and you need to learn to be a better wife to him or he wouldn't treat you the way he does. You are messing this up!" That was the last time she would ask her mother for help. Not so surprisingly, her father said something similar.

Patrice and Harry were no good to anyone. They never had a positive influence over their son. He did have a half-sister named Amanda she had recently met. Amanda was the person to actually sit Cilicia down and give her the raw true story of the family. Cilicia had always wondered why Jeremey had a sister who was only seven months apart. She assumed at some point that Harry cheated on Patrice and had a baby out of wedlock. What she found out was there was cheating, but not how she assumed.

Amanda's mother Vivian and Harry were married. Patrice was married to a man named Phillip. Harry and Patrice had an affair together against both their spouses. When Vivian became pregnant with Amanda, Patrice had already divorced Phillip and shortly after she became pregnant with Jeremey on purpose. Cilicia had the entire story backwards. Patrice married Harry when the kids were 9 years old after Vivian had finally divorced him. These weren't Harry's only children. He had an older daughter named Myra. Myra once told Jeremey that he was illegitimate and should have never been born, since he was a love child product. This might be the cause of some of his insecurities.

Previously, Jeremey had explained how his father was controlling over his mother, which is why he didn't have respect for his mother and their relationship was strained. He would never give any details but he would say how happy he was living in Indiana with his mom and aunts. After the marriage, the family moved to Florida where Harry isolated Patrice and she had little contact with anyone else. Harry was very controlling over Patrice. In Jeremey's eyes, his mother allowed it and resented her for it. It was one of the many reasons why Jeremey was once attracted to Cilicia. Cilicia had a backbone and took nothing from no one. Now Jeremey expected her to be like Patrice and didn't like her being disobedient. These habits Jeremey later inherited from his father against his own wife and daughter.

Amanda was the only person in the family who stood up to Jeremey over the treatment of his wife and daughter. In Jeremey's eyes, Amanda betrayed him and took the side of Cilicia. Amanda tried to tell him there were no sides other than right and wrong. After that Jeremey started slandering Amanda to her friends. When Cilicia found out, she told him he was wrong and childish. She tried to remind him that Amanda was still his sister and what he was doing was terrible.

"She is a fat bitch and needs to get over the death of her mother! That happened seven years ago! Ain't nobody feeling no sympathy for her! I remember when all my friends wanted to get with her. Now they are like nah, I am good." Jeremey's words were evil. Amanda's mother had passed away from cancer when they were 17 years old. If he had spoken that way about his own flesh and blood what was he capable to do to her?

Sitting alone in a small hotel room, she put together his trifling capabilities. "First Amanda, now me and Ayanna..." It would be a matter of time before he hurts someone else that he was supposed to love.

Chapter 16

One day picking up Ayanna from daycare, Tracy mentioned that her daughter Saundra was looking for a roommate. Saundra had a 3-year-old son and was a single mother too. They lived in Hampton in a three-bedroom townhouse. Cilicia jumped at the opportunity and moved in. After being displaced in the hotel for nearly two months, they had a stable place to live.

By now Cilicia heard from Lisa that her husband Leon left her and moved in with Jeremey. She was devastated and heartbroken. Especially since Lisa allowed Jeremey to stay with them during the restraining order against him. She would say all he would talk about was his wife and daughter and how much he wanted them back into his life. How much he messed up and wanted to make things right. What she really did was let the devil in her home wreaking havoc.

Cilicia still had the key to her old apartment with Jeremey. There were times when she needed to go over there to get the stuff that had to be left behind. As she entered the apartment everything, was a mess. The once tidy and pleasant place had turned into a garbage dump. There were chicken bones on the floor, wrestled beds, dishes of half eaten food all over the place, dirty clothes piled on the floor. It was all disgusting.

She walked into Ayanna's nursery and discovered he had torn up the room. Her crib was turned over, curtains shredded, decorations were broken, the baby books were torn and her clothes were hidden throughout the house. Cilicia started taking pictures of everything. As she walked through the mess tears streamed down her face. She began to fear him coming in there while she was alone. She called his supervisor to let her know what she had witnessed. Candace called him into her office. "I am on the phone with Cilicia and she is telling me that you wrecked your baby's room. She is going to be removing the furniture from the apartment tomorrow. Did you do this Jeremey?"

"No I didn't do this. She is lying. She is lying like she lies about everything. Why would I do that to my daughter's room? She is my daughter and I love her," Jeremey responded back in his most sincere tone.

Cilicia could hear him and knew he would lie. He always lied. He always played the good guy and switched the blame to the victim. Well she wasn't in the mood for games today. "Please Candace check your inbox. I sent you over some pictures of the room. I implore you. I am not lying."

Candace clicked through the photos in horror. "Jeremey, you lied to me! You did do this! How could you do this?" The photos were disturbing. "Cilicia I will ensure that he will not be on the premises when you remove the furniture and you are free to take anything out of the home that you need. I am very sorry." Cilicia breathed a sigh of regret and relief at the same time.

"Jermaine, I am sorry to bother you but I need your help…" Cilicia explained what happened and he believed her. He didn't need the pictures or any proof. She arranged for a storage facility and a moving truck. Jermaine told Tyesha, who then met up with Cilicia, to make sure she was okay.

When she returned the next day a group of college guys that shared an apartment on the first floor approached her. "Hey, you used to live on the third floor with your daughter, right? You have a baby girl. I remember her."

Cilicia was a little taken back by the guys. They had never spoken to her before. "Uh Yes, I lived in Apartment 3E why?" She was curious as to what they had to tell her.

"Well we wanted to let you know that we know you drive the silver Honda Civic. A few times, in the middle of the night, we would catch some guy always trying to break into your car. Later, we realized that he was your husband. We ran him off but he would come back and go up the stairs like it wasn't him. Are you okay?" The young guy reached out to her. Clearly, she had been crying.

"Um no, not really. I moved out with my baby. I just need to get my daughter's things out of the home. I am just trying to get everything straightened out." Cilicia was too tired to act like she wasn't upset.

"Hey, anything you need. We will gladly help you. You need to stay away from that guy. He is crazy! Don't worry. Just knock on the door and we will be here to help in any way we can," his roommate said and put his hand on her shoulder.

That is exactly what the guys did. When everyone witnessed the mess, they didn't know what to say. Jermaine believed her but he didn't imagine this. "Oh my God!" He was pissed off. He called Tyesha to tell her that she was to stay away from Jeremey and sent her photos also. "I don't trust that bastard with anything!" The young guys didn't say anything, but the horror was written over their face. The guys moved the furniture while she searched through the home looking for Ayanna's clothes. He had hidden them in draws, cabinets, under the bed and other places. It was madness, but it was over.

Jeremey would send strange and cruel text messages to her, especially after everyone found out about the nursery. He no longer spoke to Clark for helping out Cilicia. Whoever lent her any favor during that time was an enemy to him. He was barely giving any money to help support Ayanna even though Cilicia still only worked part time. She didn't understand how his friends could still support him after what he had done to her and his daughter. Everything that she accused him of she proved time and time again. His lies were just that. Lies.

A few of them reached out to her. Calling her all hours of the day telling her that Jeremey was sorry and wanted her back. The conversation would normally have ended with Cilicia cursing them out and hanging up the phone, which led her to appear as if she was some angry black woman and she could care less. Most of their numbers she had blocked by then. When she sent them proof for her side of the story combating his lies, they would defend him and make excuses.

Living with Saundra wasn't what it was all cracked up to be, but it was a stable place. Cilicia spent the majority of her time cooped up in her room with Ayanna. She only left to go to the kitchen to cook. Her bathroom was attached to her room also. Saundra had a boyfriend and they fought every single day. All they did was argue all hours of the night. Cilicia wasn't a fan of his. His normal conversations normally consisted of aliens and she avoided him like the return of the black plague. "What in the *hell* does she see in him?"

Jeremey had taken his crazy to extra levels. Cilicia's elderly neighbor warned her that she would see him driving through her parking lot at various times, but mostly at night watching who comes in and out of their house. She told her she needed to be careful and she believed he was stalking her.

Cilicia hustled at work to work extra hours and overtime. She worked so much that she never had a forty-hour paycheck. It was always seventy-six hours to eighty. Her company wasn't sure how she was doing it. Volunteering to work when someone else didn't gave her the extra hours needed to maintain a healthy living. If they were not at work she took their shift. She had a child to feed and that was her only focus. After a few months of costing the company more money than allotted, they hired her for the full-time security position. With her own position open, she was able to recommend Jermaine for the job. He had the same background as she did in security. It all worked out quite nicely.

After a huge blow out with Saundra's boyfriend, Cilicia came home from a Reserve weekend to find that the door had been broken. She called Clark to fix the door which is when they found out about the fighting. Saundra's parents had not been aware of the boyfriend drama. As a result, they shipped Saundra off to North Carolina to be with family and offered the townhouse to Cilicia. She gladly accepted. Clark, at this time, was making her feel uncomfortable. He had begun flirting with her so she kept her distance. She wasn't sure what he told Tracy, but when she would go by to drop off the rent checks, she was greeted with an attitude. It was then she decided it would be best to not be bothered with either of them and mail the checks instead.

When Jeremey found out she had her own place, he would come by in the middle of the night banging and screaming at the door. A few times her neighbors had to come out and defend her by threatening to call the police. He would reluctantly leave.

"I want to see my daughter! You cannot keep her from me! I know you have someone in there with you! Who is in there with you?" Jeremey was once again yelling profanities at her. It was 2:00 am. "I know you are in there! You dumb Bitch!"

"Leave that woman alone! Get out of here before we call the police. Its 2 am! Lady don't you dare open that door! This man is crazy!" Cilicia felt bad but she was glad her neighbors defended her. She was too scared to open the door on that night or any other night.

Cilicia had planned to take Ayanna who was now one-and-a-half years old to the Washington DC Cherry Blossom festival. She had heard about it during her Drill weekend with the Reserves. She was stationed at Andrews Air Force Base in Maryland. The morning of, it poured down raining so the two was stuck in Hampton once again. Her phone rings… It's a private number. Cilicia hated private numbers. This went on for about five minutes.

"Hello, who is this?" Cilicia answered the phone cautiously. She had a feeling nothing good would come from this call.

"This is Chyna, Jeremey's friend." Cilicia had heard that he had moved another woman into the home after he kicked her and Ayanna out.

"So, my husband's girlfriend is calling me? What do you want?" Cilicia went from cautious to annoyed yet curious.

"I just want to make sure you aren't getting back together with him. I am not trying to waste my time with no man that's not going to move forward with me. I know he's been spending more time with his daughter and you—" Chyna was cut off mid-sentence.

"Wait, you call me to ask me if I am getting back with *my* husband. Oh, you are just as *crazy* as he is. If I were to want him back, he would be mine. Who the hell do you think you are calling me disturbing my Saturday with this foolishness? And the nerve to be using my anytime minutes for this stupidity! I really hope Jeremey knows you called me. You don't know him like I do. If I were you I would start packing!" Cilicia thought the situation was rather comical. The joke about the anytime minutes went over the girl's head. This only furthered annoyed Cilicia. She thought it was a good joke.

"Oh well no he doesn't know. I called you but I don't need to pack or nothing, it's going to be fine. I just needed to make sure for me." Chyna had no idea what she had done.

Cilicia sat on her bed and looked at her daughter. *Wow didn't see this one coming.* She laughed again. Not much surprised her anymore. "Jeremey now you knows better than to bring anymore drama to me."

"Yo, I am so sorry. I don't know why this Bitch called you. Oh my God! Are you on your way over here? You don't have to come over here!" Jeremey started screaming in the background. "Get the fuck out of my damn house! Are you crazy? Bitch you called my wife!"

Cilicia was now laughing to herself "This dude *really* is crazy. He got me on the phone pleading with me and throwing her out!" She was sure no one was going to believe this one! As a matter of fact, for the most part all her life she dealt with people not believing her "tall tales." Sometimes fiction is easier to grasp than reality. "Jeremey deal with your bullshit over there and leave me out of it. Y'all are crazy as hell!"

"Cilicia, you don't know how sorry I am. I didn't know she called you. She got your number from my phone," he paused. Chyna was saying something to him in the background. "Bitch I said get the fuck out of my damn house!"

Cilicia hung up the phone on the both of them. She called Lisa to tell her what was going on. Her husband Leon was now also living with Jeremey. From what she heard they had turned the place into some kind of married men bachelor pad. "Girl what are you going to do? Are you going over there?" Lisa asked Cilicia.

"Go over there for what? I am not dealing with those crazy people. My grandmother always told me that you fight for what you want. Girl I don't want him! There is nothing to fight for. I will talk to you later and let you know everything."

"If that chick comes to your house let me know. I will be over there to help you whoop her ass. She is just as crazy as he is!" Lisa and Cilicia laughed.

"How are you, hon?" Cilicia wanted to make sure her friend was doing well. They were in the same boat.

"Girl, thanks for asking. No one ever asks me that. I am taking it one day at a time. I never thought Leon would do this to me. I still love him, but I am learning to let go. I wanted to have children with him, but I am happy all we ever had together was this dog! And for Jeremey of all people to do all of this." Her voice cracked holding back tears. "That man sat on my couch crying over you for two weeks and now he and my husband are living the single life. It's like I welcomed the devil in my home."

"I am so sorry hon." Cilicia could hear her friend's voice crack and it hurt her heart.

"Cilicia let me further warn you even though I know you know already. You watch that chick Latoya. Even after all this time I hear that she is still talking about you badly. I have run into people that told me that you are still a hot topic and your name is still in her mouth. I never liked that chick." Cilicia thanked her friend for the warning. She had heard the same rumor too. It was making its way around the small circle. It had been months since Cilicia had spoken to Latoya even though she still called from time to time. Lisa was one of the few people who saw Jeremey for what he was. Nothing good.

Later that day Jeremey called Cilicia back to apologize. He wanted to take her out to lunch and sit down with her. Cilicia agreed only because what he needed to tell him needed to be face to face. It would be for her benefit not his. She dropped Ayanna off with Lisa. There was no need for her to witness her parents going at each other's throats.

"Thanks for meeting with me. I know today was wild. I am really sorry about that." Jeremey sounded sincere. Cilicia didn't care.

She ordered her food which was the most expensive thing on the menu. "Listen to me good. I only met you here to tell you this to your face. I didn't want the airwaves from the phone to mess with your sense of comprehension. I don't care what you do or who you do it with. We are not together and you are not what I want, but I promise you that if there is a next time for that Bitch to call me, I will whoop her ass off of principal. I don't want you. She and everyone else can have your sorry ass. You don't love me. You don't love our daughter. You don't take care of your daughter. You don't impress me, but I will whoop her ass for principal alone."

Jeremey sat there in dead silence. A part of him wanted Cilicia to be angry and hurt. That would have showed that she still cared, but it was clear at that moment she didn't. Cilicia continued… "You come to *my house* screaming and yelling all through the night embarrassing me to my neighbors and you are laying up with some stank-named-bitch named Chyna? What the fuck is a Chyna anyway? What is she?

241

A Stripper! You have a lot of nerve. Don't come by my place again screaming and acting crazy in the middle of the night or you will be greeted by the Hampton Police Department! And another thing, I need you to listen to me loud and clear. Get you a quality Hoe. One who will wash your drawers, cook your food and clean up your nasty ass apartment. I kept that place immaculate. Do better! Get you a Hoe that will suck your little dick and shut the fuck up about it. Get you a Hoe that knows her place. That knows she's a hoe and understands that I am the wife. I will be divorcing you as soon as I can. VA law mandates a one-year separation. This October will be one year. I suggest you wait by the mail for your papers. I am tired of you and all your *shit*. You leave me and my baby alone. If you don't want to be a father, fine. I am not going to deter you or enable you. Know this for sure, I don't want you at all. I don't give a good goddamn what my mother has told you. Your dumb ass friends will stop calling me and you will not call my family!" Cilicia said what she needed to say and walked out leaving him sitting there alone.

There were a few more run-ins with Jeremy although nothing as major as before. One evening he came by to see Ayanna and refused to leave. He wanted his family back. It was the same story he had been telling her ever since the Chyna incident. "I have been really messing up! Leon had all kinds of women coming in and out of the house. I feel bad that I did that to Lisa. She was nice to me and let me stay there after we had that fight. You don't want anything to do with me and I barely know my daughter and Chyna is crazy! You know I went and got a bank loan for her for $2,500 that now I have to pay back because I had to throw her out. I only gave her the money because she has a record for stabbing her ex-boyfriend in the hand with scissors. I don't know what's going on with me. I need you to help me, Yo. I really do." Jeremey was sitting on the floor talking to his feet. He looked defeated.

"So, you barely give me anything for our daughter and I struggle from day to day but you gave her $2,500? You are crazy J. You are crazier and selfish than I had ever thought. You and Leon are some tired ass hoes. The both of you together over there messing around with random bitches. You both had good wives that took care of you and held y'all down. Now you are running a damn brothel and giving away money in the process instead of making profit! Get out of my house. We won't meet here anymore for anything. We will meet in mutual public locations from now on." Cilicia turned and walked away.

"It's all your fault! If you had not left, we would be making all kinds of money. I am not giving you shit. You need to learn that you do *need* me and then I will help you out!" Jeremey was back to his old self just that quickly. He grabbed her arm.

"Let go of me Jeremey or I promise you, you won't leave here the way you came. Don't you every put your hands on me again!" Cilicia was not playing and he knew it. He had lost. He could not control her anymore.

"You will never get another man! You are a single mother. No man is going to want to deal with you and no child. You fucked up now! You will be alone for the rest of your life. And when I get another family, Ayanna won't be a priority. She won't even be a factor. When she grows up, I am going to tell her that we are not together because you are crazy and insecure. I love you, I really do, but I am not going to put up with this shit from you!" Jeremey came up with anything he could to try to hurt Cilicia and get her to change her mind.

"You know when you say you love me it is not different than you calling me a bitch or saying fuck you or I hate you. It all means the same damn thing. Absolutely nothing. There is nothing you can say to me that will make me want you. You always said that you liked me because I was different. Now it seems as though you want a woman like you mother! Are you resentful because I stand up to you over Ayanna and that is something you always wanted Patrice to do for you? You need to find someone just as docile as her! And if you do get remarried and have more kids, if you want nothing to do with Ayanna, that will be your fault not mine and your loss. As for me not finding someone to be with and *actually* love me the way a man ought to,

Sweetie, you are mistaken, because I am cute!" Cilicia had enough of his pettiness. He lost his wife. He let go of his grip and stormed out of the house.

Chapter 17

October had finally come. Cilicia had been waiting for this month since their first altercation last year. She had been researching how to file for divorce and since Jeremy's behavior was so erratic it was best she went the route of a lawyer. In her research, she found that sometimes when children are involved the judge could order a couple to do marital counseling. She feared anything that would delay the process of ridding him as her husband.

A few months prior, she came up with the idea to go to counseling. Not only did she not want it to bite her in her ass later on, she really thought they had needed it. At this point, she couldn't stand Jeremey. There was still Ayanna to think about. They would be parents together regardless. "I think we should do marital counseling before I file for divorce." Cilicia had no reason to lie at this point. You only lie when there is something to hide or as a flawed way to save something broke.

"I agree! We need to work on our marriage," Jeremey responded. He obviously didn't hear anything she had just said and heard only what his brain wanted him to hear.

Cilicia set the whole thing up. She picked him up from work and they walked into the doctor's office. Dr. Castle asked, "So what brings you two to my office? We can start with you Jeremey." Dr. Castle was an older white woman with gray hair and kind blue eyes. Cilicia already felt comfortable with her.

Jeremey answered in a proud voice, "I am here to get my family back. My wife and I are separated and it kills me every day that I am not with them." Cilicia was immediately annoyed. He had regurgitated the same damn lie he had been spewing the past year.

Dr. Castle noticed the shift of emotion from Cilicia. "And you Ma'am, why are you here? It says here that you are the one that made the call."

Cilicia paused for a moment. "I am here because I don't like him. I don't like any part of him and we have a child together and I want us to be better parents to our daughter." She couldn't take one more lie and she surely wasn't going to add to it.

Dr. Castle looked at Cilicia and Jeremey. "Well I can vouch for at least one-person in the room who is being truthful. Cilicia why don't you like your husband?"

Cilicia took another deep breath "Because he is mean to me and our daughter. He screams at us both. She doesn't even call him daddy. When he is around her, he refers to himself as *that nigga*. It's terrible. Ayanna doesn't even call him 'Daddy' she calls him 'Jeremey'. He runs around telling these lies about how he wants his family back, but he is laying up with another woman that he threw us out for. He is a liar and I can't stand him."

"Is what she's saying true Jeremey that you are with another woman right now sitting here telling me that you want your family back?" Dr. Castle was confused. None of this was making any sense and she now understood Cilicia's frustrations.

"Well yeah I do, but that doesn't mean I don't love my wife. I have needs. I need to be taken care of and I found someone willing to do that for me. I still want my family though. Why is that so wrong?" Jeremey raising his voice to the therapist.

Dr. Castle then asked, "Cilicia how did you find out about this other woman?"

"Oh Doctor, there has been more than one woman, but one in particular well... She called me one day and told me. We had a full conversation about it."

Dr. Castle turning her attentions to Jeremey. "It's wrong because if you really wanted your family back you would not be living with someone else. You can't expect that your wife is going to accept that kind of behavior from you or anyone else." Dr. Castle then said to Cilicia, "When you were in the house how was it for you and your daughter?"

"Lord, that is such a loaded question, but in short it was misery. He was never home. When he did come home, all he did was argue with me and yell at Ayanna. It was to the point where I stopped fighting back so he would be yelling to himself. He would rip my scarf off my head really quickly to see if I would flinch. He would pour large cups of water on my head if I did something that he didn't like and deemed disobedient as if he was training a dog! He had nothing to do with our daughter and nothing to do with me. He would embarrass me in front of our friends. At one point, he offered to switch spouses with another couple. We were thrown out after the big fight we had when he told me he wanted nothing to do with us and threw her in the air and into her crib. I had to call the police. No, I don't want to be with him, but we have a child. He is not a good person. All he does is lie about me and I don't care anymore, because eventually everyone will see his truth for themselves." She stopped to take a breath. This was her time to finally get her feelings out and someone would actually listen to her. "He wasn't like this when we were dating. It was as if once we got married, I turned into a possession and not a person anymore." That was the most Cilicia would be able to speak for the entire session.

"Jeremey, is this true what Cilicia is saying? What changed for you after you all go married?" The doctor's voice was calm and even. Her hands sat in her lap with her fingers clasped. Her ankles still crossed and her posture still broad.

"Well, some of that is true, but the water was funny. It was all a joke! She can't take a joke!" Jeremey heartily laughed. "And what changed after we got married? Everything had to change. She was a wife! A wife listens to her husband and does we he says."

After that the Doctor asked him if he abused alcohol or drugs. He was deeply offended. She then explained then that would be a reason for his erratic behavior. It was that moment Jeremey showed his true colors. He showed his entire rainbow of truth and all of his crazy was exposed. He cursed Dr. Castle out as if she was some random hooker on the street. Cilicia sat quietly. She didn't look at either of them. Dr. Castle had changed her stance with her feet planted securely on the ground. Her once clasped hands were now pointing in Jeremey's direction. She wished she was looking out of the window of a car so she could secretly cheer the joggers as they ran by. Even after the terrible meeting, Dr. Castle invited them back the following week. Cilicia was the only one who showed up to the appointment.

"Ma'am, will your husband be joining us this afternoon?" Dr. Castle asked Cilicia who was sitting in the office in the chair across from her. Jeremey's seat stayed vacant. Dr. Castle was back to her previous tame and mild mannered self.

"Ummm I am not sure. I have not heard from him." Cilicia was telling the truth. After the appointment, he didn't answer her text about returning to anymore sessions.

"I think you are doing the right thing by not staying with him and subjecting your daughter to his abuse. He sat down and looked me in the face adamantly telling me he wanted his family back. You sat there and told me you no longer wanted to be in the marriage and yet you are here and he isn't." Dr. Castle shifted in her chair. "This is my advice to you. Get your divorce. You are young, you are beautiful, and your daughter is beautiful. You have time to start over and make a new life for you and her. The only way we could change him is if we shoved him back in his mother's stomach, birthed him and raised him all over again. He needs more than couple's counseling. He needs one on one therapy. I saw through his game as soon as he got in this office. He wasn't able to make me think you are being some crazy villain. No young lady, you go and live your life, and in the meantime, get you a boyfriend!"

Did Cilicia hear correctly? Did her marriage counselor tell her to get a boyfriend? She laughed all the way to her car with her paperwork that they had tried marriage counseling to add to the divorce package. She had received her confirmation. Her marriage was definitely over. Now all she needed to do was make it legal.

The lawyer's process was easy. She had gotten a referral from a coworker and as an added bonus saw a coupon for the office of Sawyer and Sawyer in the penny savers coupons that came in the mail. The biggest hurdle was confirming his new address. Apparently, Jeremey was also watching the calendar and moved from the three-bedroom apartment without telling Cilicia. When she checked to make sure everything was in order, she was surprised to find it had been cleaned out and he had moved.

She went to the leasing office to inquire about the vacant apartment. "Oh, there you are. We have been asking about you." Cilicia was confused but went along with the program.

"Oh sure, that is why I came down. Can I ask you a question can you show me my forwarding address please?" Cilicia asked slyly.

The apartment representative pulled out their folder. "You don't live here anymore do you? I haven't seen you go on walks with your baby in about a year. Earlier today your husband came in with a woman, but we know who you are and we knew who she wasn't." The representative passed her the folder. "Here is your address Ma'am, have a nice day!" That was it! Cilicia had his new home address and place to send the divorce papers too.

She gladly paid in full $495.00 to the attorney. Her lawyer didn't trust that was his correct address and to be sure she also sent the papers to his parents' house and his workplace. Cilicia loved that her lawyer was so thorough. She had made the right decision. She stopped to pick up Ayanna from daycare. She was such a happy toddler running and smiling toward Cilicia. "This will all be over soon baby. It's just you and mommy now. I won't let anyone hurt you." Ayanna had been the spitting image of her mother. She had received all of her features from her mother. The only thing that set them apart was Ayanna's beautiful dark coco brown skin. She was the image of love she had always dreamed of. "I wish grandma could have held you at least once lovely."

Cilicia was now hopeful towards her future. Jeremey called her furious when he got the papers at his new address still wondering how she found out where he had moved to. He tried to act as if he didn't know Cilicia was going to file for divorce. She paid him no mind. "Just sign the papers. I am not asking you for anything. I didn't even ask you for child support. I am done with you." That is all she had to say to him. The relationship had long been over since it began really.

Jermaine gladly met her at her lawyer's office to act as a witness to the marriage and the separation. He wanted her divorced just as badly as she needed to be. To prove they were separated for the one year she submitted the hotel receipts as well as the lease from her new home. Being brutally honest with herself admitting they should have never married him in the first place.

Her health was still a concern. About 6 months after she gave birth, the tumors appeared bigger and multiplied. This would be a new battle she would have to face. During their marriage, her periods unregulated terribly. The periods would last for sometimes three weeks straight. At the time, Jeremey didn't believe her and would make her change her bloody menses products in front of him. She was humiliated. He would stand there as she showed him the soiled pad to prove she wasn't lying. It took him over four months to sign the papers, but he signed it. He tried to fight it, but she had tied up all the loose ends and left no loop holes. So much went on in that marriage, but now it was all over and welcomed freedom. Free to do what she needed to do for the welfare of her daughter. "Please Lord heal my heart."

CORRINE

He kissed me
He kissed me so deeply
I melted
I physically melted in his arms
In his warmth
In his charm
In his
Manliness
And he accepted
The best of my femininity
On his tongue
And we became profound
We became something so much more
Than ever before
We intertwined like
Vines
In meadows of lilies
My flowers bloomed for him
And as crashing waves
Unceasingly
Increasingly
He gave me all the pleasure
I've ever needed
And I didn't know I did
I didn't know
I could give
My flesh
As it deepened in moistness
Just for him
I let go all
Inhibitions
That I held so dear
And he accepted

He rejected
Only the notion that I was not perfection
His blessing
My release
Figures between sheets
He gleaned
On me
In me
He stroked
And he stroked
And he stroked
And he spoke
Yes, he spoke to me
In ways I had only heard
With giggling chatter
From other girl's stories
But this is mine
And now I am free to tell
To speak
Freely if I felt the notion to do so
I catered to him
Made him feel as if he
The only man that not only every mattered
But
Ever existed
My Adam
My new beginning
In my Eden
His Eve
We
Unhinged from all torments of reality
We
Deserve to place the world on hold

Embrace our curves
In natural form
I'm beauty
To him and he alone can dwell within
My deep
My deepness
His weakness
And even still
I recall the earth shattering
Gaze that I gave right before
He spoke my name
It lingered
Like fingertip tickles
On skin
It lingers
Like the memories of him

Chapter 1

Corrine was a hard worker her job was easy and she didn't mind working. She has always been far from lazy. Newly divorced and a single mother at the age of twenty-five she was rather young for her situation. While most people her age was still going out and partying to the sun came up, Corrine traded that lifestyle for motherhood. She loved being a mother to her 1-year-old baby. Ariana was the joy to the Corrine's heart.

After dealing with the abuse of Ariana's father Jeremiah, she didn't want to be a relationship. Her focus was work and her child and not in that order. She didn't go out very much. She had no family within the 8-hour radius of which she lived. She was essentially alone in Virginia with her child, although she had been through worse things in her life.

One day at work when she was walking around securing the building, Corrine had landed a job on Langley Air Force base as contractor. Unfortunately, it was the same base where Jeremiah worked too. She hardly left her building and would go straight home after work, in an effort to avoid her ex-husband. "Corrine I would like you to meet our new employee Chris. He will be working in the facilities branch. You guys will be working closely together on some problems that arise in the building when dealing with the security system," said Chris' supervisor Mr. Bell.

"Oh great. Nice meeting you Chris welcome!" Corrine gave him a warm sincere smile. Most people in the building really liked her. There were only a few bad apples that didn't think a woman should be in a security section. Most of the guys she worked with were her friends so they made sure she was taken care of. Chris was cute in an unconventional kind of way. He was not tall. Well not to Corrine who stood at 5 foot 10 inches. He was shorter than her, but average height for a man. Normally anyone who was shorter than her was just short in her opinion. He wasn't very slim but by no means was he fat or even thick and his hair was cut short. His smile seemed shy. He didn't say much to her. Just a nod of the head. He was dressed nicely. Corrine kept on with her building checks.

By the end of the week Chris had warmed up to the section. The facilities branch always hung out with security. It was just how the day would go. The security office was on the main floor and the facilities section sat on the second floor. "How are you liking it Chris?" Ray, another facility monitor, asked him. Ray was good people. He was funny and sometimes he could be a little crass at times but he was dependable and knowledgeable.

"Oh yeah, I like it here. The people seem cool and I don't mind the 10-minute commute either. I am originally from Maryland, but I took this job in VA," Chris replied sitting in the swivel chair.

"Cool man! I am from DC. I go home every once in a while, too. We are from right down the street from each other," Ray said cheerfully. Just then Corrine entered the room. She had just got done escorting personnel who didn't have the proper clearance for the building.

"Hey everyone! Hey Chris hanging out with us today?" Corrine sat down in the chair across from him to check her emails for the day. She was always out of the office doing just what he said she was doing.

258

She was deemed the unofficial "escorter" for those who didn't have a clearance for the building. She didn't mind. It got her out of what she called the "fish bowl". The one side of the office was made of mostly glass that created a huge window. When people walked by, it made them feel as if they were a live aquarium.

"Oh, Hey Corrine! How are you today?" Chris asked her. He always seemed uneasy around her. She noticed and made her feel a little self-conscience about it. She turned her back and checked her email. The conversation wasn't long. Chris didn't stay and left the office.

A couple of weeks later Chris overheard Corrine telling Ray her daughter would be going on two-week vacation. Staying one week with her mom and one week with her father's parents. "Damn C what are you going to do? You know that child is your whole world and please don't go out with those lames that had you out there with the stinky clothes and roaches." Ray laughed hysterically. Corrine found it funny but refused to laugh. Her love life sucked and everyone knew it.

"Gosh Ray, can we let that go?" Corrine chuckled "Chris, pay him no mind. He is a fool and you don't have time for fools I am sure" she joked.

"No, no I think I wasn't to hear this one. Go on Ray. What's this I hear about the stank dude and roaches?" Chris was curious while Corrine was flushed in the face.

Ray, still laughing, starts telling the story. "Okay man, see there was a guy C went out with. She left here talking about he was going to a blind date to a book store. We all know C is a nerd so it was not that big of a deal for us. This girl will read anything twenty-five times if you let her. Don't let the cute face fool you. My sister is a straight up nerd." Corrine rolled her eyes. It was true but he didn't have to stress it. "So, this guy goes into her friend's phone and sees her picture. He has the friend call up Corrine. Corrine is like, okay, I am going to the book store you can meet me there. Now Corrine does not date, but we were all getting on her about her moving on from her ex and what not. That dude was a damn terror so she, you know, was a little hesitant to go out with anyone new."

"Oh my God! Ray stop telling *all* of my business, dang!" Corrine was annoyed and Ray kept going as if she had not interjected.

"So, she goes to the book store. She has no clue what dude looks like. She sees a guy pull up in a SUV. She thinks that is him. The guy jumps out the ride in gym clothes. He opens his trunk to a pile of clothes and starts putting them all over the sweater gym clothes. C has an attitude now and is disgusted. The guy's name is Quincy. He walks up to her and tries to give her a hug. As soon as he put his arms up, C smells his stank pits. She dodges the hug." By now the whole office is hysterically laughing at Ray physically reenacting the whole scene. "Needless to say, the date lasted ten minutes and the guy still calls her to this day. Hahahhahhhaha. How do you go on a date stank? *And* he tried to hug her goodbye! I bet you can still smell him, huh C?" Ray was hysterical.

Chris looked at Corrine and laughed. "This can't be true. He had on stank gym clothes?"

"Hahaha, Yes he did. Very funny." Corrine mocked her coworkers. "It was the worst ten-minute date I think anyone can have. I have his number under my DNA, listen, Do Not Answer. He told me he didn't have time to take a shower when he got done playing basketball and didn't want to be late"

"Well I am sure you would have wanted him to be late rather than musty," Ray laughed again.

"Ummm, maybe we can all hang out since you have your mommy-free break coming up. You can dodge all the Quincy's in VA," Chris said jokingly.

"Nah man, you can count me out. My girlfriend is too jealous. Corrine is too pretty to hang out with. She's my sister and all, but my girl is crazy," Ray said as he stood up. "If she ever saw me out with her she would have my head on a platter and I would be on the 6 o'clock news." He laughed, but he was serious. "My girl is the type that touches the hood of my car to see if it's warm. If it is, she knows I had just been out. I need to park and get that thing cooled down before she gets home from work!" He walked out of the office to head home.

Ray wasn't lying. His girlfriend was just what he described her to be. Absolutely insane. No one in the office understood why he was with her in the first place. "The sex just can't be that damn good!" Luke their supervisor said, shaking his head watching Ray hurry to the parking lot to get home. "Ain't no way I would let a woman run me like that! Especially an unattractive white girl. If you date outside the race, get you a good one. Not some fake wannabe rocking braids and beads. He might as well date a black woman! Guys like that kill me."

What Luke was saying behind Ray's back was nothing that wasn't said to him to his face. The entire security office had expressed their disdain for his relationship numerous times. Mainly because they knew that Ray deserved better than that. At some point, Ray had slept on every last one of their sofas because of their many fights and her kicking him out. Normally their fights were over something silly. He used more miles driving than usual in a day, the hood of the car was warm when she got home, and he didn't call her when he was on his way home from work on her days off.

"Well I guess it's just me and you, huh?' Chris said nervously "Don't worry I will take a shower. So, what happened with the roaches?"

"Oh, I am not telling you that mess. You will have to wait for Ray." While laughing at her previous statement, she followed up with a question of her own. "Soooo is this a date or just a friendly outing?" There was nothing worse than being on an outing and figuring out halfway through the order that it was actually a date.

"It can be whatever you want it to be. I don't want you to be alone at all during your mommy-free time. I want to take up all your time." Chris liked Corrine. He had been watching her and noticing her for the last few weeks. Her style was cool. It was silly for the most part, but quiet. She had even shared a couple of her poems.

"Oh, it's my choice if we date or not? Interesting. I say we see how it goes. How about that?" Corrine was curious and it had been a long time since someone had intrigued her.

Chapter 2

Chris did exactly what he said he would do. He spent every waking hour with Corinne. He liked her even more. The first date did not go perfectly at all. They were both awkward and a bit sloppy. They went to dinner at a local restaurant. Chris had it in his mind that it was going to go well, but destiny had a different agenda.

"Yo! Why is this waitress so damn rude?" Chris was frustrated and everyone in the ear shot could tell. He wasn't exactly whispering his discontentment. "I mean she didn't even give my proper order and then gets mad at me about it! Who does that?"

Crystal wanted to laugh, but she held it in. He was actually cute all frustrated. "It's okay Chris, maybe she was having a bad day. You never know. It will be fine. No worries"

"Ugh maybe you are right, but she is still pissing me off. Whatever happened to the customer is always right?" He paused for a moment. "Damn, I have been bitching for twenty minutes. I'm messing up huh?" His question was sincere, but he was high strung the majority of the time. He didn't seem that he was aware of that character trait.

"Well yeah, it's been about twenty minutes, but I am not bothered by it in the least," Corrine said breezy.

"Are you always like this?" Chris quizzed.

"Always like what exactly?" Questioning his question.

"Carefree…" He let that word linger for a minute.

"No, I am human. I try to be, but why make a strained situation worse by adding fuel to it. Besides, I am not on a *date* with the waitress. I am on the *date* with you. She is not my focus of the evening," Corrine said and smiled. She had yet to tell him if their outing was just that or a date.

"For real? We dating?" Chris said beaming. She had just made his day and he laughed a genuine sweet laugh.

The rest of the meal went somewhat smoothly. The waitress kept messing up but Chris took his time to try to place his attention on what was Corrine. He wasn't sure how a man could treat her the way her ex-husband did. She didn't bring him up often. He heard Ray talking about it one day when she was out escorting. All it did was intrigue him to get to know her for himself.

Chris was just out of a situation also. He was married for a few years with twin girls as a result. His wife, however, cheated on him with his mentor at the time. He was still devastated and dealing with a lot of the trauma from that relationship. Corrine was refreshing as a breath of fresh air. When dinner was over, she gave him a hug and thanked him for the amusing evening.

"Corrine, tomorrow you are busy. I don't know what we are doing but we are doing something." Chris smiled and closed the door to her car. She nodded with a giggle and drove away. "Damn, so that's Corrine."

The next day at work they didn't change their routine. There was no mention about the date and that they were to meet up that night. It was easier that way. People are too nosey. Especially her coworkers.

Text message:

Corrine, meet me at my house. I will cook. All I know how to make is fried chicken. Sorry.

She met him at his apartment. He had a small one-bedroom apartment with barely any furniture. "Sorry, she got the furniture in the divorce."

"Stop apologizing and give me my chicken," Corrine teased. She opted to sit right on the floor with some pillows. Material things never impressed her much from anyone. It was the heart, the character and how people treated others that mattered. Right now, Chris treated her sweetly and he was offering her his hospitality. "Next time, I will fry the chicken. Deal?" She held out her hand to shake on it.

"Wait you cook too? Oh man, this can't be real. Are you real? Like for real, are you real?" Chris was genuinely excited about that cooking fact. "You just don't know how many women these days don't know how to cook! They barely know where the kitchen is! You are so dope!"

"Well thank you very much kind sir!" She jokingly gave a curtsey. "It's a deal. Tomorrow night I will cook for you and don't be late!"

Night number three was great. She made him lasagna, which he ate two plates of. "C, this is so damn good! Thank you so much. I eat chicken a lot." He ate some more pasta. "I am not being too greedy, am I?"

"Hahahaha no you are perfect. I love to see people enjoy my food. I love to cook!" She loved that he loved her cooking. She hoped she could cook for him more often. Something was telling her he was thinking the same thing. The biggest issue these two had so far was his obsession with Narnia and hers with Lord of the Rings.

"Okay its official you are not perfect. If you were perfect, you would always choose Narnia!" Chris thinking if this was her flaw then he could definitely live with that.

"Narnia sucks always and forever Middle Earth!" Corrine responded with arms flailing gesture.

"Fine how about the next four nights that is what we do. We watch all of it! We will debate again which one is better." Chris had to be creative. The two weeks were up, but he still wanted to spend time with Corrine. The days went by and they just enjoyed each other's company. This was new territory for the both of them and they welcomed it with open arms.

Chapter 3

"Lord of the Rings is still better!" Corrine in her mind won the battle that went on between them. At this point they had forced each other to watch it three times over and neither one of them were budging. They had been dating a few months. Movies, dinners, TV nights, inside dates and outings. They were inseparable in their own little world.

"You're crazy! Okay, okay we can agree to disagree," Chris said his face was one inch from Corrine's. He paused. He looked at her for a second. "You are so beautiful." She loved his compliments. The men in her past didn't waste too much of their time giving them. As if the reassurance of it all would empower her and enable her to take a step for herself. It only embedded their insecurity. It was the first time in a long time anyone had called her beautiful and she wasn't sure when the last time anyone bothered to look at her in that way.

Corrine caught his gaze and reciprocated. Chris brushed her hair from her face. They leaned in and kissed. It was sweet and slow. The more they kissed the deeper it got. His tongue explored her mouth for the first time as if a sailor drifting with just a map and compass. He couldn't pull away from her. He gripped her tighter. She kept her eyes closed. She would always keep her eyes closed for every kiss thereafter. His hand slid to her waist and laid her on the carpet where they were sitting. She allowed him to. The connection was instant. He didn't want to stop, but he did.

He lay next to her for a minute in pure silence. He reached down and held her hand. "Wow you kiss like your poetry." Chris was mind-blown. He wanted Corrine, but he wanted her to want him too. She sat up. He was a bit disappointed. He figured she was getting ready to leave. He walked to the door. "Look C, I am sorry I shouldn't have."

Corrine cut him off. "Stop apologizing, I told you and you are at the wrong door," looking in the direction of his bedroom. Chris looked as if his heart was going to jump out his chest. He took her by the hand and kissed her with all the passion he had stored up inside of him. He noticed her his first day at work. He thought she was the most beautiful woman he had ever seen and now he was kissing her in his apartment. Now he was about to make love to her for the first time.

It had been a while since the last time Corrine had been with anyone. Her and her ex-husband stopped having a sexual relationship way before the divorce papers were even filed, but she was ready and she wanted it to be with Chris. He led her to his room. She was nervous. He could sense her slight hesitation. He laid her down on the bed and kissed her again. Like the living room the decorum was sparse but it was his and she liked him. She liked him enough that when he took off her shirt she didn't resist. She welcomed him undressing her. She wasn't sure if she had been kissed so sweetly before. She had thought about all her first kisses up until that point and nothing could compare. She was older now. She accepted her body more and her confidence was showing. No more did she cower behind, leaving items of clothing on as she did before. She was completely nude. He leaned up just to look at her. He always looked at her sweetly. That look would be her weakness. The sincerity in his eyes was hard to come by. She had seen it once before. In a brief time period from another long-ago lover, but this was different. That was placed in the category of pure lust. This was different.

She lay under him touching his dark brown skin with her fingers. He was kissing her slowly everywhere. Paying careful attention to every part of her. His lips on her neck lasted for what seemed forever. If forever could just last a little longer. Further down along her path, he stopped at her breasts which were small but supple. He flicked his tongue on her nipples and they hardened with each lick. She moaned and so did he. He wasn't aware of how much he would love the sound. Her sounds. Her voice.

Pausing briefly at her naval she squirmed from the tickling sensation of his tongue. There had only been one other who had given her body this much-needed attention and that was hardly in comparison of what she was experiencing now. It was years ago, and they too had a friendship that evolved into more. It was only for a short time. They were young barely 20 years old. It was during a breakup with her boyfriend at the time. Andre taught her things about herself that she didn't know. He traveled lower. She gasped at the delight of him placing his warm moist tongue on her lily. He salivated the more she became wet for him. She remembered some advice she heard when she was younger "Never let a man have sex with you without tasting you first!" This rule came second on the list right under "Always use a condom." She didn't need to coerce or ask, he gladly did it. Her ex-husband hated to perform the act. Since he made so big of a deal about it she didn't bring it up even though it bothered her. It was a selfish act. Although Corrine was considered the primary pleaser, she still appreciated when a man would take the time to feast on her. This was Chris' lesson. He taught her that her needs mattered too.

Her body shivered with his head between her thighs. He pinned her down as her strength grew with each flick of his tongue on her flower. She gripped his sheets as if her life depended on it. Her legs tightened. He didn't stop. It only energized him. She was nearing her climax and he needed to taste every drop. Nothing would be wasted.

He wanted her to always remember. He wanted his beauty to always come back for more. He would do whatever it took to achieve his goals. He would be her best.

Corrine was spiraling and couldn't contain herself. For the first time in her life she didn't want to. She wanted to release every last bit of anything she had held deep within her. This would not be one of those many nights she would cry herself to sleep. She would enjoy this man and give him the gift of her. Chris didn't want to stop and she didn't want him to. He kept going past her climax until she peaked again. She was ready for him. He was beyond ready for her. There was no more nervousness from her. He had lost his inhibitions by his third beer. He put on a condom and entered her so deep from the first stroke. She was tight. It had been a long time since she had had any kind or form of sex. In reality it had been a long time since she had been properly kissed. Now her walls were snuggly wrapped around him. He was a perfect fit. She came. Calling his name over and over. She wasn't one before this night to do so. It took a lot of effort to make her call out in passion. Normally, she was the pleaser. Normally, she was the doer. Normally, she was the initiator or it just didn't happen. But that night everything changed. She was open to the world of ecstasy that had been hidden from her for years.

Her legs gripped his waist. He kissed her while he stroked over and over again. They created magic. They created something so special that it would be hard for words to ever describe. It compared to nothing she could ever dream of. After her three previous lovers, the dream quelled. But now with Chris in his room, the dream ignited and became life. This was love in the making.

After it was over they lay there exhausted heavily breathing trying to catch their breaths. "Are you okay? Do you want me to get you anything?" Chris asked looking at Corrine.

"Well I could take more of you, but other than that, nope." Corrine would have never thought to say anything like that before this evening. In that instant, she had changed. She was less resistant to being filtered. Somewhere between her skin and his tongue she became unhinged.

"If you want more of me you can have me." Chris was serious and she took him up on his offer. It was just as good if not better than the first time. He bent her over from behind for a different view. It wasn't very often she had sex this way. Before it was normally missionary. Before it was normally ordinary. Chris was nothing close to ordinary.

He wanted her to stay, but understood that she had to go. She had to pick up Ariana from the babysitter. "Hey Chris…" Corrine called out to him.

"Yes C?" Chris simply replied.

"What did you think when we first kissed tonight?" She asked.

He paused. "I thought… I hope you wanted me as much as I wanted you." He kissed her again. "Hey make sure you let me know when you get home. It's getting late and I worry about you," Corrine nodded and she left.

Corrine made it home and let him know she was safe. "I only want you safe C," was his reply. That night she drifted off to sleep in her own bed and she did not shed a tear. It was different and it was nice. She had not experienced nice in a long time. She hoped it wasn't a fluke.

Chapter 4

Corrine woke up that next morning as if the evening had been a dream. She couldn't remember the last time she had slept that well. It wasn't until she checked her phone and saw the text from Chris telling her how much he cherished last night and he hoped she did too. She smiled at her new reality. Hope.

When she got to work, there were only two stolen glances between the two. Even though they were now beyond just friends they didn't want the office knowing anything. It was never spoken. It was never discussed. It was always implied. She wanted to keep her job environment as professional as she could. The bedroom and behind closed doors was a different story.

Corrine saw Chris storm out of the building in a hurry. She knew something was seriously wrong. It was beyond the normal annoyance on his face. She wanted to go after him but realized from the front camera system, he appeared to be arguing. She assumed it was his ex-wife and figured he would need some time alone with that. She sent him a text asking if he would like to come over. But this one was different. It wasn't the normal hey-I-am-frying-chicken text.

Cell phones were not allowed in her workspace. When she got to her car at the end of the duty day, she was greeted with her own drama. A series of mean and spiteful messages from her ex-husband. He called her names she never wanted to repeat. Jeremiah was upset about the divorce even though he had moved on with yet another girlfriend. She silently cried to herself. The next message was from Chris saying he would be by for dinner.

By the time Chris got to her house, it was about 6:00 p.m. He knew dinner was a little early at her house since her daughter had an early bedtime. Ariana refused to take naps during the day so she needed adequate rest to keep her little self-going. He loved how she raised her daughter and the happy toddler showed it with her smile. For dinner, she made baked barbecue chicken wings, baked mac and cheese and string beans. They were both a little quieter than usual, but still enjoyed each other's company.

She had just put Ariana down to sleep. It was 8:00 pm. "Chris can you do me a favor?" Corrine asked a bit uneasily.

Chris noticed she too was isolated and hoped it had not been any regrets from the previous night. "What's the matter C? What's going on?" Even though he had his own situation to deal with, he wouldn't discredit her concerning gesture.

Corrine replied, "I know this is the time you normally head home, but… can you just… stay with me tonight. It's okay if you don't want to. We don't have to have sex. I just need you to hold me."

Chris was a little shocked she had asked, but elated nonetheless. "I will do anything you want me to do. I will hold you all night long."

She got up and cleaned the kitchen putting the leftovers away. She then took her shower. She had just picked up some cucumber melon body wash from *Bath and Body Works*. Her shower was longer than normal. It had been a long day. When she met him in bed she was wearing a short tank top and her panties. She lay on his chest.

273

"Damn you smell good," he said thinking out loud. He only realized it when she said thank you. "Hey C, are you okay? You have been quiet all night. Is this about last night?" Chris wasn't one to let things fester, so if she was having second thoughts he wanted to know now.

"Last night was unimaginable. I loved last night. I have no regrets. It's not you. I got some messages from my ex today and it hurt. I don't know why he hates me so much." Corrine was whispering. It wasn't so much the hate towards her that was being expressed it was that it was being transferred to their daughter. Nothing hurt her like her child being hurt. She was so delicate. He had never seen her so fragile before and all he wanted to do was hold her to keep her together. "Normally on nights like this I cry myself to sleep, but I just wanted you that's all...Just you."

That brought relief to Chris. Not that she was heartbroken, but they were still in a good place. He was no longer worried about their relationship and with her admission. He told her about his conversation with his ex-wife threatening to take him to court for more money and less visitation. He loved his girls and would do anything for them. Corrine showed him the messages. Chris read in disbelief as they were threats that she'd hope she die.

"Baby I am so sorry!" He just wanted to take the pain away. He wanted his own pain to go away. He kissed her. Not like last night. This was something different. He kissed her tears as they streamed down her face. He kissed her past her pain. He took off her clothes quickly. He needed to be inside of her. He needed to feel her warmth of his body wrapped around him. He needed her to be his peace and that is exactly what she became for him.

Chapter 5

After that night, they spent most nights together. He didn't like her alone after he figured out what she was dealing with. He was falling for her and couldn't tell her. He couldn't let her know. Not after his wife had done what she did. He wanted to trust her and she hadn't given him a reason not to. He also heard from Ray one day that she had issues with her ex coming by in the middle of the night. It had been a while since he did it, but he was ready for him if he happened to pop up again.

They continued their relationship in mostly secret. She had met a few of his friends one night when they visited from Maryland. She didn't know they would be there. When he opened the door, it was a room full of people. The guys just kind of sat around quietly staring at her. It was a bit much for her to take in at first.

"Chris I didn't know you had company," she stated a bit astonished. "I could come back later if you want?" Corrine was heading right back out the door even though he had invited her over when he jumped up and lead her back in the apartment.

"Hey guys this is Corrine. Corrine these are my friends. Friends be on good behavior please!" Chris had a smile on his face, but he was serious. The bunch had a good time and somehow, she managed to fry them all chicken.

Corrine laughed, "You duped me Chris!" She was washing dishes.

"No, no I didn't! I just simply didn't tell you my boys would be here *and* I didn't tell you you'd be cooking for an additional five people *and* okay I might have duped you but they love you." He smiled. She loved his smile.

There were times after that when his best friend would come with him to her house to hang out. It was all just so relaxed and so easy. He would walk in, take off his sneakers, run give her kiss and grab the remote. They had a routine.

She loved him. She didn't say it. She has always been a more than words type person. She had expressed it in her poetry to him. Only very special people received personal poems from her. She would normally send them to his work email when she knew he was at his desk with the subject, "A little something to brighten your day." On the nights he didn't come over for dinner, she would sometimes pack him a lunch plate and leave it on his desk. She got into work before him so it was rather easy to do. She liked making him smile. Corrine knew he wasn't ready for an intense relationship, although they would slip into one periodically. She loved loving him but he wasn't fully accepting of it.

Chris was growing distant and Corrine's heart hurt. The issues with his children's mother were escalating and he was spending more time in Maryland going to court. She wanted to support him, but he made it hard for her to do so. Corrine was surprise he took her advice to send the twins matching love plants for a Valentine's Day gift from 1-800 Flowers. Other than that, he closed her off and shut her down. They would still see each other from time to time and she missed him dearly. She decided it would be best to give him the space that he wanted. For a moment, their relationship grew to be purely sexual and she didn't like that. She too started to pull away. If they had met at different times in their lives it could have been the greatest love affair the world had ever known. There is only so far a couple can go when dealing with each other's broken hearts.

The nights grew colder for Corrine as it had been for some time. She would always stop and remember him though. They wouldn't say much to each other at work and the lunches she left on his desk were few and far in between. She felt as though her love was rejected. They even had a few arguments, which she hated. She never liked conflict and for the most part would try to avoid them. She wasn't sure of why the hostility was towards her but her patience for that dwindled with her last relationship. Whatever had ignited had dimmed and their time was coming to an end.

"Is that all you want me for is sex? If that's the case, you can go home Chris!" Corrine was upset. That was the only time he wanted to see her or so she thought.

"Is that what you think? That's not it at all. You just don't understand!" Christ was aggravated. He didn't know how to explain to her his hurt. Sex was just a way to get comfort and the only comfort he wanted it from was her, but since he wasn't doing anything else, Corrine was being made to think that was all he wanted.

"You don't talk to me anymore. What is the matter with you? Is it your ex? We can get through it together Chris! I am not her!" Corrine started crying. She hated crying. *Never let them see you cry.* She wasn't doing a good job with her father's advice.

"Listen if you are going to cry I am going to leave! I don't need this from you or anyone else." Chris walked out of her bedroom to the front door. He couldn't leave. He didn't want to leave, but didn't want to hurt her. He was confused. He turned around and hugged her. She was standing close to the front door. The master bedroom was only a few feet away. The two other rooms were upstairs along with a full-sized bathroom. Her daughter was sleeping. "I am so sorry baby. I am just all fucked up right now. I don't want to hurt you," he said as he kissed her. Even though they weren't in a good place, the passion could not be denied. It is a passion that would always be there. Even if due to certain circumstances it couldn't be expressed.

"You are so easy to love…" the words echoed from Andre spoken to her five years ago. Maybe he was wrong. It seemed as if loving her was hard for everyone to do. Her thoughts were interrupted.

"Baby, ride me." Chris wanted to be inside of Corrine so badly. It was hard to say no to him and she obliged. Straddling his lap, he eased in her with a moan. This is what he wanted so badly. This is what he needed. She rocked and swayed on top of him in her own rhythm she created months ago. He gripped her shoulders pressing them down to control the force from beneath her. If he could just have her just like *this* every day.

Corrine gripped him tightly and he responded with a stronger hold. "I am sorry baby," he whispered in her ear. She didn't respond. She wanted to forget the altercation altogether and bask in the moment. It didn't stop the tears to lightly dampen her cheeks. A part of her was still sad, but she appreciated this time with him. She appreciated sharing intimacy.

It was months later and Corrine was moving. She decided that this was as good as any time to reach out to Chris. She tried calling him, but it went to voice mail. She had asked him to meet her at her house, but he never showed. On her last day of work, she left a letter on his desk. She confessed her love for him and wished him well. "All love affairs are not meant to last forever, but at least I can say I had one for a little while." If anything, the situation with Chris taught her another valuable lesson. Honesty. She yearned for it. No matter how brutal the truth, a lie just would not do on any level. She had so many failed relationships built on false appearances and lies that she no longer wanted to or would tolerate them. It didn't work out obviously, but Chris set a standard.

His passion and his sincerity even when he was being an asshole will always intrigue her. It allowed for their sexual encounters to be nothing short of explosive. Every kiss was love and every stroke was adornment. He did cherish her and lavished in her beauty for a short while. He may have not been "the one," but she needed those qualities. They were just two people emotionally broken. Emotionally unavailable wrapped in an emotional circumstance. She missed being able to love him. She would simply love him from afar.

CONSTANCE

My life
Had come full circle
Betrayal
Heartbreak
But at its core
At the nucleus
Of it all
Love
And one might wonder how
How could I love beyond
The very things that broke me
In the first place
Faith
Where I know
That I am
Who I am to be
Not because
You say I am
I am the meaning of my name
I am the embodiment of royalty
And joyfully
I can be full
Wisdom
Now flows from my lips
Only due to harshness
I have lived
I have learned
And even now
I learn
And I grow
And I cry
And I smile
Because under this crown

The majestic beauty
I am simply human
And even though
As time went on
And days grew long
I have been stifled by my own fear
I breathe
I breathe so deeply
That is the blessing
So please
The next time you see me
Point to me
I will lend out a hug
Because I know you
Like I
Have a story to tell
And you
Like I was
Hide behind your own
Cell
With fear
Bonding to the walls
See me
Reach out
And please
I ask you
Call me Queen...

Chapter 1

Constance entered The East Pole on East 65th Street in New York City. It was her favorite restaurant to dine in for lunch on warm summer days. Especially when she was alone. She loved the quaint and tastefully decorated restaurant. She didn't really need the menu. She had ordered the same thing every time she came. She was such a creature of habit at times. When she liked it, she liked it and that was all that mattered. The sun was shining and the breeze was sweet. She even spotted a few butterflies fluttering along the way. She remembered her grandmother's card. "A butterfly landed on the windowsill and that is good luck for you and me." She desperately missed her. It saddened her that the card was misplaced, but she still remembered the words.

"Would you like to sit inside or outside?" The hostess asked.

"Oh, it's so beautiful. I would like to sit outside if that is okay." The hostess leads her to her table for one facing the street so she could see the people walk by to and fro. Constance replied, "Oh, and I am ready to order." The waitress approached with her pen and pad. "I will have The East Pole cheeseburger, duck fat chips and pickles please. Thank you."

"I will put that in for you, Ma'am." The waitress walked away.

Constance loved the vibe of the city. For some, it was too much. Too many people. Too busy. Too hectic. But for her, it was beauty. She would wonder what people's stories were. Where they were headed. What were their dreams? She liked to think that all New Yorkers both born or traveling for a spell, had a dream.

She wore a cute black strapless dress that hit her right at her calf. It had grown to be her favorite dress. It was casual and comfortable. It would always draw attention and compliments. Probably because she was so tall and noticeable. The dress was form fitting, but not unreasonably tight. It was a nice day, but not nice enough for articles of clothing to cling to unwanted areas.

The tall brick buildings seemed slightly bigger on the sunken patio. She loved the huge lime green door next door to her table. It was so bright and cheery. The waitress came with her food. While eating, she reflected on her life. She thought back to all of her highs and lows. The accomplishments and failures. Some too disastrous to be called simply a failure, but she made it through it all. "Thank you Lord for always protecting me," she prayed. There was no other way to describe how she had gotten through some of her events that occurred in her life.

Constance did not reflect often, but doing so kept her grounded and humbled. In most cases, the reflection made her take a hard look at herself and where she had been. It left her more grateful than vengeful. The last thing she ever wanted was bitterness to grow within her. There were times when she fought herself to stop it from happening. If she had a fear, it was that.

Those nights she had to hold the elevator door when her mother was in the apartment. She was protected. She was loved and she was covered in favor. It was nothing but angels that kept her safe walking through the Bronx at midnight to get to her beloved grandmother's house after her mother had abused her. As a child, she had always believed that angels were stars. The fireworks on her birthday made her imagine if the stars had aligned just for her with beautiful colors and marvelous spectacles. Even at 26 years old she still found herself looking up to count the stars. To see her angels.

It was, at first, hard to admit but God was still with her when her first boyfriend violated her and raped her. We all have free will and we choose to do things that are not of Him and choose to do things that are. Even so, she had not had any diseases from those encounters. God allowed her to survive deployments and foreign wars. She was comforted when faced with adversity against her race and gender.

She was allowed to have a baby. She was actually allowed to be a mother and the strength to carry and give birth to a beautiful baby girl. She remembered her grandmother and all of her countless hugs. She remembered the love. Her beloved was the first person she felt and saw love from. She was her example and prayed that she was blessed if she could only be a fraction of the woman she was.

The heartbreak she endured from her father leading her to broken relationships and a selfish marriage all helped her to be wiser. Somehow only somehow was she able to still yearn for true love even after all of that. There were times it seemed as though she was living in a movie and not her realty. Some days just didn't seem real. Some days she used to wish they never happened. But right now, in this small patio looking at the dreamers and lovers go by she was excited. Excited that after she paid for her check and got up from the table she would be considered a dreamer and lover too.

She missed her lover. The only real lover she had experienced in her life. He was yet another man to break her heart. They both made mistakes and she couldn't blame him for everything. It just wasn't their time. It didn't seem like it would ever be fully their time and she accepted that. Every now and again he would too send her a random email of a song lyric from their days together. Everything just made since. She hummed to herself *"I just wonder do you ever, think of me, anymore, do you..."* Ne-yo's classic song, *Do you?* Every lyric when they parted ways spoke to her heart. She very well knew the answer to that question. Some things just don't go away. He still made her smile.

Letting all of it drift away, she was to embark on yet another journey of love from a man she had adored for years. She had just sent Ryan a letter written by her own hand disclosing every secret she had ever kept in her heart. She vowed that if she were to indulge in love again, he would have to be accepting to all of her. The good and the bad. He had willingly confessed her love for her and her daughter.

Constance had finally accepted her own crown. It took 25 years to acknowledge it. It took 25 years to understand its existence. Her own personal crown. With her back straight and head held high she wears it gracefully. Look closely and you will see it there. It is beautiful. Over the years, Constance grew, learned and evolved from every stage and major events in her life. It was as if she had to become a new person to face whatever challenges that were ahead. Her wisdom and discernment was increasing. Although it still had a way to go, she always wanted to remain teachable and fluid. It is as if derived from lotus itself. She too has risen amongst the muddy waters only to be purified. One day sat and read the meaning of the lotus. It made sense why that was one of her favorite flowers. She too was a lotus. A rare kind not yet discovered by many, but noticed by some. Maybe this was the reason she had faced so many battles and conquered so many storms in her life, because as the lotus rises in the morning so will she.

The journey continues...

Acknowledgements

Thank you for taking the time to read my first novel. I am so excited to share this moment with you! It was on my heart to complete this book not just for my own benefit, but to help anyone out there who may be going through hard times. Please know that you are not alone. Please know that you are loved regardless of what others have told you and maybe beyond what you have told yourself.

Thank you for the very special chosen few who knew about me writing this book. To me it is more than a book, but a journey about triumphs over heartache. It shows individual strength and personal achievement. Not every story has a happy ending. Some stories end with the acceptance that life itself is a gift. No matter how troubling times can be. Appreciate the time people lent to you. It is one of the few things we cannot get back. I am so thankful for your support, concern and love.

Thank you to anyone who was inspiration for this literary piece. Without you it would have been impossible to create and share this tale with the world. Thank you to those that have ever uttered the words "I love you," thank you for every hug and every smile. You are too appreciated. My spirit is so filled with joy as I think of you. You are very special to me. Stay blessed.

Until next time loves

About the Author

Call Me Queen is Cyrene's first novel. After years of writing poetry, her first literary love, she decided to expand her love for words and storytelling. She hopes to continue her literary path creating more heartwarming and thrilling novels. Cyrene currently resides in New York City where she is originally from.

Made in the USA
Middletown, DE
18 March 2017